For April, who has worked countless hours as I strived to make Haddie real for people outside of my friends and family. These stories would not exist, at least in this form, without April.

In Memory of David Farland.
I've never met someone so passionate about mentorship and writing. You are loved and missed.

INFRARED

BOOK FIVE OF THE ANGELSONG SERIES

KEVIN A DAVIS

Inkd
Publishing

CONTENTS

INFRARED

This is *Infrared*, Book Five of the AngelSong series and the final story of Haddie and Thomas.

The Unceasing close in on their final moments, threatening the world. Haddie, Thomas, and their teams are not going to let that happen.

This is a story of family and sacrifices.

PART I

When they first accompanied me, I thought there were only shades of white with no color, then I learned my brain couldn't fully accept the depth of hues that make up their world.

CHAPTER 1

HADDIE SLIPPED on her shirt as David worked the motel coffee pot. The scent of coffee wafted around her as the machine hissed. *He's going back to work today.* Even this early in the morning, a door in the hall thudded and wheeled luggage squeaked past.

"English Breakfast?" he asked as he held up a pod. He wore dark blue boxers with a red line along the band. His right shoulder and arms were bruised. Tall and fit, she imagined he had put up a fight when they'd kidnapped him. He'd shaved off the stubble, though she'd sort of liked it.

"Any black tea is fine." Haddie walked up behind him and rubbed her hands across the muscles of his shoulders. She'd miss him, but she planned on driving back to Albuquerque to meet Dad today.

David's clothes were folded neatly beside the television, just under the picture of the cherry blossoms blooming in Japan that he'd been excited to find in their room. He'd placed his shoes and socks neatly at the base. Her pants draped over the chair, one sock was visible on the floor, and a boot leaned haphazardly against the air conditioner. *We're so different.* They hadn't talked about his kidnapping or her powers all night. It had been a reprieve from everything that threatened to tear them apart.

She wondered why he drank coffee this morning, but when she scanned the options there seemed to be only one tea available. He'd saved it for her. *Sweet.* As her tea sputtered and brewed, David turned to her, ignored the purpura dotting her face, and kissed her.

Why can't this be my life? "I'm going to miss you," she said.

He nodded and kissed her again. David tilted his forehead against hers. "Can you clear the warrant? Is there anything Andrea can do?"

Haddie stared down his chest and said, "Maybe." *Not Andrea.*

Dad planned on going after Bruce. If they stopped the madman, destroyed him, would that end the FBI's hunt? Did they have information linking her to Bruce's people they'd killed? David's shock at her murder of his kidnapper hurt. She'd been protecting herself and saving him. *Does that make me a monster?* The innocents who had died at the rave bothered her the most. Had she become callous to killing the coerced and Bruce's thugs?

They pulled apart as the tea finished brewing and the coffee maker became raucous. They'd passed an ice machine on the way in, but she didn't feel like putting on pants to prepare her usual tea.

David abandoned the conversation which had left her brooding. "I'm meeting with my director this morning. I think they just want to make sure I'm fit for work."

He'd given the police and his office the same excuse for his absence: he'd been distraught about the FBI and Haddie and had gone for a two-day hike. *He's still at risk.*

The FBI or Bruce's men could find him, but they hadn't shown themselves over the past day, so perhaps they'd let him be.

Haddie twisted her hair into a tight knot as he stood drinking his coffee. Her tea was too hot without the ice, so she placed it by the television. "Be careful."

David snorted. "You need to be careful. I'm assuming that you're not done yet, since you're headed out of town."

She nodded and took a deep breath. "I'm glad you don't hate me."

Smiling, he put down his coffee and wrapped his arms around her. "No. I'm scared of you and worried about you, but I love you." His used a teasing tone, but it hit too close to home.

Haddie closed her eyes and buried her face in his chest. *I don't want you to be afraid of me.* Her tea had cooled when she finally let go of him.

They left the small room in the early morning twilight. Fumes from the nearby rumbling I-5 mixed with the earthy scent of mulch and trees. Cars filled most of the parking spots, and the diner next door already had some patrons.

Haddie fought tears as they hugged but managed a smile before they kissed good-bye.

David climbed into his rental, gave her a nod, and started the Prius. Sitting in the driver's seat of the Highlander, she sagged and waited for him to leave ahead of her. *I'm not going to cry.* When would she see him again?

She pulled out her phone and texted Liz, "On my way."

Liz replied quickly, "I'll put tea on."

When Haddie arrived at Liz's house, the sky had just started to lighten in the east. Reds and oranges colored wispy clouds. *I should check the weather.* She didn't look forward to another long trip to Albuquerque, and certainly not with Cooper. Not that he bothered her as much as before, she just couldn't get past his personality.

Liz opened the door dressed in a blue and green blouse, navy slacks, and with her hair actually under control. "You look like crap," she said.

Haddie raised her eyebrows. "Really? No 'good morning'?"

"Obviously too late for that." Liz smirked and led the way into the downstairs sitting room. "Tea's steeping."

The house smelled like fried potatoes and coffee; the kitchen had a pan in the sink. "Did you cook this morning?" Liz ate granola bars for breakfast, if not cookies.

Liz shrugged. "Sorry. I would have left some if I was sure you'd be here on time." She pulled a mug from a cabinet, put it back, and grabbed a glass.

"You made breakfast for Cooper?"

Liz didn't answer; instead, she let the fridge grind ice shavings into the glass.

Haddie walked over to the teapot. A rich oolong, probably Da Hong Pao from the flowery, earthy scent. "Thanks for the tea."

"You sure about this?" Liz handed over the cold glass.

"Tea?" Haddie smirked. "About the trip? No. But Dad is geared to go." Part of her didn't care if Bruce planned on destroying civilization. *He's a madman.* Haddie and her dad had ruined a lot of his plans. *Killed his people.* She shook the thought away.

"What?" Liz asked as she studied her. "What's bothering you? Other than diving back into this mess."

Haddie poured the hot tea slowly into the center of the ice and felt the warmth swirl through the glass. "Am I a monster?"

Liz snorted with a laugh. "Didn't we already do this? I

told you 'no' then. Same now. You've had to do some horrible things, but it has gotten rid of much worse."

They had gone over this after the raves, and somehow Haddie had accepted her role in all of it. *How had I become so cold?* David had shown her how horrifying her power was. Even today he'd said he was scared of her. *A joke — was it?*

Pushing gently past Haddie's glass, Liz gave her a hug. "I'm sorry for all this. However, you saved me — us, and so many more."

"Thank you. That helps." Haddie blinked away tears. *What is wrong with me this morning?* She'd been punchy since she woke up.

Her phone buzzed in her pocket, and Liz let her go.

Terry texted her, "Where are you?"

Haddie raised her phone. "It's Terry."

"Livia still pissed?" Liz smirked.

"As of last night."

Terry had fabricated a half-lie about the whole situation, and his girlfriend thought he'd been on a jaunt with Haddie and Dad.

Haddie texted a reply, "Liz's. Getting ready to go."

"Can you stop by my apartment? I've got a list of properties, but I don't even want to send a picture of them." Terry had moved to a new level of paranoia since the FBI had talked to him a second time.

"Okay." It meant a detour, but they would need the list. Bruce's corporation out of India owned a lot of Texas properties, some within range of Terry's encryption. The tracking clustered around Amarillo. Dad thought Bruce would be there in Texas.

Liz picked up a plastic bag from the table. "Is Terry going with you?" She handed her package to Haddie.

"No. What's this?"

"Extra bandages for Dale's wounds. Make sure to use the antibiotic and keep everything dry."

Haddie scoffed. "As if I'm going to be changing his bandages."

Liz blinked and frowned. "You can help."

Did Liz like Cooper? "Yeah, maybe. If he needs it."

Satisfied, Liz patted the package. "Good." She jerked and headed across the kitchen for her phone. "Almost forgot. I've got to send you a link."

Haddie sipped her tea. "On how to change a bandage?"

"No. Polyphonic overtone singing." Liz leaned against a counter and typed into her phone.

"For the car ride?" No one wanted to hear Haddie sing. *Perhaps if Cooper gets annoying.*

Liz giggled. "No. You don't hate Dale, do you? This lady teaches you how to sing two tones at once."

Haddie blinked. *Why?* Her phone buzzed with Liz's message.

"So you can do both of your things at once." Liz bobbed her head from one side to the next to emphasize her words. "Protect and attack."

CHAPTER 2

THOMAS WALKED OUTSIDE and took a breath of the spicy desert air. The sun still hadn't risen over the Sandia mountains. Few cars and trucks were scattered in the parking lot beside the building. Small clouds drifted in blue sky, and the breeze came down from the north. He faced southeast, toward Texas. *Where are you, Bruce?* Terry had said that communication had been sparse, but out of Amarillo. Thomas had hoped there would be one property to focus on, but it seemed there were too many to target. He'd enlisted three people who he knew to be seasoned investigators, and they waited for his word to begin. Trig had been able to get him eight mercenaries out of northern California, and they were due to arrive outside Amarillo tomorrow.

By then, Haddie will be here. He still hadn't emphasized to her how much he wanted to find that nursery. *She wouldn't understand.* He'd seen too much about Bruce to let those kids grow up under his teachings. She'd been a little terse in their last round of messages, likely due to the trouble with her boyfriend. He was lucky to have Kiana, though she watched him like a hawk after his last excursion.

Biff entered the parking lot from the street carrying two bags of breakfast. A broad smile stretched across his face as he spotted Thomas. He had picked them all up some clothes the day before. Biff sported a turquoise shirt with a black section over the shoulders that had been embroidered, his hair was styled back like an Elvis wannabe, and he had a strut to his walk. His Texas disguise.

Thomas turned back to their motel room and entered, leaving the door ajar. "Biff's back with breakfast."

Kiana stepped out of the bathroom, tying off the end of a braid with a small red band. "Wearing that ridiculous cowboy hat?" She had on a pair of the jean shorts Biff had bought and a yellow button-down tied at the waist.

"Not yet." Thomas flipped the cover up on the bed and smoothed out one side in a stroke. The room didn't have much in the way of seating. Most of the patrons were likely truckers or traveling businesspeople who wanted a television or a computer desk. Before television, rooms at inns had been smaller, but usually had chairs. Sometime early last century the beds had gotten bigger, and chairs had all but disappeared.

Biff pushed open the door and posed for a second with both bags. "Breakfast is served."

Thomas tilted his head and put out his hand.

Yanking back the packages, Biff strode over to the small desk to put the bags down. "The lady had waffles, I believe."

Kiana stood with a crutch under one arm and her other hand on her hip. With a frown, she glanced at Thomas. "How did you live with him all those years?"

"He's showing off." Thomas shrugged. "Mornings are always the worst. He gets worn out by afternoons."

Kiana took her food and sat at the edge of the bed

beside Thomas. "Bruce is going to be expecting you. He knows we found him somehow."

"I'm hoping he thought I signaled Haddie in some way."

She tilted her head and shrugged one shoulder. "Maybe."

Thomas took his container. "Thanks." He did worry about Bruce's plans, for him and the world. He had Terry working on information about the recruitment of the Unceasing. It might very well be their best plan, though it could be a long game to get inside and get intel out. Security would be heightened after Albuquerque.

Kiana had agreed that no matter what, she'd sit outside and handle communications. If things got rough, she might renege, but it was the best he could hope for.

Haddie was a different matter altogether. She'd flat out refused any chance that she'd play it safe. *If I go in, she's going to follow.* Because of that, he had to be very careful, while trying to beat whatever timeline Bruce had. *I can only hope he's laid up.* What were the chances that Kiana's hit to his chest had been fatal? From Terry's analysis, someone was using their encryption protocols in Amarillo. Could Bruce's operation and plans survive him?

Kiana held a piece of waffle in the air as she spoke. "Trig's bringing portable transceivers?"

Thomas nodded. "Yes." The eggs were good. Fresh, not some batter. Salted, but not overmuch.

"Armament?"

"More than enough for us and his men. He's got two ex-military who have sniper experience as well."

"You know I like that." She cut into the oversized waffle with the plastic knife.

He waited to see if she pushed to join, but she didn't. Worrying about Haddie would be enough on his plate. *I need Kiana safe.* What he could marshal right now wasn't enough. He had Trig looking for more, and Crow insisted on calling some of his contacts. The three investigators in Amarillo were his. They just needed a location.

"I'm going to suit up and visit Crow today." Thomas wrapped a piece of his rye toast around some eggs.

"Be careful. Who knows how far the FBI are casting out to look for you."

"You'll do the eye bandage again." It worked against facial recognition and gave him an edge of sympathy from the staff.

"I understand. Crow was your man."

And I risked him in all this. Now Biff. And Haddie. Thomas rubbed his hair back. "Still is. He'll be okay in a couple months if he rests." He pointed his plastic fork at her cast. "We need to get your leg looked at after all that running around without a crutch."

Kiana's beads clattered as she swung her head up to him. "It'll be fine."

"I hope so." He sighed and dug at his eggs. They had a rough trip ahead of them. Hopefully, he could keep everyone safe.

CHAPTER 3

HADDIE DROVE AWAY from Liz's house with Cooper in the passenger seat. He wore his black shirt from their last trip, without the silver detective's star. Liz had loaned him a pair of her sweats which fit his waist, but left his calves showing. His bandages scented the Highlander with sharp antibiotic.

In all the time on their last trip, they'd never been in the front together. Terry had gotten along with Cooper well enough. *This will be awkward.* Does Liz really like him? His scowl set his jawline tight, and his eyes always seemed dark. He'd shaved, and his black hair had been freshly washed and brushed back. He was okay for an older man, but Liz did have odd tastes.

"Are you sure you don't want me to take the first shift?" He held a travel mug, and the light scent of coffee fought the ointment in his bandages.

"I'm stopping for a moment." She hadn't told him about Terry. Not that there was a reason not to, though being back in Eugene made Cooper seem a little darker. The city reminded her of his days as a detective. *Warning me and hounding me. His job.*

Terry planned on meeting her at a corner where he could make sure he hadn't been followed. His conspiracy theories had grown since his return, and he planned an elaborate path. *Like when we first met Aaron.* Her chest hollowed at the thought. It hadn't been that long since he'd saved Dad and lost his own life. She'd bludgeoned a man to death with a hammer that day. *What have I become?* She felt heavy and tightened her grip on the wheel.

"You've killed people." She stared ahead, even as they were slowing at a light.

Cooper coughed. "Yes."

"How do you deal with it?" she asked. *Stupid question.*

He nodded, remaining silent too long for her comfort. "That's a really good question." Cooper stared straight as he spoke. "When it comes to taking a life, there are three kinds of people that I know of. Those who enjoy it, those who will die before they can do it, and you and I are in the third group. We react to protect ourselves or others. A sniper or a drone operator might kill to protect family or country. There is no enjoyment, even in vengeance. We pause a part of us that will regret it and act in defense. Then later, that remorse will return in varying degrees. Soldiers have the worst of it, as there is no space between for reflection. It seems you have been a soldier for a while. I'm sorry for that."

Haddie raised her eyebrows. Cooper had hardly ever spoken that much, and his words made sense. They gave her some small comfort. David was likely one who could never kill. Bruce, despite what he'd told Dad, probably enjoyed the power of killing. *I'm the one who can, then suffers from doing it.* Dad had mentioned something similar, and it had helped for a while. She let out a breath. "Thank you."

"I hope it helps." His tone dropped, almost saddened. "I don't know how you can do — the things you do. However, I'm glad you were able to destroy those creatures. The demons, you call them."

She didn't respond. Her guilt did end with them. They were created to destroy, and she felt it. Dad had said that Dylan had made them. What did that say about *his* heart? Like Lady Erica's coerced, Dylan would not be making any more demons.

Cooper cleared his throat. "You've mentioned angels. I'm assuming it is a nickname, like demons."

Haddie stiffened slightly, because the term came from Meg. She didn't want to discuss her or Sam with Cooper. *I still don't fully trust him.* "Yes. A nickname."

"What are they?"

Haddie frowned. They reminded her of her powers, present and almost describable, but she didn't understand them. *I don't know.* It hadn't bothered her until this moment. Each time they were around, they just were, and she trusted them. They cared. They helped, just not always like she might have wanted. *What are they?*

"I'm sorry. Never mind." Cooper turned to her, shaking his head.

She imagined he thought she didn't want to answer. *I have no answer.* That troubled her. They had healed her and given her energy when she needed it most. They meant her well; she could feel it. Meg said they followed her. But — they weren't really angels, not in the gowns with wings sense.

She pulled up to a quiet residential intersection and a shadow peeled off a wall and approached the Highlander. *Terry.* He wore a hoodie and red sneakers. She made out his grin as he got closer, and she rolled down the window. There was no one behind them.

He leaned in and palmed her a thick envelope. "Here." Terry brushed a random strand out of his eyes and leered at Cooper. "Hey, Inspector. Nice nickers."

"Thanks, Terry." Haddie took the envelope. "Let's hope this gives us a lead."

He grimaced and bit at his lip. "Sorry I can't come." He seemed ashamed, as if he should be risking his life with them. "Livia would kill me."

Haddie chuckled. "She might still."

Terry looked relieved to move off the topic. "I think she's considered it. I worried her." His eyes tightened. "How's things with David?"

"Better." She shrugged. "He hasn't dumped me yet."

"He won't." Terry glanced over the hood as a door slammed in the early morning of the neighborhood. "We got your back, Buckaroo." He tilted his head. "Gotta go. Be safe." He loped back to the sidewalk.

"Bye, Terry." Haddie turned right and checked her rear view. No cars moved out of driveways.

Her guilt over killing the kidnapper faded, but now they were headed into a far worse situation. Bruce would be expecting them. *He has to be.* More of his people would die, and possibly at her hand. She didn't doubt that destroying Bruce was better for the world. *Why me?* Why Dad?

She turned east through Eugene to the highways that would wind down to Albuquerque. I-5 made her feel too exposed. Her wig would stay on this time, no matter how much it pulled. The FBI were still looking for her. Hopefully Dad stayed hidden. It would take over a day to drive to him with just the two of them to take shifts.

She didn't have much choice, as Dad would go without her. He'd been on a suicide mission before with Bruce; he wouldn't stop now. *I can't let him go alone.* More than ever, she relied on Dad. *I can't lose him.*

CHAPTER 4

Bruce leaned back in his hospital bed as the nurse finished her wound care. The medical staff were all Unceasing, but they had been uncomfortable from the start with his care of the gunshot. He had explained his healing abilities and dismissed their concerns. Antiseptic and alcohol reeked in the room. Stanton, dressed in his navy Brooks Brothers suit and face glowing yellow, waited against the window for the nurse to finish and leave the room. *I won't stay in this bed much longer.*

The woman closed the door slowly, studying him with tight lips. Some feared him, others came close to worship. Either way, he'd need to keep the two nurses and the doctor here permanently and out of the public domain. Few of the Unceasing knew who he truly was.

Stanton stepped forward as she left them alone. "Your contact at the CDC is checking in on rescheduling a meeting."

"Not a high priority at the moment." There was still work to be done before New York happened. Thomas had been a waste of valuable time. *I never should have tried.*

Dylan and the barracks were a loss that couldn't easily be overcome.

His lung healed as quickly as expected, but not fast enough for him to get out of the bed for another day or two. Communications needed to be relocated to New Mexico from Albuquerque to a smaller, but secure, facility in Grants. His troops could never be replaced.

The room felt warm despite the air conditioning. *I never should have let my guard down.* He blamed for the loose defenses. Of all places, the Coyote Canyon facility was the easiest to secure. Bruce had expanded his perimeter here in Amarillo, but the flat terrain required a different type of defense grid. For now, he couldn't close off access roads that cut through his territory.

"Have Elon come in and report."

Stanton barely nodded as he typed one-handed onto the tablet. The man served tirelessly, and he had the sharpest mind for logistics. He'd been a CEO for a small grocery supply chain out of Utah that Barbara had absorbed.

"Where are we on the resupply of munitions for the northwest end of the corridor?" Bruce couldn't let Albuquerque loosen his hold on New Mexico. It was vital to his path up to Denver in the early stages and later for California.

"Even with using the Ahmedabad budget, we have six months before we are back to required capacity. That includes the calculations for delays post New York."

The military industrial companies would be hard pressed in a couple weeks to keep up with demands. Bruce had lost key control in three of the corporations after Lady Erica had died. It was a loss that cost him more dearly after Albuquerque.

"What would I lose to reduce that to five months?"

"Northwest India would be the least damaging to your plans, considering the weakening of Ahmedabad. Jamnagar and Bhuj."

Too much. They'd have to hope that their contacts kept anyone from noticing the arms movement. In six months, US security would be at its height. "Check in with all of our State, CIA, and DOD contacts. Have we located the missing FBI?"

"No. Assume dead?" Stanton asked.

Bruce nodded. That would have been the daughter's work. He still hadn't unraveled her involvement in Albuquerque, but she'd been able to shield a small group from his powers. A significant feat. She might have proved a formidable asset. *No. I need to let them go.* They would be scurrying around looking for him at this point. How Haddie and the detective had tracked them down the first time remained a mystery. Elon would have to deal with that.

"I've printed out the local maps for Grants and replaced Albuquerque in the war room. Your contact in Amarillo cleared the land use issue with the local council, and the trucking company is relocating starting next week." Stanton had left the minor topics for last, though Bruce would have eventually asked about them.

Elon opened the door and stepped in with a nod. "Reporting, sir." Lady Erica's yellow glow blurred his blue eyes, and sweat stuck his blond hair to his temples. He'd let it grow too long. He wore his khaki uniform neat, though, and he'd cleared some of the dust off his boots before entering. Despite three squads of men, he rode the perimeter himself every sunrise when he could.

"How tight is our network in Amarillo?"

"You're concerned that Albuquerque will happen

here?" Elon's eyes glinted, and his lips curled into a smile. "Bring it on." He stiffened after a moment. "We monitor every access point eight miles out, with redundancy. I've got Unceasing physically at seven exits along I-40 and I-27. One communications portable is fully connected to all the city cameras, local law enforcement, and three private security networks. Facial recognition scrubs all those feeds and social media originating for a hundred miles from here. We've got your list of twenty-seven profiles, and if one shows their face, we'll know."

The manpower seemed adequate. There wouldn't be any new Unceasing recruits coming from Albuquerque.

"Have you determined how Thomas got word out to his team?"

Elon frowned. He hadn't liked the task in the first place. "Someone got sloppy. I don't show any communication out of our network that wasn't authorized."

By someone, he meant Dylan. Unlike Stanton, Elon didn't consider the Noveilm to be gods. He'd never gotten along with any of them.

Thomas wouldn't have messaged Bruce if he knew the location of Dylan in Coyote Canyon. His team would have hit or attempted infiltration. They only knew of the site after Thomas arrived. The equipment on the helicopter would have identified any electronic devices. Had Dylan been sloppy? He had had a penchant for social media, and Bruce had allowed the indulgence. *A stretch.* Could the Seroveilm be involved? As far back as Bruce's ancestral memories had gone, they had never returned to Earth.

"Move quickly on any information regarding Thomas or his daughter. We can cover it up afterward. Use chemical restraint on one or both of them if possible; if not, kill them."

Elon smiled.

Bruce leaned deeper into his pillow. No matter how fast he healed, his chest hurt. *Thomas and his daughter won't be bothering me here.*

CHAPTER 5

HADDIE DROVE the last shift down I-40 ignoring the stench of the fish that Cooper had been eating. She'd opened the window a couple of times, but the midday heat made her sweat. Thick clouds had dotted the southern horizon for a while, but overhead the sky shone light blue. She couldn't tell if Cooper was sleeping; he barely seemed to and rarely snored.

They'd lost four hours on the trip to sleep at a rest stop in the pitch black of the early morning. It had been Haddie's shift, and she'd argued for the break.

Haddie exchanged quick messages with David. He obviously did not like using the burner. Terry had checked in, as well as Liz. Terry had mainly complained about school and worried about Livia. Liz slid the conversation over to Cooper, and Haddie had reluctantly given him Liz's number. What could she possibly see in the man?

"ETA?" had been Dad's only text. She'd sent him updates, but he stayed quiet. He'd be busy organizing his people. Kiana planned on going to Amarillo with them. Considering the cast, it didn't make sense. Sam and Meg had been alone for a while and would probably have welcomed the company.

Haddie blinked when Cooper spoke. "Should we see if they need us to pick up anything before we get there?"

"No. They've got Biff." Despite Liz's search, the Eugene police could have extended their BOLO for Cooper outside the county. *I just want to get with Dad and find out the plan.* Her lips tightened. She'd tried to stay quiet and not take her frustration out on Cooper. Everything he said, she wanted to argue about. However, she had acquiesced and let him pick up some clothes yesterday.

Dad's stunt with Bruce bothered her. She hadn't expected him to risk himself like that and suspected that it might have to do with herself. He'd made the decision when the FBI and Bruce's goons were closing in on her. *That's not fair.* If he had died, probably just gone missing, it would tear her apart. Had he thought of Kiana? Her jaw tightened and she released it, taking a deep breath.

She'd been too beat up and worried about David to talk to him about it. *I will now.*

Albuquerque traffic filled the highway, and they slowed as they crossed to the eastern edge of the city. When they arrived back at the motel, it looked the same as the day they'd left.

They parked, and Cooper jumped out and stretched. He almost seemed to be smiling.

"Happy to be done with the drive?" she asked.

He scoffed. "Yes, if it means the singing will stop."

"I was practicing."

"You need more practice." He smoothed his mustache. *Was* he smiling?

Thomas opened the door to a room that was neater without all Terry's garbage. Kiana lay back on the bed with a book at her side. She wore an orange-red blouse that almost matched her beads. She smiled as Dad opened the door wider, offering to let them inside.

"You look better," she said. "Face is clearing up."

The purpura looked like acne from a distance. Haddie tried to smile at Kiana, while keeping her frown for Dad. She led Cooper in and jerked her head at Dad. "Can we talk?"

He rubbed his light hair back and nodded. "Sure. What's up?"

She waited until the door closed, then looked up and down the second-floor walkway. Finally, she leaned on the railing. "We never would have known."

"Known what?" He tilted his head. His purpura ran like an odd beard along his jawline and speckled his bent nose.

"If Bruce had killed you. We were only guessing where you were. It could have been Portland, if the FBI had gotten to you." She raised a hand to gesture in frustration. "I would have kept looking, Dad. Forever."

He shook his head. "It was a worse plan than that. I likely would have gotten you killed. You would have done exactly what you did; come looking for me." He took a deep breath. "I'm sorry. I could have dragged us all into a disaster."

Haddie stared at the cars in the lot below her. She hadn't expected him to agree. "Why then?"

"I wasn't thinking straight. I should have locked you down and taken you away myself. Crow obviously couldn't handle you."

Was that the flaw in his plan? *That I'm uncontrollable?* "What about Kiana? Did you even think about her?"

Her voice had risen, and he looked back at the door. The air conditioner rattled under the window, and water trickled onto the cement but dried before reaching the edge. "Wasn't fair to her either. Bad plan all around."

Did he regret that it didn't work, and that Crow didn't keep them out of it? Or that he'd jumped into the mess? "So what exactly are you sorry about?"

Dad interlaced his fingers and turned his attention to the horizon. "That I didn't communicate clearly with those who care about me. I might consider the same attempt, if the opportunity arises. Bruce is a danger to all of you. Meg, Sam, Liz, Terry, David. What risk would you take to save them?"

Haddie's heart raced. His first comment infuriated her. She knew the answer to the question at the end. He did too.

In regard to killing, Cooper had mentioned reacting to protect others. That third type of person. Would that include those who would die for others? Could she really blame Dad? *I nearly died for Liz.*

She closed her eyes. "So, what's the plan?"

Dad put his hand on her shoulder. "Let's all of us talk about it."

She bobbed her head in a nod. Hadn't she just been arguing that point? Haddie snorted and followed him inside.

PART II

The Seroveilm share their minds with music, at least that is how I understand it, and I found my own voice to take part in an incomprehensible conversation.

CHAPTER 6

MEG ROLLED her shoulders back and smiled up at the tree-tops and the sun that brightened green needles. The air smelled of pine, flowers, and warm grass. The evergreens sprayed a thousand shades of green against a deep blue sky. Each needle held a variety of hues.

Haddie's black Pitbull, Rock, played with her puppy Louis while sniffing at the trunks and diving through the high grass. White flowers collected determined bees.

Outside felt better than inside, but the other animals couldn't come out. There were hawks and coyotes. Sam worried about Louis.

She heard their music first. *I'm here.* The greens and whites brightened around her. Rock and Louis returned, though they didn't seem worried. *They never are.* Only Sam got concerned about the angels. T didn't really believe her, but they rarely came when he was out.

Three dots grew in the woods to her right. Meg stepped toward them. It didn't change how far away they were. They raced toward her, growing in shape and clarity. Their songs blended and danced about each other, creating a melody that made her smile.

The tunnels grew with ribbons of light that rippled to the surface and sped away. Her eyes darted from one strip to the other, and she giggled. *My angels.* They knew she enjoyed seeing them and came to her partly for that reason. Wings of light feathered out, both hiding and brightening the woods behind. She could almost see faces in the motion, but she didn't need to. They knew her and she knew them.

Meg's face drooped. *Sadness.* They knew that Aunt Haddie would be sad. *Like the Sad Man?* thought Meg. Even the music seemed to linger on deeper notes.

They would be there for Aunt Haddie. Meg would help.

She brightened. *Yes, I'll help.*

Aunt Haddie did important things. The angels liked her and wanted her to do what she did.

It would be okay in the end and fixed.

Meg smiled. *Yes, okay.*

CHAPTER 7

HADDIE STEPPED INSIDE at Dad's prompt; the room smelled like the leftover pizza in a box beside the television. She eased onto the edge of the soft bed. Cooper sat in the office chair at the desk. Kiana had disappeared into the bathroom. Part of Haddie wanted to lean back and get some real sleep, but her heart fluttered with anxious excitement. She pulled Terry's envelope out of her back pocket and handed it to Dad.

He nodded and opened the flap. "We've got five investigators already in Amarillo, three separate teams. We would have had four, but we lost one after the police and emergency crews moved in on Dylan's ranch. They bailed, but contacted Crow." Dad sat down beside her. "After we left, Bruce's people torched the southern training facility."

He pulled out the two pages with a couple dozen listings. All had Amarillo addresses.

Kiana hobbled out of the bathroom, face washed and smiling. "Did you read him the riot act?" she asked.

Haddie scoffed. "Yeah. As much good as it would do." She did feel better, having gotten it off her chest.

Dad studied the listings and opened his phone, typing in addresses. "Terry was good enough to put acreage on here. Two parcels are big enough to hide operations. I'm guessing the four hundred acre one is where we should be looking."

He pulled up a satellite view of the terrain. Haddie leaned in. Open farmland stretched beside back roads. The land looked gray and dead, but there were dots that she imagined were trees. A trench led through the property back to a winding waterway with streets and houses on each side. The city itself lay far to the north.

He zoomed in to a house with a small pond at the back of it. Nearby was a light-roofed building that could have been a garage and a much larger building with two roofs that had peaks in opposite directions. *A barn?* He entered another address, and it bordered the first.

"I'm going to have Biff stop along the way and pick up some equipment. Laptop and printer. We'll set up at the closest motel and coordinate surveillance. I'm not going to rush just because of his threats about New York. It might have been bluster in an attempt to impress me. It's hard to tell." He searched another address. "Either way, the last of Trig's people won't be there until tomorrow. We can arrive in less than five hours." He tapped the screen, then started typing. "Bruce has bought up a lot of neighbors, probably to keep his activities unnoticed. I want to take a drive down this back highway before we get settled at a motel. It helps if I can place the landscape in my mind."

Haddie sighed. At least Dad planned on a careful approach this time. No suicide missions. "Trig? Have I met him?"

Dad looked up. "Yes. You were still in high school, eleventh grade maybe. He and his boyfriend at the time brought out those guns for you to try on the range. You'd only been shooting a 9mm Sig and wanted to try other guns."

Haddie blushed. She'd been interested in a boy who shot a revolver, but she hadn't told Dad that. Trig and Beetle had brought automatic rifles. "I remember them. Trig is bald with a beard. Tattoos on his arms and rings on his fingers. Beetle had a red bandanna and hair as long as yours — was."

"Yep. Trig is more than sleeved now."

"I was deaf for a weak."

"Dramatic that long, at least." Dad returned to his phone and continued searching addresses.

Kiana had settled on the bed behind them, her colorful cast propped on the mattress. "I suggested we pair off, boys and girls, for the ride." Her lips rose to a sly grin. "Me and you?" she asked Haddie.

Haddie glanced at Cooper as she spoke. "Definitely." Her cheeks flushed. She hadn't meant it to seem like she couldn't wait to get away from him, but it came out that way.

Cooper shrugged though his scowl didn't soften. "No hard feelings. I could use the break, too."

Dad chuckled. "Kiana's done with Biff's antics. Can't say I blame her."

Kiana tilted her head. "There might be some truth to that."

Haddie had been a little brusque to Cooper, especially this morning. Hopefully she'd get some sleep tonight. Dad would likely get her a room by herself. She didn't intend to share with Cooper or Biff, and he'd want Kiana with him.

"Where is Biff?" she asked.

"Getting lunch. He should be back by now." Dad nodded his head toward Cooper. "You get ammo?"

"Yes. Liz, Haddie's friend, bought me some."

Dad grunted. "Good. Someday, when this craziness is over, I'd like to see you and Kiana compete. Not sure who I'd bet on."

Kiana hit him with a pillow. "Better be on me." She leaned up. "Cooper, you mind doing me a favor? Biff left a couple slices of pizza here last night in case we wanted a snack. I couldn't get him to throw it out this morning, and I'm tired of smelling it."

Cooper stood up and grabbed the box; his eyes flicked from Kiana to Haddie.

When he'd left, Kiana asked, "Everything okay with him? I'm still concerned we're going to find the FBI or police showing up whenever I see him."

Haddie reached up and stopped when she felt the dry hair of the wig. "I don't know whether to trust him or not."

"He'll be fine," Dad said, eyes on his screen. "I understand the need to find the truth. He got a taste of Bruce and wants to know more about what the man's up to. Besides, I had men watching Liz's just in case he decided to meet with any of his buddies. I wanted to see what he said about the ammo."

Kiana snorted. "Thanks for keeping me in the loop."

What else was Dad working on that he hadn't mentioned? He always did that. Her frustration from earlier rekindled, but she kept quiet. Cooper returned a minute later as Kiana began commenting on stats from Amarillo that she looked up on her phone. Evidently, none of them had ever been to the city before, except Dad; he didn't mention when.

Ten minutes later, Dad had finished his searches and

had started listing the equipment and people Trig brought with him before Biff kicked at the door.

Haddie raised her eyebrows and peeked out before opening the door.

Biff smiled broadly. Multiple bags hung from each hand. "I missed you, Girl. Damn. You're as ugly as T now."

Haddie swore at him. "I haven't missed you."

CHAPTER 8

Thomas rolled down his window an inch, letting in the spiced desert air. The sun had dropped in the sky behind them, but the heat still felt like midday. The plains stretched out with only a few man-made interruptions. In Texas, you could almost forget about society and busy cities, if you had the right vantage point. Along this back highway, there were signs of irrigation, fences, and electric poles. A nearly cloudless blue sky stretched to a distant horizon with tan grass to his left. *Are you out here, Bruce?* They would pass close to one of the properties on the list. Within sight, though not along its border.

The people he'd hired would work aerial surveillance but keep out of Bruce's territory. They'd even chartered a plane to do a pass along the north. Thomas would get more than enough from the air to start, without risking a direct pass in a vehicle. Even this short trip had reminded him of the flat, grassy plains that he'd be dealing with. A number of gullies and ravines made up some of Bruce's holdings, but he wouldn't be living there.

Thomas texted Kiana, "Pick us out a quiet motel in

Canyon, that town we came through." They'd driven south from Amarillo along I-27, as it gave them easy access to this highway. He leaned to get a view of the Highlander that Haddie drove.

Eastern red cedar and plains cottonwood made up any copses outside the grass and farms. Plenty of roadside flowers grew from the pole and wire fences to the edge of the asphalt. The road had no center line and just enough room to pull off on the side. Ahead, heavy power poles marched north and south, bringing electricity to the smaller roadside poles that fed the occasional farm. A trailer and a windmill stood out on a field to the north, and the road intersected another under the wires. To the left would take them toward Bruce's territory. They would keep straight for a bit, then turn around, head back to a motel, and set up communications.

Biff swore as the left front tire blew. The wheel wobbled, and the rim bit into asphalt. Biff braked and swerved, trying to keep the truck on the road. The blown tire flapped.

Thomas dropped his phone as the truck swerved. The right tire lipped off the road and bounced into the dirt. Dust flew in the window, and he made out the echo of a rifle.

Someone had shot out their tire. *Bruce.*

"It's an ambush." Thomas grabbed the handle above as the rear right tire left the road and the truck tilted.

In the mirror, he couldn't see Haddie but hoped she had figured out what happened and would get clear of the shooter.

Ahead, there wasn't another car in sight. Biff yanked on the wheel, driving away from the road and aiming them toward the field to the south. He stopped braking.

Good. Follow us, Haddie. Off road with a flat wasn't

optimal, but it might put some distance between them and the shooter.

"You see anyone?" he yelled back to Cooper.

A dull thud sounded against metal. Biff grunted. He leaned forward and tightened his grip on the steering wheel.

Hell. Thomas reached back for his gun. Biff had been hit. The gunshot echoed outside.

With three tires off the road, they slid out of control. Biff grimaced as he turned the wheel.

Metal screeched as a fence pole ground into the grill. The truck lurched to a stop, wedged against the post. Steam hissed. A thud sounded from the front as another bullet sunk into the front left panel near the ruined tire.

Cooper swore as a window popped in the back.

A dark truck drove from the south along the crossroad and turned toward them, kicking up a trail of dust.

Thomas stuffed his gun between his legs, reached over, and unlatched Biff's seatbelt, pulling him down in almost one motion. Blood soaked his side. "Let me get you out."

Biff's right arm twisted under him, still trying to reach his gun.

The rear passenger door opened as Cooper climbed out. Two more bullets tore through the back of the cab, shattering glass.

Thomas flinched, ducking down. *They aren't firing at me.* They would have had a clear shot.

Two more vehicles sped toward them from the north, one on the road, the second through the field. At least one sniper and three trucks full of soldiers.

Thomas unclasped his own seatbelt. He could drag Biff out of the truck; they'd be safer in the grass. He couldn't check on Haddie, not and save Biff.

Cooper fired at the truck coming from the south.

"I'm dragging Biff out, cover me." *Cover Biff.*

Opening his door wide, something slapped his neck. He reached up and found the feather end of the dart. Yanking it out, he growled. His tone rang. The truck from the south disappeared.

However, the shot had come from farther back in the field. *Back near Haddie.*

CHAPTER 9

A BULLET RICOCHETED at Haddie's feet as she ran toward Biff's rental truck. She faltered and searched across the empty field to the north. Someone had shot the glass out of the back of the truck where Cooper had been sitting.

Kiana yelled from the passenger side of the Highlander. "Damn it, Haddie! Get down!"

Another bullet dug a cloud of dust from the side of the road as she veered off in a crouch. The grass smelled like hot hay. They hadn't been firing at her at first. Dad had used his powers on the lone truck coming from the right. The other two vehicles had almost reached the paved road. The dust they kicked up plumed behind them. There were two men holding on in the bed of each truck, but they weren't shooting.

A third bullet thudded into the grass in front of her. She came to a stop. Haddie needed to get to Dad; he'd be slipping into his visions and vulnerable. Whoever was shooting at her didn't want her to reach him.

Kiana fired three quick rounds at the sniper atop a

trailer. He might have been the one shooting at Haddie. His rifle skidded off the side.

How did they know we were coming here? The route hadn't been planned until the gas stop outside Albuquerque. They'd told no one.

Cooper fired into the grass field to Haddie's right. Another sniper?

She couldn't see Dad anywhere near Biff's rental. *I don't see Biff, either.* Her chest tightened and her neck chilled. Jaw clenched, she started for their truck again.

Her wig tugged, and a red-tailed dart spun out of it. There were too many directions to focus on. They were surrounded.

The two trucks that approached came to a stop. A silver Ford skidded in the field across from her. Two men jumped out of the other at the intersection under the power poles.

Above the gunshots from Kiana and Cooper, a roar came from Haddie's left. Smoke billowed off the truck in the field. Haddie turned toward them, ready to use her powers. The two men had stayed in the bed. One aimed a rifle but didn't fire; the second aimed a larger weapon.

The explosion happened behind her, near the Highlander and Kiana.

Grass and dirt sprayed in the air. A fence post dangled, trapped with wire. *Kiana.* The windshield of the Highlander was cracked. The sound of the stone glancing off it was lost with the bedlam. Dirt and grass roots rained down on Haddie.

They had missed the Highlander. In the dust, she couldn't see Kiana.

Growling, she turned toward the truck in the field. The men had dropped down, busy working, possibly reloading. This left the driver looking at her through dark sunglasses.

Her tone rang out and the Ford vanished. Smoke and dust swirled around it.

Pinpricks of pain crawled up her cheeks and the tops of her arms. Haddie swayed toward the Highlander. The cloud of dirt covered where Kiana had been. No gunshots came from her direction. Dread poured cold through Haddie's chest.

Bullets tore into Biff's rental, smashing through glass. Cooper dove behind the rear wheel, and she could see him reloading as he inched toward the tailgate. Metal glinted as strips shredded off the roof. They fired high. They didn't want to hurt Dad. *This is a kidnapping.*

Her visions engulfed her with flames. Her skin burned, and her dark uniform smoked from the heat. Inside a burning building, she choked on a lungful of smoke and kicked a door. Flames sucked into a room where a woman in a white nightdress huddled with two small children. Flames on the outside of the house lit the glass. Dad's voice yelled, "Run!" His tone rang out, and the wall behind the family evaporated, exposing a dark night and letting in cool air.

The next vision seemed to be the same firelit night. A man in a garish red uniform with a rifle with an attached bayonet lunged at her. The blade caught her right armpit and slid down against her ribs. Dad's tone rang out, and the soldier disappeared.

The last happened in darkness without any firelight as she braced against a log barricade. The sound of horse hooves pounded toward them. Starlight glinted on metal, buttons, and weapons alike. The soldiers rode in a tight pack toward a nearly defenseless village. The attackers fired in an even volley, and the defenders returned sporadic fire, too little to stop the soldiers. Dad called out, and half a dozen red-uniformed soldiers vanished.

Pain raged across her skin, and her heart pounded in her throat. In the bright blue world of Texas, somewhere behind Haddie, Kiana coughed. Gunshots fired into metal ahead of her. *Dad.* Gunpowder had overcome the scent of hay. Steam leaked and hissed from Dad's vehicle.

Men, shadows, moved near the truck, and Haddie dropped her hands into warm grass. The light forced her to blink. *I need to get to Dad.* Pressed against hard earth and knots of grass, her knees didn't want to move.

To the right, a blue truck approached, trailing dust down the dirt road toward the intersection. *Too many.* Haddie focused on the shapes around Biff's rental. Could that be Dad or Biff? They knelt this side of a ruined fence near the passenger door. Steam wrapped around them. Cooper rolled down and fired at the shapes. From one of the figures, a muzzle sprayed gunfire, and bullets tore into the quarter panel and bumper. Haddie winced as Cooper lurched back behind the tailgate.

Close to Haddie, Kiana fired two quick shots, and one of the men grunted.

"Do you see him?" Haddie's voice came out in a dry croak.

"Get down, Haddie." Kiana lay prone nearly under the fence. Leaning out, she took two more shots.

Haddie wanted to stumble toward Biff's rental to find Dad. Cooper waved her down. Dropping to her elbows, she crawled through tall grass toward them. Her heart pounding, she felt on the verge of passing out as pain slowed every move. The men had receded, and the gunfire stopped. A spout of steam leaked from under the hood, but she couldn't see any other movement.

The rumble of the approaching blue truck disappeared behind Biff's, likely joining the other in the intersection.

Automatic gunfire tore into Biff's rental. The truck's tires squealed as they spun out across pavement. Cooper slid under the bumper and began firing as the attackers raced north along the dirt road.

"No!" Kiana yelled. "I think they've got Thomas."

Had Dad been hit? *The dart.* This had been an ambush to kidnap Dad. *And me.*

Random bullets thudded into the rental, some ricocheting off the asphalt. Using the truck as cover, Kiana crouched and hobbled to the passenger side without her crutch. Both doors were open. "They took him." Her voice cracked. "Biff's been hit."

The bullets had stopped. They were satisfied with Dad.

Cooper scrambled up and ran along the passenger side to Kiana.

Haddie staggered to her feet. Clouds drifted like the battlefields she'd witnessed from her visions of Dad. One near the Highlander drifted toward her. A smaller wisp circled where she'd made the truck of men disappear. A longer persistent tan plume followed the trucks that left with her dad. *Returning to Bruce.* What would he do? If he wanted Dad dead, he wouldn't have used darts.

In the field to her right, light glinted. She sucked in a breath and froze. Not a reflection against some weapon, it hung loose and spinning over the far road. The dust from the last truck drifted against the backdrop of a bright blue sky. The glimmer hung in the middle of it. *An angel.* It faded as she watched, light splashing off its edges. *They're watching.* Why didn't they help? Could they? Haddie blinked and the shimmer was gone.

"Biff?" Kiana leaned into the truck.

Haddie stumbled to her feet. Had they killed Biff?

"No!" His voice echoed out of the truck as she approached. "I've got pressure on it. Leave me."

"We're not leaving you." Kiana motioned Cooper toward the open passenger door. She hobbled back and studied Haddie, possibly checking for a gunshot wound.

Biff's voice turned serious. "Listen to me. I need medical attention. Hospital. None of you can bring me in with a gunshot wound. You'd be arrested."

Kiana frowned. "Biff . . ."

"Leave me. I'll call 911 if I get reception. Otherwise, take my phone and report the attack. I'll say I got caught in crossfire. Innocent victim. This is my rental truck. They'd start looking for me anyway." He cleared his throat. "I don't think it's a deep hit, but I don't want to start moving around, except to get in an ambulance. Take my gun."

Haddie peered over Cooper's shoulder. Biff lay wedged on the floor, hand at his side with his knees up at the steering wheel. The dash hung apart in wires and plastic, shredded from bullets. The seats were chewed with fluff sticking out of white holes. *He's lucky to be alive.*

"Cooper, grab your stuff and T's. His phone is under my head." Biff smiled at Haddie. "Wipe down where your dad might have touched." He frowned. "Don't go after them until Trig gets here."

CHAPTER 10

HADDIE RETREATED along the highway where they'd been following Dad minutes before. She fought slamming on the Highlander's brakes and turning around, but Biff had been right. Bruce's men would not only expect her to chase, but plan on it. They might already have reinforcements following.

The Highlander reeked of gunpowder from Kiana and Cooper. The passenger side window had a small crack that matched the web of broken glass on the windshield.

Kiana's left thumb hung on her ear, and she fidgeted with Dad's phone in her lap. *She's as worried as I am.* What did Bruce plan to do with Dad?

It had been just as hard to leave Biff behind. Kiana had argued that the attackers might return, but he'd persuaded them. If anyone, they'd be looking for Haddie.

"How?" Cooper asked. "Who knew we were going to be on that road, in that spot? They had snipers positioned to blow out our tires and shoot the two of you with tranquilizer darts."

Haddie's jaw ached as she clenched her teeth. She

almost suspected him. He hadn't given her any reason, but she knew it couldn't be Kiana or Biff.

Kiana sighed. "We could have been spotted. Bruce knew every one of us, except maybe Biff. Who knows how efficient his intelligence is? An ambush like that could be set up in fifteen minutes. Air surveillance could determine our route." Her voice dropped down to a mutter. "Tranquilizer darts are damn dangerous."

"None of it matters. They have Dad." Haddie's knuckles whitened as she gripped the steering wheel.

"It does matter. I want Thomas back as well." Kiana shifted and dropped both hands to her lap. "If Bruce is tracking us, then we have no chance of setting up a rescue. He'll move on us before we have a chance, or when we make our move. We have to assume the worst."

"I'm not giving up," Haddie said, jerking her head to glare at Kiana, but the woman stared out the window.

Kiana's face was dark, and her voice rose. "Neither am I." She took a breath, dropped her tone, and spread her fingers in the air over her legs. "When we get back to the town, we'll try to get out of sight and regroup. Let me call Trig." Both hands moved to Dad's cell in her lap, and she raised the phone hesitantly.

The road turned left with the only other option a dirt drive to the right. "I'm sorry." Haddie sighed as she slowed and turned. She couldn't change what happened. Bruce likely had an army similar to the one in Albuquerque. They had to play the situation safe, despite her pounding heart. She regretted not being strong enough to stop more of the ambush. *It happened so quick.* Even after all her concerns over killing the kidnapper, she felt no remorse for the men who'd tried and succeeded to take Dad. *I would kill them all.* She shivered, knowing it was true.

"Trig?" Kiana swallowed. "This is Kiana. Phoenix fire. Hound is down."

Haddie raised her eyebrows. A code? Dad had never given her a pass phrase.

"I'm traveling with Haddie and ex-detective Dale Cooper. Biff is waiting on medical care at the ambush site. We might have eyes on us. We need to disappear. Can you help us?"

Lights flickered ahead in the far distance and became blue and red as Haddie watched. Hopefully, the ambulance for Biff. She waved her hand and pointed toward the oncoming vehicles. A road branched off to the left and she gestured that she should take it. Kiana nodded. Mailboxes lined the asphalt, and a dirt road with plenty of tracks turned into the tan fields and disappeared against the horizon.

"Okay," Kiana said and dug in her pocket for her own phone. "217 and 87. Say the name again?" She cocked her head and started typing on her phone. "Got it. Ten minutes. Biff's ambulance is passing now. Can you get someone in place to check on him? None of us can get near . . ." She listened and then hung up Dad's phone.

Haddie did a three-point turn. "What's the plan?" She held her breath and waited for two police cars and an ambulance to fly by, kicking up a wall of dust.

"We'll switch into one of Trig's vehicles and disappear. They'll monitor to see if we're still under surveillance."

"Left?" At Kiana's nod, Haddie pulled back onto the highway.

Dust hung in the air, but no one followed them down the empty road. Maybe a plane or drone? Her heart felt like it sank into an empty chest. Leaving Dad became real as they drove to find a place to hide.

Kiana navigated them through the farms and plains to Canyon, the town they'd come through on the way south from Amarillo.

They pulled into a gas station with a white awning and bright red logo and striping. Haddie recognized Trig's bald head and stiff beard pumping gas into an old, blue Chrysler Town and Country minivan with dark tinted windows. On the back window a stick figure family included a dog. His hand leaned against the top of the roof, and he discreetly thumbed to the empty parking spot on the other side of his pump. He wore a black vest that hung loose over a hairy chest and stomach.

A woman with brown hair tied in a braid washed the windshield and moved to return the squeegee. As Haddie pulled up, Trig finished pumping, and the side door slid open to reveal two more people inside.

A man with light brown skin stepped out and crossed the island to open Haddie's door. "Leave the keys. Get in the back of the van." He had a slight Hispanic accent.

Haddie grabbed her water bottle and phone before sliding out. She hadn't expected to change cars. "Hey, Trig."

He rubbed the back of his neck, eyes flicking around the street and parking lot. "Hi Haddie. Inside."

Trig's people started piling into the Highlander. Haddie started to sit until Trig gestured toward the far back. Air freshener and stale food clung inside the SUV. How far would Trig take them? Did he already have a place planned? Dad hadn't locked down a motel for them before his little side excursion. Everything fell apart around her. *I need to do something.*

Cooper followed and was motioned to the far seat with her. Trig closed the door after Kiana settled in, tossing her crutch on the floor.

As he climbed into the front seat, Kiana spoke. "Thanks, Trig. What's the plan?"

"Marco and his people will bury your Highlander in a parking garage in downtown Amarillo. I don't have people to spare to keep an eye on it right now." He started the SUV. "If they've got people in the air, we might be able to make this work. The rest of my people are taking positions and will look for anyone following me."

They pulled out of the gas station as the Highlander backed up. Canyon appeared to have a lot of cream-colored stucco buildings, few over one story high until Trig drove them through a university with spacious green lawns and three-story classrooms. A college dorm? Too many people. The roundabouts and long drives would make it easy to spot anyone following by car, though.

Kiana typed quietly on Dad's phone.

Haddie leaned forward as Trig drove them around a curved end of the road and returned through the school. "Anything from the investigators?"

On the screen, the same landscape from earlier showed with the house, garage, and brown-roofed double barn. The photo showed six shipping containers behind the barn and three more in a row between the house and the garage. One more sat closer to the pond than anywhere else. Trucks, farm equipment, and four-wheelers were parked around the property. Had one of those trucks brought Dad from the ambush? Was Dad in the house?

"Is this photo before, or after?" Haddie asked.

"Before. I've asked them to schedule another fly over. This is from a charter plane." Kiana flipped through pictures and stopped at another view of the same area but from a greater distance. "Look at this truck."

A semi was backed into the barn as if unloading or loading. "Deliveries?" Haddie asked.

"Maybe. They'd likely come from the same route that we took. I've asked for some stationary surveillance along the route."

Trig slowed and turned into a drive. They pulled into a motel that Haddie recognized from their trip out of the gas station.

She swiveled in her seat to find the red and white awnings nearly across the street. "This is right by the gas station."

The small motel formed a U-shape with the open end to the street. A handful of white and gray, one-story units had parking close to the overhang. It looked like the kind of place where Dad loved to stay during their tours on their bikes, if they weren't camping.

She pushed away the dread of losing Dad. Trig headed for the back and cut close by a parked, brown Ford pickup toward a thin man in a black T-shirt who stepped out of a parking space in the corner. He opened the door, nearly under the overhang, and pointed to the room directly ahead of them. The air conditioner rattled and dripped a dark gray stream across the sidewalk. The water dropped to the asphalt and disappeared.

Trig hopped out and opened the door for Kiana. "Let's talk this through and figure out what the hell just happened."

Haddie followed last into a room with its little floor space cluttered with cases and two beds. It felt small with everyone inside. They'd be stuck here, trying to make a plan and getting intel. She didn't want to sit and worry about Dad. *We need to do something.* Trig closed the door to what felt like their jail cell.

CHAPTER 11

THOMAS ROLLED over and spit the grit out of his mouth. A flickering yellow light splashed off rust red walls. A shipping container? Sewage reeked in stagnant, hot air. His body ached, more from using his power than the drugs. His prison extended about eight feet wide and as tall. The light that hung above didn't reach the far end. *How did you find me, Bruce?* He hadn't told anyone about the trip out by the perimeter. Somehow, the man had known.

Biff had been shot. *Haddie. Kiana.* He tensed, wanting to lash out in anger. *They took my damned boots.* Thomas forced himself to his bare feet. His sheath was still wrapped around his lower calf, but they'd taken the knife. Sweating, he patted his empty pockets.

He spotted the silhouette curled up on the floor and his pulse quickened. *Not a guard.* A dull glow hung on the man's head, muted with his face turned toward the rusted steel. *Coerced.* Thomas took a deep breath and studied the back of the man. Matted blond hair spilled onto the dusty floor. The prisoner's T-shirt looked like it had been originally plain white, stained gray and brown. He appeared to be wearing business slacks without a belt and had blackened, bare feet.

Why would Bruce put me in with a coerced prisoner? *A spy.* At the moment, the figure reminded Thomas of Haddie's friend, Josh. However, this was no lanky surfer. His muscles were toned as if military. The man would try to get Thomas to talk. *Befriend me.*

The steel walls were dented and pitted in spots. Dark holes marked seams and ceilings where cameras or microphones could hide. Air came from somewhere. A five-gallon pail sat by the edge past the man.

Thomas gave the figure a wide berth and stepped along the side into the darkness. A light hum sounded near one end, and he crept toward it, checking back to see if the man stirred. The air moved in the container. A dark square contrasted against the door. The container had to be forty feet. A light, tepid breeze with a petroleum scent wafted through a vent. *They're pumping air in.* He leaned against one of the double doors. It creaked but didn't budge.

The man moaned and shifted.

Thomas moved to the second door and rested a shoulder against it. Bruce would want to talk with him, or else he'd already be dead. Biff had been shot. The rest of the kidnapping blurred into gunshots, vision, and pain. There had been an explosion. The drugs had taken time to work, and he'd hoped to escape before he awoke here.

He didn't have time to sit around. If Haddie and Kiana had survived, they'd regroup with Trig and try to get him out, likely with a hasty and dangerous plan. Bruce would expect him to try and break out — make one of the walls disappear.

"Who's there?" The shape had hardly moved, but the head had turned, and the glow was brighter, exposed.

Thomas sighed and walked toward the man. Perhaps he could use Bruce's plan to get information.

The man scrambled to his knees and scuttled across the floor to the back corner.

"Name's Thomas. Do you know where we are?" He stopped and stood three paces from the man.

They could have put a lid on the five-gallon bucket. The silence did him little good. He slid down against the wall and stretched his legs.

"What's your name?" he tried.

Bruce's man obviously wanted to make a show of it. Thomas sat for a few minutes, wasting time while he waited for the game to begin. He could open a hole in the side, but they would expect it, and it would likely get him nowhere. After this charade, he'd probably get a meeting with Bruce. If the opportunity came again, he'd kill him. *I can't worry about the nursery anymore.* Did they plan for a long captivity? *Am I bait for Haddie?*

"Do they let you out of here?" he asked.

"I can't reach her." The voice came so pitifully, it almost seemed real.

Did he mean Lady Erica? Josh had been obsessed with the woman who coerced him, but Haddie had been able to redirect him, somewhat.

"Lady Erica?"

The man bolted to his knees. "You know her? Has she come for me?"

If this was an act, the man had a good reference. "I've met her once," Thomas said.

"Take me to her." The man didn't command it, but pleaded.

"Where are we?"

"Underground." The man pointed frantically to the sides and ceiling. "But the door, they put food in. They brought you through there."

"When?"

The man shrugged. "Where is she?"

Would Bruce put me in a cell with a coerced? Perhaps he kept the man with hopes to turn him toward the cause. If it weren't a ruse, better to keep the man searching for her. "I don't know. When do they open the doors?" They had to change out the bucket of sewage.

"At night." The man stood, agitated; he was of average height with a solid build and fingers that looked dirty or bloody, but he was otherwise unharmed. "We need to find her."

Why would Bruce put us together if the man weren't a plant? They were likely being watched and monitored. *Did he think I'd open up to this man?* No, but I'd pump him for information to escape. *What I ask will be the key.* Trig would plan a rescue attempt, but likely take forty-eight hours or more. Hopefully, he could convince Haddie and Kiana to keep out of the way. Probably not, but as long as they were in the middle of a strong team, they should be okay.

The man scampered to the doors and slammed into them. If this were a sly interrogation, it was a long con. The man had tried to get nothing out of him. *Maybe Bruce just wants to annoy me. Wear me down.* It would take more than this.

With a sigh, Thomas rose, leaned against the wall with his arms crossed, and thudded his heel against the steel wall. No echo. It could have dirt on the other side. He strolled to the end were the man pounded and pried on the doors.

As Thomas approached, blue eyes studied him warily amid a yellow haze. He pounded on the door with the man.

Hollow. The front wasn't buried. However, they'd be watching.

HADDIE SAT on one of the beds as Kiana set up the laptop they'd bought. One of Trig's people had brought a stack of pizza and drinks. Despite the enticing aroma, she couldn't quell her stomach enough to eat. Dad had been kidnapped over two hours ago. There had still been no word on Biff. Trig and Cooper had moved some of the containers to make room around the small desk and chair for Kiana.

Cooper, who'd been closest to Dad during the ambush, sat on one of the containers and relayed most of the details to Trig, filling in some of the blank spots for Haddie as well. Cooper made no mention of her or Dad's abilities. Kiana had given him a stern look during the start, which might have helped.

Trig's phone rang, and he motioned to Cooper before taking it toward the bathroom. Haddie raised her eyebrows, surprised that he wouldn't take the call in front of them. Dad hadn't told Trig they were doing a drive by, or had he? She flushed, unsure whether she was ashamed of not trusting Dad's friend or worried.

Cooper scowled as well, though he didn't look at her. He stood up and wandered over to Kiana. "How's it look?"

"I'm using Terry's gateway. Slow as hell." She frowned. "I can't keep doing this."

"Doing what?" Cooper asked.

"Thomas." Kiana shook her head.

Haddie swallowed, feeling the pain. *David feels it too.* Did he worry about her now? She pulled out her phone and stopped. *Am I going to lie?* Telling him about the ambush would be the last thing he needed. She took a breath and texted, "We've arrived. I love you. I'll check in with you tonight if we're not busy." *If I'm not creeping around the enemy's camp.*

Trig came back and leaned on the wall by the door, eating a slice of pizza. "I've got four more people coming in tomorrow night out of California. People I trust."

A chill ran up Haddie's neck. *This will take too long.* Dad's plan had been to take time, but now his life was on the line. "I want to sneak in on one of their delivery trucks."

Kiana spoke sharply. "That's not a good plan. Thomas would never agree."

Trig laughed. "I wouldn't send one of my own people into an armed camp alone."

"What's your plan?" Haddie asked with touch of sarcasm to her tone.

"Assess the strength. Count the manpower. Determine the patrols and surveillance they have. Test the perimeter."

"Days? Weeks? Sometime before they kill Dad?"

Kiana closed her eyes and sounded less sure of herself. "If they'd wanted him dead, they wouldn't have used tranquilizers."

Think before you blurt things out, Haddie. "I'm sorry. I'm worried about him, and I know you are too." Haddie swallowed. She stood up from the bed, with no room to pace. "They've got to be watching the perimeter, like they did in Albuquerque. Kiana, you and Dad drove straight in to rescue me."

"With them chasing us in an armored troop carrier the whole way. All I saw were trucks and four-wheelers in the picture." Kiana itched at the edge of her cast. "I'm guessing they have the same level of munitions as they did in Albuquerque.

We can't wait weeks or days. "First, I get in through the delivery truck. Two, I hide until night. Three, I check in and you create a distraction. Four, I either get enough information about their camp that we can attack, or I find Dad and get him out."

Trig shook his head. "That is a horrible plan. First, you have no idea when or if there will be any deliveries."

Haddie raised her eyebrows. "Good point. Let me text Terry." She gestured to Kiana's laptop. "Can you send Terry a picture of the truck? I'll see if he can hack in and get information about the companies that deliver there."

Kiana folded her hands in her lap. "It could be days before they have another delivery. How is Terry going to get that information? Haddie, you're not being logical."

It could be days. At the thought, Haddie's chest tightened, but she kept her voice calm and sure. "Then consider this plan B. Trig, keep working on getting your information. It'll help my plan either way." She nodded toward Kiana's laptop. "Can you send me the picture as well?"

Her phone vibrated mid-message to Terry. David texted, "Thanks. I appreciate you checking in. I love you. Be careful."

She swallowed. *Careful might not be the word for what I'm planning.* "I love you," she texted.

Kiana turned and spoke as she worked on the laptop. "You're acting like your father. Stubborn. Unreasonable. Single-minded with no thought about how this affects anyone else."

Haddie sat back on the bed and finished her message to Terry. *I'm stuck here.* She needed space. Too many people. *I need some sleep.* She began removing her wig. Maybe the plan wouldn't work. "Where's Cooper going to sleep?" she asked Trig.

He laughed, shaking his head. "You really are just like T. We all disagree with your crazy plan and you're just going to wait until we get it all ready so you can do it anyway. I'm not sending you in alone. Not happening. You're not going."

Cooper coughed. "I'll go with her."

CHAPTER 13

BRUCE WATCHED the video feed from where he sat at his desk. His full-bodied Nicaraguan cigar filled the room. His office had a comfortable couch and two stiffer chairs on the other side of his mahogany desk, but Stanton stood quietly at the door. It had never been a requirement, but the man had a reverence. Unfortunately, it extended to Dylan and some of the others, but there was no true conflict, just the annoyance of Stanton's occasional fawning over them. That shouldn't prove an issue anymore.

From his window, Bruce could see where the container had been buried, back by the beginning of the gullies. *How long before the daughter comes looking?* She had help; that much was obvious.

The wounded driver had been identified as Biff Smith, Daren Whittaker originally, though he had a legal name change a few years back. He was the owner of the garage business that Thomas had built. Men watched the hospital, but no one had shown up to check on the man.

Thomas spoke over the monitor. "They must have to empty this bucket. Do they come in here?" The cameras in the container caught three angles of him sitting against the wall, acting relaxed.

He's a caged animal, but won't show it. Bruce smiled, then stiffened. *Do I just enjoy torturing him, or do I hold on to some reservation that I can turn him?* The daughter might be more pliable. Either way, he couldn't have them damaging his plans any more than they already had.

He tapped his cigar into the tray. "Check again."

Stanton nodded and typed on the tablet. He waited for a moment and then shook his head. "They have not found them. They have reviewed the footage three times. As you know, their vehicle was located. However, there is no trace of the targets nearby, nor any lead on who helped them."

She'll come. "I want all squads out tonight. Focus on the perimeter, but make sure Epsilon is guarding the second ring around our guest."

Albuquerque had been devastating, but his best human troops were here. He didn't want to risk Epsilon except in a full defense mode.

He drew on his cigar, blew out in a focused puff, and watched the smoke curl around the screen. *I should put a bullet into Thomas and call it a day.* They'd been lucky to identify Thomas when he'd come through Amarillo. Luckier still that their little caravan had driven directly toward Bruce. It had made a quick ambush possible, if not completely effective.

Since the losses in Albuquerque, there was more work than ever to accomplish before New York. Thomas and his daughter proved to be a distraction. *One I can't afford right now.*

CHAPTER 14

Haddie sat up on her bed and squinted at Kiana tapping on the laptop. The aroma of pizza lingered, and hunger tugged at her stomach. She'd fallen asleep feeling nauseous and woke famished.

"Anything?" She winced and slid off the bed, heading for the pizza box on a container.

Kiana shifted her chair around. "Depends what you're looking for. We've got more images of the compound. None of Thomas, though I suspect that lone trailer which is gone now. Our count for troops is over fifty including ten demons. And — one delivery."

"Another delivery?" Haddie paused, hand inside the pizza box. Cold, plain cheese, but it smelled delicious.

Kiana nodded, then rubbed her ear. "Please think this over carefully before you jump on this. I know Trig will help you, no matter what he says. I'll help you, no matter how bad an idea it is. Thomas will be pissed. Bruce will be waiting for you."

Haddie stuffed another bite down and nodded. She had

no idea what she would do if she made it inside. Asking for suggestions would make the plan sound worse.

"Where exactly do you plan to hide? Inside the back, aren't they going to find you when they unload?"

That had been the plan. "Yes." They'd unloaded equipment at Dad's garage before with a ramp that the guy walked down. She imagined the same. She and Cooper would sneak out while the driver dropped off the load.

Kiana frowned. "Okay, then what?"

Haddie drew in deep breath. "They'll have to guard Dad, so I'll be looking for a heavily guarded area. If it's night, then it'll likely be lit up."

"This is not well thought out, Haddie."

"I know." She stared at Kiana. "Maybe I can blow some things up. Cause a distraction. Then Trig comes in and we get Dad. Maybe I find Dad, release him, and we escape. What I can't do is let him die there while we watch." She finished off her slice and went for another.

Kiana winced and turned back to her laptop. "Your phone buzzed earlier."

Haddie spun halfway to the box and grabbed her phone off the nightstand.

Terry had sent a message. "Actually easier than I thought. Zero security. I've got a truck coming down I-40 now with a delivery for your location."

Haddie's pulse rose, and she checked the time. He'd sent the text an hour and a half ago. "Where is it now?"

She tapped the phone to keep it from timing out as there was no response. *Midnight.* Terry rarely went to sleep this early.

Her phone went dark, and she sat down with it in her lap. "I know you think it's stupid, but I have to try."

Kiana didn't turn. "Worst part is, if I didn't have this

cast, I'd go with you. I can't see a way to come at Bruce. He'll see us coming for miles and have plenty of time to set up defenses."

Haddie's phone vibrated, and she fumbled picking it up.

"Sorry, with Livia," Terry texted. "Let me check."

Again, Haddie sat staring at her phone.

"Terry?" Kiana turned back and wiped her face, her eyes moist from crying.

"I'm sorry."

Kiana shrugged. "Not you. I'm mad and scared. I want to do something instead of sit here with a cast on my leg." She gestured toward Haddie's phone.

"Terry found a delivery. I might have missed it." Haddie grimaced and shrugged.

Almost smiling, Kiana shook her head. She tugged at her ear and her lip moved as if she might say something, but turned for a soda on her desk instead.

Haddie jumped when Terry replied, "On break at a truck stop off I-27. Scheduled to deliver at 7am." Haddie stood up. She hadn't missed it. Better yet, the truck just waited there for her. One of her many problems had been how to get inside. Most of her ideas sounded like a stage-coach robbery.

"What?" Kiana spun to face her.

"It's at a truck stop, probably for a few hours. Doesn't get to Bruce until tomorrow morning."

"Haddie . . ."

"I'm doing it. If I have to walk to the truck from here."

CHAPTER 15

Haddie jumped as a clink sounded when Zipper, the woman who'd been washing the windows at the gas station, picked the lock. Trig carefully lifted the handle, keeping pressure on the door. The truck smelled of familiar grease and diesel. Haddie adjusted her pack and readied herself to climb in. *We'll be locked in.* Her heart threatened to pound through her chest. The tight hooded cowl made her sweat.

"The app will track your location. We'll know where you are at all times." Trig nodded toward the open door. "Don't die."

Haddie grabbed the side of the door and pulled up. "Thanks." Her gloves were thin, but warm.

The back of the truck looked out at a barren farm, but the bright lights of the parking lot clearly lit Trig as Cooper climbed in behind her. The door closed, the metal latch ground, the lock clicked into place, and they were left in darkness.

Haddie turned on her flashlight and scanned the pallets. Canned goods, from the print on the cardboard boxes, were all wrapped in plastic that shone under the light. They had hours before the driver might come back out to his truck from the nearby motel. Then the trip to Bruce's ranch. *Past where they took Dad.* If the truck got there on time, the sun wouldn't fully be up for another half hour.

She stepped through the stuffy container and tugged on the backpack. Trig had forced them each to carry small emergency oxygen tanks along with a cordless drill, tubes, and a carbon dioxide meter. The C4 weighed two and half pounds. *I don't want to think about that.* Trig had forced her to carry the Sig 9mm at her side. Cooper had taken three weapons and more ammo. Every addition they'd made to her load had added to her nervousness. Even now, she felt like she breathed too fast.

They climbed between the first two columns of pallets and found a place where Cooper could hide. Haddie found a spot farther back, between boxes labeled green peas and chicken stock. The truck carried enough food to feed an army. The piles loomed so high that she could only see over them when she stood up. Air seemed sparse. *I'm not trapped.* She could get out if she needed to and used her powers.

Haddie practiced finding a notch between the stacks to see the back doors. She'd braided her hair tight, and the cowl fit snugly around her head and face. Everything Trig had given her to wear was black — and hot. Even the thick socks with soles, meant for stealth, felt warmer than her boots had.

After a couple hours, some of the other trucks had already moved, but she jumped when their driver opened the cab door at the front. The air felt thick. *But empty.* She leaned against a pile and fought her rising dread.

The ride jostled her against walls and plastic wrap. A pallet shifted, and panic forced her to stand. She waited, ready to leap onto the tops, until they reached what she imagined was the highway. *Too early to be panicking*. The engine groaned as the driver shifted through gears. Traffic raced past.

Before too long, dirt roads rattled her to the bone, but she knew that meant they were close. Her heart raced faster when the truck came to a stop. Men's voices called from outside. They had a Texas accent with a cheerful tone. *I expected someone harsh, and military*. Shifting gears, the container reversed, and she turned to peer into the darkness.

When the truck stopped, her face pressed into plastic.

The Texas voice continued at the front of the cab near the driver, and the door opened there. Keys jingled, and both voices passed the side of the trailer. She held her breath. *Calm down, Haddie*. The lock clattered against the back, and she jerked.

Keys jingled. A rank smell leeched into the container like bad meat. As the Texan spoke, someone laughed. *This will* work.

The back door opened, and light wedged inside. Not sunlight. Large fluorescents hung from trusses along a metal ceiling.

"Barry, right? C'mon, let's get some coffee while the boys empty it out." The Texas voice trailed away.

A forklift rumbled in the background, moving toward Haddie. A sharper voice without a Texas accent called, "Get in there. Clear it."

Footsteps clambered on metal, and Haddie froze, her heartbeat pounding in her ears. Did they know? Kneeling, she peered through her thin crack between piles.

A camouflage hat appeared, and a man sighed, swearing under his breath. "Up all damned night and now this BS."

He didn't sound like he actively searched for them, more like he'd been sent to make sure no one was hiding there. Either way, he'd find them. He laid a rifle on a stack, two pallets away from Cooper, and wiggled through the opening. Barely looking, he glanced to each side.

This wasn't some kidnapper about to kill her, but he would expose Cooper in seconds. One of them might shoot, unless Cooper surrendered. *They'd find me right after.* Haddie hesitated. Gunfire would make sure more people died. However, if she made the soldier disappear, the others would wonder where he went. *This is bad.* Trig was right. If she did do anything, they needed this man's clothes.

Rifle still not at the ready, the soldier slid and swore between pallets before he squeezed through the piles that hid Cooper.

The man jumped when Cooper hissed, "Haddie."

She winced, then whispered, "Sorry." Her tone rang in the air to her ears alone, deafening in the confined space.

His reactions were too slow. She intentionally only pushed against his flesh, selfishly leaving everything else. It felt more like murder than anything she'd ever done.

His fingers faded off the gun before he shifted, his shaded face disappeared, his hat toppled down, and his clothes rumpled into a wad at Cooper's feet.

Shame flushed across her cheeks a fraction of a moment before her skin prickled with pain. Cooper scrambled into sight and grabbed at the clothing. She shivered as the pain tore at her arms and face. Her tone seemed to echo in the distance. She leaned her head against the stack in front of her and dropped into the visions.

Whatever war Dad had fought brought her scenes of vicious cruelty on the part of red coated soldiers she'd grown to hate. The last left her on the verge of retching when the dim light of the container came back into view. The forklift rumbled toward them, engine echoing inside the confined space.

Cooper shrugged into a camouflage shirt. He spoke in a whisper. "Haddie. I'll give you the all-clear. Be ready to move. Grab my pack." He already wore the dead man's hat.

His actions disgusted her, but she'd killed the man with the intention of using his clothes as a disguise. *I am a monster.* She shook the thought from her head. The men her dad had fought were monsters who tortured and maimed for pleasure.

"Haddie?"

She nodded and pressed a palm against warm steel. Needles of pain dug into her flesh and her hips groaned. "Yes."

Cooper stood and continued past her, moving with the rifle loosely held as the soldier had. He carried the pants at his side. He stunk of the foul decaying reek that came with what her power did to flesh. She could only imagine what the inside of the clothes looked like. He'd left the boots behind, and she stared at the sock that draped over the side. *I'm here for Dad.*

The forklift reached the edge of the truck, and the floor shifted. Metal scraped on metal, then against wood.

She startled when Cooper yelled, "Clear!"

He'd turned in the darkness at the back and held the rifle so it crossed his face. After a moment's pause, he hurried toward her. Somehow, he'd put on the pants while he walked. He paused at the shoes and yanked out the socks. "Ready?"

"Yes." She squatted behind the pallet.

He barely shoved the boots over the soled socks and

made for the edge of the truck. "You're good. Hurry. To the right."

Haddie slipped through the piles and grabbed Cooper's pack from the floor. They had made it inside, though one man had lost his life. What did she expect? Did she think that Dad could just be freed and they'd sneak out? It likely would come to people dying. *And I don't want it to be Dad.*

CHAPTER 16

THOMAS JUMPED from where he'd been dozing against the wall. His companion curled up against rust red walls and didn't stir. *That's Haddie's tone.* Would Bruce hear it? *Dammit Haddie.* He hoped to wait until they came in for the reeking sewage, but he needed Bruce to think it was him.

What the hell are you doing here, Haddie? Trig wouldn't have had time to set up an extraction. *They won't even know where I am.*

Turning to the far corner, Thomas growled. His tone rang loud, though the man didn't stir.

The upper corner disappeared, and along with it, the earth for a good six feet. Pre-dawn gray shone in the sky. A moment of fresh air flooded in. The opening held for a brief moment.

Sand and earth collapsed above, and the light disappeared. A cascade of soil poured onto the floor, finally waking the man.

Thomas leaned against the steel wall and prepared for the pain and visions.

The prison light nearly matched the sun filtering into a dark forest. He could make out the group of six that faced him, and he knew one of them. Ghanem. The tall man had the same powers as Barbara, who Kiana had shot. As he sang, lightning crackled out of the ground and leaped at Thomas.

He growled and brought out an altered tone that he recognized. It forced the lightning away, like a bubble extending from him. The one Haddie used. Frenzied electrical lines thickened around the edges, igniting the grass and slowly circling him. The scent of ozone and smoke filled the air.

The five who accompanied Ghanem lifted their bows.

Thomas rolled through his own circle. Shocks flung him to the side, and he groaned. His tone echoed in the forest. The five archers vanished, leaving Ghanem standing alone.

The next two visions seemed mundane compared to facing off with one of his own. Gruesome and horrifying, his ancestor tortured the innocent, but nothing new.

He still leaned against the wall of the container. The other man had risen to his feet. At least if Bruce were watching, he would believe he heard Thomas, not Haddie.

The man raced to the hole and dug, hurrying the earth down into the pile that he stood on. It flowed freely from above. There would be guards on the surface, snipers trained on this location.

"Be careful," he said to the man. "They'll be waiting."

"I have to get to her."

Could this man be like Josh? Unattached and without purpose except for Lady Erica? "Yes. We have to survive. She would want us to live, wouldn't she?"

The man dug slower, but didn't stop.

Metal grated as someone unlatched the front door.

Thomas turned to face them, but the man left his pile of sand and raced forward in a wild frenzy. Had they seen the dirt move above, or had Bruce alerted them?

Dim light silhouetted the guard as the door opened. Faint highlights marked the weapon in the man's hands. The rifle had been pointed down, but as the cellmate continued to pummel toward the man, the muzzle lifted.

"Devil in hell." Thomas couldn't determine if the prisoner was a spy or some hapless leftover from Lady Erica. If it were the latter, he couldn't let the man be killed because of Thomas and Haddie. "No," he growled.

As the silhouette backed away from the door and pointed the gun, it faded.

His tone rung in the tight confines, and Thomas reached for the wall. His skin felt shredded immediately, so soon after the last use of his ability. Nightmarish visions took him back into the twisted path of his ancestor.

He returned with one knee on the floor and his palm against warm metal.

His cellmate had disappeared, but outside, grunts and shuffling sounded through the open door. Thomas fought the burning of his skin and joints that resisted as he stood. He stumbled as he moved. Stiff knees joined with ankles and hips that ached at his weight.

There had to be more than two guards. *I'm not that lucky.* However, from the dim light outside, it was early in the morning and Bruce might have his patrols on the perimeter overnight. He might have guarded against an attempted rescue, more than a breakout. *No, he would expect me to try.*

Outside the door, a slanting ramp of sand led up to a tan tarp. The guard pinned the blond cellmate to the dirt and pressed a long bowie toward his throat. Bruce's soldier had the better position, but turned as Thomas rounded the opening. An automatic rifle lay in the dirt beside the container, tucked under the crumpled silver tubing that had been venting air into their prison.

Without losing momentum, Thomas stepped into a swing that caught the guard square in the eye. The other prisoner used the dazing impact to turn the knife and sink it into the man's lung. The move confirmed to Thomas that his cellmate certainly had military training.

Too easy. The tarp above them hung loose at one corner, but nothing seemed to move outside. The fresh, cool air mingled with the stench left from the guard Thomas had killed. *This is a trap.* His cellmate could be the plant he suspected, or Bruce could have something else in mind. *What choice do I have?* He could go back inside and play out the prisoner role, but what benefit did that gain him?

Go with it. At least they were outside the container. He could play out the hand and see where it led.

As the guard gasped last breaths, Thomas took the man's sidearm and grabbed the rifle. His cellmate started for the tarp.

I could let him go. If it weren't a ruse, they might be kept busy with hysterical bait. "Wait," Thomas said. If the man were ex-military and like Josh, then he might be reasoned with; a spy would play along. "Think. If you run off without prep, you'll never make it to her. Swap clothes." *Before they're too bloody.* The two men were close in size.

The other prisoner stopped.

The guard's hand shook as he reached toward his shoulder for his radio switch. Thomas slammed the butt of the rifle into the man's forehead, then reached down and plucked the ear bud and mike off the unconscious man. *These might be useful.*

Patting the man's pockets, he found a cell phone and turned it on. *Unlocked and full bars.* How was there any reception out here?

CHAPTER 17

DAD'S CLOSE. Haddie heard his tone as she scurried to the adjacent barn. She crouched behind a row of boxes in the cool building. In the larger building, the forklift driver unloaded the truck. The walls and ceiling appeared to be the same construction, but stood half the height and smelled like a horse barn. Stacks of provisions had been packed tightly across the dirt floor and rose to the steel trusses that supported the roof. The lights were off, but hung at the apex.

Cooper had walked in the opposite direction after she'd climbed out of the truck and ran for the most obvious hiding place, a stack of empty pallets at the front of the taller building. By the time she'd crept into the next building, he'd disappeared.

The soldier who seemed to be in charge directed the forklift. She and Cooper would both appear when they returned to the truck.

She'd moved to the side, by the outer wall. Her breathing had calmed once alarms hadn't sounded and no one had yelled as she darted into the storage area. *Where the hell is Cooper?* He couldn't have followed her directly, but she imagined he'd circle around and meet her. Enough light came through the windows in the doors so that she could see, but the rising sun only lit the rear of the building.

Her phone vibrated in her pocket, and she put down a knee to dig under her stiff vest. She didn't recognize the number, but the tone could only be Dad. "What are you doing? If I could hear you, he could hear you. Where are you?" He signed the message, "T."

"Dad," she whispered. How did he have a phone? Why hadn't he used it before? Shaking, she texted, "I'm in the small barn. Where they store the food. Where are you?"

"Was underground. We've escaped, maybe. I'm not sure what they have waiting for me on the surface. I don't know the layout up top. However, I heard your tone, so you must be close. Who is with you?"

"Cooper."

"Hell. Where's Trig?"

"On the perimeter. If I give him the signal, he'll start a diversion."

"How did you get in?"

"We hid in a delivery truck. Semi." Could they use that to escape? "Can you meet me at the barn, where they are unloading the truck?" Dad could drive an eighteen-wheeler.

"I don't know. This escape could be a trap. How much of a diversion can you create?"

Haddie glanced at Cooper's pack. "C4. 5 lbs. 4 remote caps."

"We'll hold here. Be careful. See what you have around you. Munitions?"

"Peas and carrots."

"Okay. Careful. We'll wait as long as we can. Then sync Trig with the distraction."

Haddie turned off her screen. We? Excitement pumped in her veins and the pain that she'd focused on seemed to ease.

The forklift still rumbled in the larger attached building, so she might have time. The door closest to her lay three stacks down. She shoved her and Cooper's backpacks at the end of a row.

The sun had just lit the tops of telephone poles outside, but the sky had turned blue. No one moved in the paddock outside, and tilting her head from one side to the next against the window, she saw only unending plains and a hint at a road passing by. The latch to the door turned easily; if it was locked from the outside, she would need to wedge something between so she could sneak back in.

Cooper's face popped in from the left side of the building, and Haddie squeaked. His scowl deepened, and he opened the door. "You need to stay inside. There are patrols." Fresh air brought the distant whine of a four-wheeler.

He pushed in as she settled her heart. His clothes reeked from the man Haddie had killed.

"I've talked with Dad. We need to make a diversion, then we'll try to steal the semi and bust out of here."

Cooper touched his mustache with black, gloved fingers and then shook his head. "How — did you talk with him?"

"He broke out, I think with someone else. They were underground. He's waiting for us to create a diversion, including Trig, then we all make for the truck. I'm not sure who's phone he's using." Haddie frowned. "Where were you?"

He jerked a thumb at the back. "I couldn't just follow you. If that officer had seen my face, he'd know I wasn't the same man he sent in. I went out the side and followed the building around the back." He nodded his head in that direction. "There's a container back there marked with a flammable caution. Let me see if I can plant some C4 back there without catching any attention." He sounded distracted, as if thinking about something else.

Haddie led toward the wall where she'd stashed their packs. "What about the rest of the C4?"

"I'll find a place for them." He stopped. "Wait. I've got it. Do you have those surveillance photos?"

With a gloved finger, she scrolled to the aerial photo and recognized the barns where the truck had docked. Shipping containers and farm equipment were parked close behind. She enlarged the area.

"Stop, scroll up." Cooper hovered too close for his stench.

She passed three more containers before coming to the edge of the pond and the last container.

He pointed to the last one. "That's gone." He shifted the screen down. "These are portables with equipment — a satellite dish and antennas. But that one up by the pond. Not there." He scrolled back to their barn and enlarged a bulldozer behind the trailers. "They might have buried that container by the pond."

If that were true, Dad would have to get past the house and those portables to reach the truck. Haddie zoomed out. *That's too far.*

Cooper started digging through the packs.

They would have to draw as much attention to the barns as possible to get Dad past the house. Maybe Bruce was at one of the other properties he owned. That would be a blessing.

Through the back windows, she could see one of the

trailers; they didn't appear very close. *How exposed would Cooper be?*

He handed her four remote controls. "You keep these." Cooper turned for the door.

"Why?" Her vest started to feel warm and confining.

He shrugged. "In case I get caught." He tapped the rifle strapped over his shoulder. "You'll know."

PART III

We, the Noveilm, pose a threat, as ours is the path taken by so many of those foes who would impose order upon creation and thus destroy it.

CHAPTER 18

BRUCE CHUCKLED and tapped his cigar in the tray. Stanton stood close, his tablet ready. The monitor had gone quiet as Thomas waited for a response on his phone.

Bruce glanced out the window past the pond and plains where the sun had risen to light up the pines. *It had to be the daughter.* As hoped, Thomas had called for an extraction.

He motioned, and Stanton moved the tablet within reach. Bruce tucked the cigar in his teeth.

"Status?" he typed.

His communications officer responded immediately, "Squads have pulled back from the perimeter, but we're monitoring."

Bruce waved, and Stanton moved the tablet. Three full squads had been pulled back to the compound and tucked in the gulch behind the pond to avoid surveillance.

They'll only see one squad. Bruce smiled. His Epsilon squad he'd packed inside the house, as a last resort. *Do you suspect, Thomas?* Once the reinforcements breeched the perimeter, and the daughter had been identified, then he could tighten the noose. It would be over before noon, most likely.

He tapped his cigar into the tray. "Soft boil and toast."

Stanton nodded and typed on the tablet.

"I'm going to have to kill them, Stanton."

There were a good many others who revered the Noveilm. Bruce would rather not make a spectacle of it in front of them, but they were loyal to him.

"It is a shame." Stanton's voice carried no emotion. There had to be some, deep inside.

She'll come. "I wanted to have him join us, even the daughter. We are too close to New York; they might reconsider."

"Understood."

He puffed on his cigar. *It is a shame.* He'd been lucky to have Dylan for so long — he added a sense of support. Barbara, too. Lady Erica had been a wonderful asset, but required so much attention and maintenance.

Thomas could have been the brother in arms Bruce wanted. A warrior. *Let it go.* Part of him still wanted to hostage the daughter and force the issue. It would never work.

A tap sounded at the door and Stanton answered, returning with a small breakfast platter.

Bruce put his cigar in the ashtray and took a sip of coffee. *Now we wait.*

CHAPTER 19

WHEN THE BACK DOOR OPENED, Haddie jumped and pressed against a pile of boxes. Her feet shifted the sand at her feet, and she grimaced at the sound. The air had already warmed, and the musky scent of a stable grew without any breeze.

She held her breath and waited, but the only sound came from the adjacent barn as the forklift continued emptying the truck and the men's voices rose and fell.

Cooper whispered, "It's me." The sound carried over the tops of the rows of boxes.

Haddie sighed and stepped to the middle of the row. She'd moved back to her original hiding spot to keep an eye on the truck. If they had finished before Cooper returned, their plans would have to change. Her heart raced, but it had been beating fast since the back of the truck had been opened.

He climbed from behind boxes along the wall. "All set."

"Based on how far they have to go in and out to get a pallet, I think they're almost done." She grabbed her pack. "I moved all the extra ammo into this pack. Left the stuff we won't need in the other." Her pack weighed much less now. "I've got an idea to take out these two. I'd like to knock them out, rather than kill them."

She opened the four remotes and arranged them in her hands, her fingers over the triggers. Then she put her hands behind her head. "You've got a prisoner — get out your gun."

Cooper shook his head. "You watch too much television. They'll call it in as soon as they see us and likely still pull their weapons. I'll end up shooting them anyway."

Haddie lowered her arms. "Do you have a plan?"

"Not a good one." His lips tightened, and he touched his mustache. "I'm counting on you and your father's abilities more than anything. First, we get Trig started. Wait a minute after that, possibly until they finish unloading, then detonate three of them. The focus should be in the back where I've placed the explosives, so we go out the front."

He gestured to their left. A series of large, garage-sized doors hung on rollers that allowed them to be slid open. Probably with a serious amount of noise. They were also exposed to the adjacent barn.

"We sneak out to the truck and secure it. Then detonate the last to keep the focus in the back. From there we can cover Thomas and anyone he brings."

Haddie studied the front bay doors. *I hadn't really thought it out.* "And, if they," she said, motioning into the larger barn, "see us?"

Cooper tilted his head with a light shrug. "Then I shoot them."

Her pulse slowed, and she felt empty as she imagined the man vanishing in front of David. *Dad needs me.* She pulled out her phone and texted Trig. "We're ready, go."

When she got a confirmation, she switched to Dad's

contact. He'd wait and move after the distraction had started. "Get ready, be careful. I love you," she texted. Her heart dropped. *What if this doesn't work?* What if they shoot him trying to get away? They didn't have a lot of options.

Dad replied, "I love you. Be careful."

She took a deep breath, tucked her phone away, and carefully picked up the remotes that would set everything in motion. Once they started the diversion, they had no other choices.

The forklift driver laughed at something, and she closed her eyes. She hated making a decision that might lead to someone dying. *They have Dad.*

Cooper led the way along the wall farthest from the unloading of the truck.

A couple of the spaces between the cardboard boxes and steel walls were tight enough that she had to take off her backpack and wedge in sideways. Each row exposed them. Anxiety tightened her shoulders. The last row blocked most of the view into the adjacent barn, so she could focus on the exits.

The two doors were massive. The one small dirty window in the middle only showed the shadowed underside of a metal roof that created an exterior pen. They moved to the door closest to the truck and, unfortunately, the barn where the forklift chugged.

His hand on the latch of the door, Cooper nodded. "Now."

Haddie plunged three remotes at once. Despite distance and the walls, the blast came as one deafening shriek. The ground under her feet shook. Thuds sounded at the rear as debris slammed into sheet metal. Glass shattered. Steel groaned at the back of the barns. Haddie glanced up at the beams, dust drifting off in waterfalls. She imagined the whole place falling down on them. A second smaller blast sounded like a firework launching a shrill whine. *Time to leave.*

Cooper slid the door aside, letting in cool, fresh air. He'd opened the latch and she hadn't heard it. The forklift operator and the officer yelled. There were voices from the front, and her chest grew tight. Almost seeming distant, the crackle and churn of fire echoed from behind the barn.

An overhang shaded the area outside the door, and dust rose from the ground. An acrid, burning scent wafted in the air. Cooper cautiously leaned out the slim opening he'd made. His head jerked for her to follow, and he stepped out.

A gunshot sounded nearby, and Haddie froze with one glove on the sliding door. Dad? Too close.

Cooper crouched down, his rifle ready. The sun shone bright across the empty plains. No troops waited for them. The only breaks in the flat horizon were electric poles and fences.

He motioned with his hand for Haddie to continue.

CHAPTER 20

THOMAS HUNG onto the hole he'd created as fresh dirt slid down onto his bare feet. The other prisoner stood at the open door at the far end. The roar outside continued after the explosions. *That was a distraction, Haddie.* Munitions? He had expected something a little less violent. *Let's hope this works.* Even if Bruce had been expecting him to escape, they might be confused now.

How long? He wanted to give time for guards to get out of position. The ground still seemed to vibrate.

Before the explosives went off, he had dug out the hole he'd created enough to see to the sky, though the ground-shaking blasts had shifted it nearly closed again. They wouldn't have long before Bruce got things under control. Did he have any competent officers? Sometimes strong military figures failed to delegate.

The upper corner darkened as smoke billowed into the sky. The sharp scent of chemical fires tinged the reek of the sewage in their prison.

Climbing the pile of earth, he crouched at the edge of being exposed and pulled the guard's 9mm Glock from his waistband. Thomas gave the signal and hoped his questionable cellmate ran up the entrance ramp.

The terrain to the north included scraggly pines and cottonwoods that grew down into a ravine. The inferno burned black and red to the south. Ahead to the east he found what he expected; a form on the ground that had turned to stare at the conflagration. They both flinched when the sound of an automatic rifle sounded behind Thomas. Bullets riddled the figure.

Thomas had time to turn as his blond comrade took out another guard lying farther south, closer to the flames. *Hell. I hope he's on my side.* Black smoke plumed into the air and spread a diffused haze at the base.

Sliding down loose dirt, Thomas winced when the sharp edge of the trailer tugged at his toe. After he dropped to the floor, he ran for the exit ramp. Haddie better be playing it safe. He would never have let her try this. Obviously, Trig had no control of the situation, but why would Kiana allow Haddie to come with Cooper? She'd survived the ambush to risk herself in a reckless, hurried attempt.

He exited the container, stalked up the ramp, and pushed through the corner where the tarp hung loose. His cellmate knelt and watched the house to the west. A pond sat behind, but there appeared to be no activity around the house. He heard voices toward the south where the fire raged. The morning sky had darkened under the smoke, and a haze hung on the ground, spreading around the tan colored barn. The semi waited in front. A good distance, but it might be possible.

A windmill stood by the house, and the light breeze clicked the blades slowly. A quiet homey sound after the mayhem.

He nodded and led the way across the field. *This might*

work. Haddie had grown into her own. She'd worked her way out of scrapes that he never would have expected her to survive. *I'm proud of her.* She balanced self-preservation and helping her friends with compassion, even for those who didn't deserve it. He'd become jaded over the years. Her mother's death had hardened him, and he'd brought her up to be a little tougher because of that. *I'd hoped she wouldn't need it.*

Thomas skidded to a stop as a man burst out of a trailer to their left. They were caught between three portables and the house. Glock raised, he paused as the man ignored them and raced to the back where he could see the fire and smoke.

Thomas lowered his gun and looked back to his cell-mate. The man had his rifle trained between the portables, but hadn't fired. The yellow haze over his eyes sent a small shiver through Thomas. He'd deal with the man once they got to Haddie. At least, he would disarm him.

The thickening smoke masked the side of the barn. The air remained clear at the front of the semi, but it wouldn't for long. *No sign of Haddie.*

CHAPTER 21

HADDIE TOOK FORCED breaths to push down her anxiety. *It's going fine.* A shadow had risen, blotting out the sunrise behind them and returning the area ahead to twilight. The stench of burning chemicals grew stronger, and smoke drifted above and around the side of the building.

Cooper edged to the corner of the larger barn and leaned low to peer under the truck. The semi stuck out from the main building, the rear wedged into its opening. Through the haze, Haddie could see underneath, and no feet moved on the other side. *We're clear.* She stepped quicker to catch up to Cooper.

Another two short bursts of automatic fire sounded from the north. *That has to be Dad.* This was the second time she'd heard it. If she had the layout correct in her head, he'd come from the north or northeast. The haze crawled around them, threatening to engulf them.

As they neared the front of the truck, the brick house came into view with two garage doors and three arched windows. She cringed, but followed. Anyone looking out those windows would see them.

She faltered at a shape in the dirt; a man in a red and black mackinaw lay face down on the ground. Blood had soaked into a black pool of mud around his head. *They probably killed the driver.* Her cheeks flushed. *This isn't my fault.* Still, he wouldn't be dead if they weren't trying to rescue Dad. She'd chosen his truck and fate.

Cooper crept along the grill of the truck and peeked around the edge.

From Haddie's position behind the massive engine and front of the truck, she couldn't see the far corner of the barn, but a small silver-white building with open stalls sat to the northeast closer to the house. From the aerial photos, she'd imagined it was a garage. The smoke had reached the back of the small building, curling around it like tentacles.

Turning back to Haddie, Cooper nodded toward the driver's door. He took two careful steps with the rifle poised at the barn where she couldn't see. He moved toward the dead driver. *Keys.* She climbed up and opened the driver's door and confirmed that the driver had taken them. *Time to go, Dad.*

She left the door open. Dad would have to drive. *I should have learned.* He'd suggested it when she was in high school.

The keys jingled and she shut her eyes. Did the driver have a family waiting somewhere? Her heart pounding, she leaned a gloved hand on the truck. *C'mon, Dad.*

Cooper handed her the keys. "Don't start it up yet." He slid to the front corner of the truck, his back against the grill, and kept his rifle trained to the northeast.

Haddie fumbled the keys and strained against the stiff vest to peer out the passenger window at the house. Why had no one come out to check on the explosions? Maybe they'd come out while she and Cooper were on the far side of the truck.

Leaving the keys waiting in the ignition, she joined Cooper, peeking past him to the barn. The reek of the fire wafted in thin smoke that trailed around them. She'd had concerns about their plan, long before they'd been locked into the back of the semi's trailer, but there had been no other option except to wait. After Dad's last interaction with Bruce, Haddie couldn't take the chance. As hare-brained as the plan had been, Cooper had believed in it. *Please, let it work.* Would Meg's angels be watching?

"Down." Cooper crouched.

Haddie lowered herself below the bumper. Shapes moved in the haze behind the open stalls. A figure climbed over one of the fences, and she held her breath. The rising sun and layers of clothes made her sweat. Her pack weighed on her shoulders. *I should at least hold my gun.* Her hand touched her holster, but she didn't pull the weapon.

Smoke swirled around and enveloped the approaching people.

Dad and a shorter man broke around the corner of the barn and ran along the front of the building. Her stomach fluttered and she smiled. *We're going to make it.*

The man behind looked like a soldier with dirty blond hair. He had a rifle.

Haddie froze. His face glowed with coercion.

Dad would know. He could see Lady Erica's effect.

She imagined Josh and relaxed. Perhaps this had been another prisoner. Haddie stepped around Cooper.

"Wait." He growled in a whisper.

She didn't, even as Dad waved her back. The two had almost reached the back of the truck.

Bruce's tone rang out to her left, from the house. Haddie

spun, searching for a target. Dark haze left the building, a mere silhouette.

Bruce pressed down on her with his power, and she resisted with her tone. Dad had tried to explain how debilitating the rage had made him. *I'm already angry.*

This had all been a trap.

Dad's tone rang out. He'd learned how to protect himself. Haddie smiled at him.

The blond man jerked his rifle and slammed the stock into the back of Dad's head. Dad's song disappeared. He crumpled to the dirt, his gun tumbling away.

"Back," yelled Cooper. His feet scuffed on the ground behind her.

Still no sign of Bruce. A shape moved in the haze.

Dad shifted on the ground but didn't rise. The sand around him glinted. With his rifle pointed at the back of her dad's head, the man who had hit him backed away.

She stumbled forward. Her jaw clenched, fighting Bruce's power and the urge to destroy the blond man. Somehow, he'd tricked Dad. *Can I do this?* She'd listened to Liz's video and practiced enough to try making two tones at once. *Overtone.*

A gunshot echoed and Cooper grunted. She turned to find him sprawled out near the driver, his rifle discarded in the dirt. He gasped a breath. *Trig's vests work.*

Dad shifted his face in the dirt.

It's on me. Haddie opened her mouth.

A shape moved in the murky gap behind the stalls — two figures. Another appeared to the left. They walked slowly and purposefully. Haddie spun toward the house. *More.* Small figures and large, at varying distances, moved toward her. She couldn't make them all disappear. Orange-eyed demons at least the height of her or Dad stayed farther back. The smaller shapes had rifles trained at them. *Too many*. At best, she could distract them — for a moment.

She spun. The figures were closing in. The blond-haired man who had betrayed Dad stepped back toward the corner of the barn. *Get up, Dad.*

Cooper hadn't moved. Had the round gone through the bulletproof vest?

The soldiers resolved into men, garbed in camouflage and holding automatic rifles. She might be able to kill some of them, but the others would mow her down, or the demons would reach her.

Bruce sauntered into a ring of five soldiers, his attendant trailing behind a few steps. The demons, more than half a dozen, waited in the murky smoke. Their forms were the more human type. *I can't make them all vanish.* She held her protective tone.

"Once again, you join us. What a mess." Bruce might have been speaking to either one of them, but he walked toward Dad.

His power did not press on her too hard, as if he didn't consider her a concern. His path took him between her and the blond man who had backed to the corner of the barn. His soldiers stepped slowly closer.

Dad's tone rose again. He lay nearly under the truck and his head shifted, as if it were too heavy to lift.

Bruce crossed between them and leaned on the container. She flushed at his casual demeanor. *Arrogant.* Did he plan on killing them? She couldn't possibly attack six soldiers and more than that many demons. The last time she'd tried it on a large group, she'd destroyed half this many and frozen the others in time.

Bruce wouldn't be affected, and he wore a holstered gun.

Haddie jolted as someone grabbed her gun. A stiff prod let her know a rifle wedged in her back. She twisted a glance over her shoulder. A soldier had come up behind her. The demons still waited a few steps behind the semi-circle of soldiers. They were prepared for her to attempt an attack. Some would die. *And so would I.*

"I think we're done here, Thomas." Bruce tilted his head.

Dad shifted, eyes on Bruce, wrists pushing on the ground, and one knee unable to find purchase under him. Blood from the hit on his head trickled down his neck. He blinked constantly.

"I'm sorry it didn't work out." Bruce reached for his gun.

Haddie shrieked. Her tone rang out, but squelched against Bruce's protective song. The rebound staggered her.

He drew a Glock from his holster. Even in the smoke, it glinted.

Leaving herself unprotected, his power pressed down on her. Her heart raced with rage; blood pressure exploding, she felt as though her brain might burst. *I want to kill him.* She growled, her tone faltering as she attempted to drag her protection up.

She heard Dad's tone belatedly shift into an attack.

Bruce casually aimed the gun.

Her tone pushed against Bruce's power. *No. Harmony.* They'd overcome Lady Erica. Dad looked up at her with a grimace, his eyes haunted and bleak. Pale blue light leaked from his skin.

She flinched at the shot.

Her dad's tone winked out.

She saw the bullet hit. Her heart stopped. His mangled face dropped into the sand.

Bruce fired a second shot. An ugly red hole appeared in Dad's hair.

"Bastard," she choked out. Her ears rang. Tears formed at the edges of her eyes. She tried to look away. She felt weak. Aching knees threatened to let her fall. Her throat tightened so that she only managed a thin croak. "Dad."

She'd done this. *Kiana. Meg.* They would never forgive her for his death. It had been a trap. *I killed him.*

Haddie fought against the thought. *Bruce did this.* "I'm going to kill you." Her voice rasping, he likely didn't hear her.

Bruce turned, rolling his shoulders in a casual maneuver against the container, and fired twice into her chest.

CHAPTER 22

HADDIE FELL on her back from the impact. *He planned on killing us both.* If she hadn't come, Dad might be alive. The miasma of smoke filled her lungs as she gasped. Tears clouded the dark sky.

Under the vest, pain blossomed across her left side. She choked a sob back. Bruce would finish her off. Even now, he pressed with his power, but her tone held the rage back.

Through the blur, she could see Bruce's assistant as he gasped. Mouth open, he faced her, clutching the tablet to his chest. His face twisted in shock and concern. *Over me?* His body twitched, as if fighting an urge to run to her aid.

The other soldiers held their ground in front of the barn, watching her. The demons lingered in a partial circle from the stalls to a position in front of the bus. Cooper lay motionless to the right.

Haddie lifted her head.

Bruce did not seem surprised. His expression conveyed annoyance, if anything. He hadn't moved away from the truck, but stood straight, his demeanor no longer haughty and relaxed. "What a mess."

He aimed for her head.

She closed her eyes. In her mind she imagined the soldiers and demons where they stood. *Intent.* She pictured her dad's body on the ground, the truck backed into the barn, and Bruce beside the container.

Haddie opened her eyes and locked onto Bruce. "Go to hell," she growled with an overtone. It rang out in the air around her.

The man beside her jerked and his head tilted awkwardly.

Behind Bruce, the bottom quarter of the truck had vanished. Tires, parts of axles, supports, and the bottom edge of the container were gone, and the rest dropped toward the ground. Metal groaned where the back rested against the barn walls as the truck and trailer twisted.

Bruce frowned at the noise and began to turn.

Pain prickled along her cheeks. Haddie's eyes trailed down to her dad's corpse. *I'm sorry, Dad.* She should have acted sooner. The soldier beside her made a wet thud as he folded onto the ground.

The container and barn walls shrieked apart as momentum crashed the truck down onto Bruce. His gun fired harmlessly into the sand as the steel container slammed him to the ground. The full force crushed him. His blood sprayed across her vision before metal blocked her view of her dad's corpse.

She hoped it had missed Dad's body. Her eyes blinked, staring at the bent top of the container. Black dust drifted off the white paint.

A bullet dusted the dirt next to her, and Haddie rolled to her side, curling away from the gunfire. It came from the direction of the barn. She'd sent a thin slice of her power through the neck of every soldier and demon.

It either hadn't been enough, or she had missed one of them.

The gunshots faded as she dropped into her visions. Again, the red-coated soldiers plagued her nightmares. Dad fought a group in a ravine with a frozen river and icicles that dripped from stone, a single soldier who stabbed into the thick coat she wore, and a pair who dragged a battered man behind their horses.

Her sense of the present returned with the clatter of gunfire and the acrid scent of smoke, the sharp tang of petroleum, and Cooper returning fire over her. He knelt where he had fallen earlier and gripped one of his pistols with two hands to fire evenly spaced shots. Facing Cooper, she closed her eyes and sobbed, not for the pain in her chest or the burning fire that raced over her skin, but her dad's anguished eyes when he knew Bruce would kill him.

A bullet thudded against her backpack, and she sucked in a breath from the pain. It immobilized her, as if she'd broken a bone. Teeth clamped, she waited for another shot to find her legs or the back of her head. Dirt sprinkled on her from the gunfire.

The soldier she'd killed stared at her in surprise. She'd severed his head, removed a thin layer across his neck. The demons too were little more than lumps in the field. Obviously, she'd missed at least one.

The blond-haired man. He'd been over at the corner of the barn, nearly out of sight. She'd failed to kill him. In her mind she'd seen each one arrayed around her, and the truck waiting behind Bruce. *Dad.* Her cheeks flushed with anger, competing against the aftermath of using her power. Had she missed others?

Roll over. Kill him. He'd led her dad into the trap. *The one I caused.*

She forced her back to move and gasped at the pain. Between the shots to her chest and back, she couldn't be sure the vest had stopped the bullets. Her skin burned from using her power.

The gunfire stopped. Was the blond-haired man dead?

"Back off," Cooper growled. He pointed his gun toward someone.

"She's hurt." A mild voice, concerned, spoke.

She hadn't killed the assistant. The way he had looked at her had been — grievous. He had feared for her safety. Why? Coerced, he should be faithful to Bruce.

"Step back." Cooper knelt.

"She is the last of the Noveilm, except the children." His tone turned plaintive. "We will be lost without them."

Trig was on his way, but this couldn't have been all of Bruce's troops. Teeth clamped, she pushed up on one elbow.

Her breath shaky, she tried to look up at the assistant. "I'm okay. How many other soldiers are there?"

He spoke crisply with an officious air. "You have twelve squads. One hundred and six soldiers and eleven technicians manning the communications."

Haddie coughed at the noisome smoke. *I have?* Did he suggest they were under her control? *Because I'm what he calls Noveilm?* It might keep Trig and Cooper alive.

"What's your name?"

Cooper lowered his gun, but didn't holster it.

"Stanton." The assistant cleared his throat. "Shall I recall your troops?"

"From where?" She winced as she tried to face Stanton. *Do I trust this?*

"You have three squads moving toward our location

from the north. Nine squads are preparing to intercept the intruders from northwest. The communication . . ."

Trig. "Have them all stand down. Stop moving, or firing, or anything." She gasped as she rolled to her knees. *Surely I've got a broken rib.*

Stanton looked like a businessman with his dark hair, expensive navy suit, and leather shoes. He swiped across his screen one-handed with an intense look. "Two squads are not responding. I fear Elon might have employed them."

"Does Elon have blond hair?" Haddie stood, her gruesome handiwork arrayed around them. She felt no remorse or guilt. Dad's body lay hidden behind the truck. Her plan had worked, but she'd frozen when her dad needed her most. She imagined the man striking the back of her dad's head, and she wanted his body here, with the others.

Stanton nodded, and still worked on the tablet. "Yes, he does. The local firefighters have been alerted to the explosions. They are in route, ETA twenty minutes. I can have the fires out and the area cleared before they arrive. I will need the remaining squads in the north to assist. The authorities will still want to investigate, but you have contacts with the local government that can recall them."

Cooper stood by Haddie's shoulder. "Why are you helping us?"

Stanton looked up, surprised. "She is Noveilm. The last."

Haddie studied his face. What twisted devotion did he have to the Noveilm? *I just killed his boss.* She couldn't trust him fully, but if Trig could get here safely, then she could relax. "Do what you need to. I want to see Dad. We're not leaving his body here."

CHAPTER 23

HADDIE TURNED toward the truck and grimaced as she took a step. *I don't want to see his face.* Smoke flowed around them with a sickly chemical scent. Her eyes watered. Breathing hurt. Her back stung the worst, though pain throbbed in her chest along her left side. A sob escaped, more from a distant self-pity than any of her injuries.

Stanton followed them, intent on his tablet.

Cooper matched her slow, stumbling gait easily. "We need to be careful. I don't trust this man, nor do I believe that local authorities are just going to ignore all of this. We should plan on a quick extraction by Trig and be done with this."

She didn't particularly care what they did. "I need to get — his body out of here."

Fuel had leaked from the cab and formed a pool of sharp smelling mud. Metal filings dusted the dirt in a swath where the bottom of the trailer was missing from the use of her power. The frame had bent from tipping over.

Bruce's legs twisted out from under the front of the

container. Three yards away, her dad's body lay unmolested by the truck. His hands and bare feet were twisted awkwardly, and the blood left no doubt.

Haddie dropped to the ground and retched.

Cooper rested his hand on her shoulder, and she pulled away.

This can't be happening. Kiana will hate me. Meg will never understand. Haddie couldn't imagine a life without her dad. He'd always been there.

The sound of four-wheelers coming toward them forced Haddie to wipe her lips and stand. "Who is that?"

Stanton stepped up. "Your men. They will take us and his body to a small cabin where the fire department will not look. The other bodies will be moved to the ravine, for the present. With your permission, I will recall some of the perimeter defense back to the compound to aid with the removal."

She looked at Bruce's feet. How would they get him out from under the truck? "Yes. Whatever." *Am I making another mistake?* The four-wheelers were close.

Cooper turned away, weapon still in his hand. "We should go with Trig."

More vehicles — trucks and four-wheelers — had started. *I don't care.* She didn't know what to do and couldn't bring herself to decide.

Two ATVs carrying three men in fatigues pulled around the front of the truck. They glanced at her nervously, but moved directly for her dad. For a brief second, she didn't want them to touch him, but she just turned away. "We'll go with them."

Stanton worked on his tablet, swiping out words one-handed. "Your outside men are twenty-two minutes out. Based on their present location, that includes time to pick up their snipers. The emergency vehicles will be here in fourteen."

Haddie sighed. "Can you give me coordinates to send to Trig? Wherever I'll be?" She pulled out her phone and avoided looking at the soldiers picking up her dad's body.

As Stanton read off the numbers, she sent Trig a terse message. What would he do when he found out her dad was dead? Would he leave her?

Cooper relaxed and lowered his gun to his thigh. "How long do we plan to stay here?"

Haddie stared at her dust-covered feet. "I don't know. I need to get Dad someplace to bury him. Oregon?"

Stanton tucked his tablet to his chest. "You have two helicopters and a jet at your disposal." He motioned her toward the four-wheeler that did not have her dad in the back. "We can accommodate most any need."

I need Dad back. She closed her eyes as her stomach twisted with a threat to retch again. Nothing would ever be the same. *What would this do to Kiana?* She stumbled toward the passenger seat and winced as she climbed in. The bulletproof vest pressed painfully against her chest and back.

Stanton slid behind the wheel. "Elon, the blond man who had been planted with your father, is not responding. He could be trouble."

"The man who hit him?" She winced as she imagined the rifle stock slamming into the back of Dad's head.

"Yes. He is one of the highest lieutenants. Men might follow him."

"Planted with Dad?"

"Yes," Stanton said. "He played along with your father. The plan was to get him a cell phone so he could call in for an extraction. We would of course know the details and intercede. However, you were already on the property."

Haddie's stomach churned. *If I hadn't been here . . .* Why had Dad trusted Elon?

Cooper scowled as he holstered his gun and climbed into the four-wheeler where her dad's body lay in the back. One of the soldiers sat in the driver's seat and drove off quickly toward the front of the truck.

As her dad's corpse jerked in the back of Cooper's ATV, Haddie leaned over and puked into the dirt.

CHAPTER 24

DALE HELD on as the soldier drove through the remains of Haddie's carnage. Thick, acrid smoke drifted over the bodies and detached heads, but it only made the scene more unsettling. *Noveilm.* No one should have power like that. Did Stanton truly worship them, or was this a ruse?

In a single move, Haddie had beheaded over a dozen soldiers, men and mutants alike. She had saved him.

His apprehension had started in Albuquerque, but now he questioned what his world would be like with people like Haddie. Stanton had said she was the last, but what about these children he mentioned?

The soldier beside him looked shaken and nervous. Because of Haddie, or was there a trap waiting for them? *They could have killed us by the truck.* The blond Elon had certainly been trying, and Stanton believed some of the men joined him. Dale rested his hand on his holster.

They traveled northeast from the barn area, driving between the covered paddock and the house. Sporting large extinguishers, soldiers worked to douse the flaming containers he'd ignited. The driver skirted around a tarp-covered trench, then continued in the same direction.

They drove to the right of an expanding gulch with tree-tops rising against the flat plains. If this were a trap, they were driving into a desolate area.

His chest hurt from the gunshots into the vest, though it had lessened from those first couple of minutes. The jostling ride didn't make it feel any better. The terrain had Dale holding firm until they reached a worn trail that headed due west. The ride turned a little smoother along the dirt track. The rising sun blinded him until they turned at an intersection. He could see Haddie staring blankly at them, or perhaps at her father's corpse at their backs.

He knew the shock she felt. He'd lived it when his son died. They'd expected his death, worried about it, but still couldn't accept the loss when the doctor came out to inform them. His wife, ex-wife, had never recovered. *I just went back to work.* What did Haddie have? Like him, she'd lost any chance to return to her life in Eugene.

The trench to their left grew thick with trees and brush before they reached a small cabin where the dirt trail looped around it. Hardly more than a room, it had a rough porch and an overhang to sit under. Evergreens grew to either side, and the ravine lay behind it.

Haddie stumbled out of her seat, and Stanton moved briskly to be at her side. "You'll only need to be here for a short while. Our contacts will have this cleared in an hour or so."

Dale hardly believed that any investigator would ignore the devastation behind the barn, let alone a semi and trailer inexplicably missing wheels, axles, and part of the under-carriage. If Trig arrived soon, he'd feel better. At least they were far away from the house and barn.

Haddie stood in the sand, still in her black operations clothes with the cowl over her head. "You said you can fly me anywhere? Today?"

Stanton nodded, almost seeming to be pleased with himself. "Yes. The helicopters are stationed at the airport, but we can have one come here. Once everything is clear."

"Plan for it." She straightened, glancing at Dale. "I need to talk to Trig first." She appeared on the verge of crying.

Stanton scrolled on his tablet. "Eighteen minutes from their present location to here. Please warn your outside man, Trig, about the emergency vehicles; we would not want any conflict there."

Cooper cocked his head and shook it lightly. A helicopter out of here sounded like the best plan. The sooner the better.

CHAPTER 25

HADDIE SAT on the steps of the porch with a glass of luke-warm water and tried to draw a lungful of fresh air. She likely had a broken rib, as difficult as it was to take a deep breath. *This isn't real.*

Cooper sat in the shade of one of the four-wheelers. He hadn't taken off his vest, so she hadn't. Stanton had promised one of Bruce's squads would be arriving to circle the cabin, in case Elon found them.

I can get Dad's body out of here. She didn't like using Bruce's men or equipment, but she didn't see a lot of other ways. *I'll ask Trig.* She looked down at her phone, unable to call Kiana.

Haddie blinked tears away, lifted her head to the sky, and looked at the blue expanse. The smoke to the south had diminished to a small line that leaned to the west. If she had just acted a few seconds sooner, she could have saved Dad. *I didn't.* She tried for a deep breath and winced. *I can't do this to Kiana.* Putting down her water, she picked up the phone.

Two soldiers jogged through the brush to the south, and Cooper stood to draw his weapon.

Stanton spoke to her loudly enough that Cooper could hear. "Those are your men. They're bringing a body bag for your father's remains."

Haddie wilted at the comment, and dropped her hand to her lap. The female soldier carried the rolled plastic under her arm.

As they reached for his body, Haddie turned away. A sob escaped, and she focused on the phone. Lead fingers typed out the number.

Kiana's tone was frantic. "What's going on, Haddie? Trig says you rerouted him to another location. We've had reports of an explosion and fire from all of our investigators."

"We . . ." A sob interrupted and Haddie sucked in a breath. "Dad — he — they — Bruce . . ." She stopped, clapping a hand over her mouth as bawled into her fingers.

"Haddie?" Kiana's tone sounded plaintive, as if she already guessed.

A loud zip sounded, and Haddie looked at the soldiers leaning over her dad's body bag. She managed to speak through loud convulsive gasps. "He's dead."

Kiana didn't respond as Haddie cried. The soldiers glanced over with a questioning look before they headed back south. Cooper returned to his seat, his gun still drawn. Each breath stabbed her chest and back with pain.

Stanton spoke. "Your people are coming."

Haddie wiped snot from her face. "I'm sorry, Kiana." She could hear engines, but couldn't see anything with the pines beside the building.

"What happened?" Kiana's tone was higher, as though she might be crying.

"Bruce shot him. I should have been able to act quicker." Large engines, possibly trucks, were almost to the cabin. "Trig's here."

"Do you have his body?"

"Yes." Haddie stared at the black plastic.

Kiana's tone hardened. "Is Bruce dead?"

A black Jeep Wrangler with oversized tires pulled in front of the cabin, lifting dust as it braked for a quick stop. Trig drove while Zipper stood on the passenger side through an open top with her rifle aimed at them, then Stanton. More vehicles idled behind, hidden by the evergreens.

"Bruce is dead. Some of his men are still out there, but the others are helping." Haddie stood.

"Helping? Never mind. Just get out of there. Bring his body back." Kiana's voice faltered. "Call me when you and Trig have a plan."

Wiping her face on her sleeve, Haddie pocketed her phone and motioned for Stanton to stay on the porch. She eased herself down the steps, veered in a circle around her dad's corpse, and took short breaths that didn't hurt too much. Trig's people were climbing out of three other dark colored jeeps. Zipper didn't take her gun, or eyes, off Stanton.

Trig glanced between Haddie, the body bag, and Stanton. His right hand leaned on the steering wheel, steadying a gun. He waited until Haddie was at his door to speak. "Is that T?"

Haddie nodded. "I should have acted sooner."

Trig's lips tightened and he looked up at Stanton. "What is going on here? They pulled back. Who is that?"

"His name is Stanton. He's helping. His orders are what

pulled Bruce's soldiers back and let you through. He was Bruce's assistant."

"You can't trust him, Haddie." Trig frowned. "I say we drop him where he stands and get out of here."

Haddie raised her eyebrows. "No. He is helping. Now that Bruce is gone, he . . ." She couldn't explain about her powers, or the Noveilm. "If he hadn't helped, Cooper and I would have never survived. He's going to be able to cover up the explosion, and everything. Bruce had some locals in his pocket, I imagine. Anyway, he can get me a helicopter to get Dad's body out of here."

"I can do that." Trig nodded toward the back of the Wrangler.

Haddie imagined the body bag stuffed in the back for a two-day ride back to Oregon. When Aaron had died, it had only been a few hours away, but Crow had driven to that hill. *That's where Dad should be buried.*

Kiana would agree. Haddie glanced at Cooper, then Stanton. *I don't really trust him.* A helicopter this afternoon would get Dad home a lot quicker. Kiana could come. *I need to call Sam to speak with Meg.* How difficult would it be for the girl?

Haddie closed her eyes. *I can't drive for days.* She shook her head. "Helicopter. Kiana can come with me. Cooper even as a guard. You can come."

Trig's frown grew harsh. "I can't let you do that. There's no reason for you to trust them — him."

Her face flushed and Haddie frowned. "I'm not asking your permission. For the moment, Stanton seems genuinely willing to help me." She couldn't explain everything and didn't need to. Kiana had some right to argue about what happened to Dad's body, not Trig. "He's proved himself loyal."

"You can't trust they'll remain loyal. We need to get you out of here."

Haddie shook her head and waved at Stanton to approach. He took quick steps off the porch and focused on her. "How long before we're clear and can get this helicopter here?" she asked.

Stanton scrolled across his pad. He typed by swiping from one letter to the next like a text. Three replies came in from different sources. "I assume we can return to the compound in thirty minutes. I can have the helicopter meet us there five minutes afterward. They're fueled and on standby."

Kiana would hate the idea.

Haddie pulled out her phone and dialed.

Sniffling, Kiana answered. "Are you and Trig picking me up? I'm ready."

"I can get us one of Bruce's helicopters. It'll get us to Oregon in hours, rather than days."

Trig shook his head and leaned down as if to speak.

Haddie continued, "It means trusting Bruce's assistant. He got us out of that mess alive and helped me get Dad's body."

Kiana coughed. "Okay. I'm lost, Haddie. I need to see him." Her tone sounded like she'd broken.

"I'll see if one of Trig's people can pick you up." Haddie hung up, knowing that Kiana wasn't thinking it through clearly.

Maybe I'm not either. Trig had been aggressive, though, trying to control something he didn't understand. *It's not his choice.* She studied Stanton. The compassion she'd seen in that moment when she'd been shot told her more than anything else.

Haddie faced Trig. "We're going to the compound, then

taking the helicopter." She nodded toward her dad's body. "I'll ride in the four-wheeler with Dad. You can follow, or go on your way. However, I'd like your support."

CHAPTER 26

HADDIE WINCED as they bounced along in the four-wheeler. Sweat poured down her chest and sides under the vest. The heat rose with the late morning sun, and the grass smelled like hay. *Am I making the right choice?*

Stanton drove Haddie. Cooper followed with Dad's body. She couldn't bring herself to get near the black bag. Trig had fumed for a while, but he hadn't left her. His four Jeeps drove in pairs on each side of the trail as if escorting them.

She'd reacted badly toward Trig and didn't like depending on Bruce's men or helicopter, but she didn't want to drive all that way with Dad. *I'll apologize to Trig.* She couldn't think straight. Even as they headed toward the last remnants of smoke, she couldn't believe that Dad was dead. Her eyes focused on the gray wisp curving to the west.

Within sight of the tan colored barn, a pair of soldiers walked with rifles on their shoulders. They stopped to watch the caravan but didn't react. Stanton must have alerted them that they were returning.

Even in what seemed to be empty flatlands, the occasional pine or brush dotted the grass. Troops could be hiding anywhere. *I can't wait to get away from here.* She could see the house with its little windmill; before Bruce, this had been someone's home with happier memories.

Soldiers knelt between each portable, watching them approach. Air conditioners hummed beside each of the containers, and equipment dotted the roofs. Besides the charred and melted remains of three containers behind the barn, the house and drive looked normal. They passed the area where Dad had likely been held captive. *All a trap for me.* Of course, Bruce wanted to kill them both. What had she expected?

Her massacre had been cleaned up. The bodies were gone, though the truck still lay on its side. How had Stanton's people convinced the local authorities to leave? A section of the truck was missing, and the containers in the back must have had munitions in them. Her dad's blood had left a muddy pool. Had someone shoveled sand over it?

Four soldiers stood in the grass along the drive. They watched the horizon as Haddie and the others pulled in behind them. Even as she stepped out, they remained alert. *They expect trouble.*

Trig jumped out as they parked in front of the house. "If we're doing this, then at least go inside while you wait for the helicopter, and have my people in there with you."

Haddie nodded. Other than Stanton at the other end of a tablet, there was little reason these soldiers should care what happened to her. *I just need to get Dad out of here.*

Trig motioned to one of the people, and they drove over the lawn and around the back of the building.

Grass grew along the walkway, and flowers decorated the brick walls. A glass entry door created a scene of a rural family home. As Stanton led the way inside, cool air breezed across her cheeks with the strong scent of cigars. She'd used the stall at the cabin, but she could use a proper bathroom. Maybe in the helicopter she could lose the vest.

The walls inside were deep reddish wood, and the foyer had a cream carpet covering the tile. The coziness ended there. Three computer monitors stretched across a long gray desk at the back window of what might have been a living room once. A single office chair waited, pushed toward the center of the room.

The pond out back was bordered with berms and brush, a tree shaded the grass outside, and chairs sat around a used fire pit. She had to step closer to see over the monitors. The Jeep parked near the tree, and Trig's two men stood behind it.

Trig's people, including Zipper, piled into the house behind them, and he led them from room to room. Somewhere to her left, Haddie heard footsteps going downstairs. The lawn outside dipped down as if to a lower-level entry.

"Are these his computers?" Haddie asked Stanton. She didn't want to say Bruce's name. A black file cabinet waited in the corner, and portfolios were stacked at the end of the desk.

He nodded. "Some. He used these for non-sensitive monitoring. Not for communication."

"He had others?"

"Multiple servers in US cities, Bangladesh, and Costa Rica." He gestured to the east. "Primary communication goes out through the portable in the back."

Gunfire sounded to the north, and Trig gestured to Zipper and one of his men.

Nothing moved around the little pond in the back.

"What's going on?" Haddie turned to Stanton. Cooper already had his gun drawn.

Stanton's fingers whisked across the tablet. "Elon is moving in through the northern gulch." His face pinched. "He had help."

"Meaning?" Haddie asked.

"I'm sorry, but not everyone is responding. I have lost two more squads; they might be helping Elon." Stanton didn't stop working on his tablet while he spoke. "If they have, we can expect the attack to come from the north and west." He gestured toward one of the side rooms and glanced at Trig. "That room is our safest at the moment. It also leaves an escape route through the garage."

Trig rested his hand on Haddie's shoulder. "I agree."

Stanton followed behind Cooper. "Elon's troops have fired on the helicopter. I returned them back to the airport until we can secure the area."

A window in the house shattered, and Trig nearly pushed Haddie into a room devoid of furniture except for a dining room table in the middle. Metal filings glittered on the wood floor. The walls were covered by maps, except for a window in the east wall that looked out at the portables. Cooper drew the curtains, and the room dimmed. Gunfire to the north intensified, and another window smashed deeper in the house.

A door to her right had been covered with a map. Trig strode to it and searched in a dark room. "Garage. Check out our options."

One of his people, a thin man with a pointed beard, jumped to the door and stepped into the darkness of the garage.

Gun in hand, Cooper moved to the door leading to the living room turned office. Most of the gunfire came from the north, but it grew loud enough that she had a hard time pinpointing it. Bullets thudded against the walls on the opposite side of the house. Stanton scrolled across his tablet. In front of Haddie, Trig stood stiffly at the table. Sweat dripped from his bald head and ran down his shaved neck to the hairs that sprouted from under his black vest.

The window across the room exploded, and a glimpse of a metal rifle stock fluttered the curtains open. Sunlight splashed in and then disappeared.

Cooper fired instantly, and Haddie winced at the gunshots echoing in the small room. The fabric tugged at two shots before one side pushed inward. A round grenade slid between the fabric and rolled across the wood floor to settle under the table. Trig turned and pushed her to the wall, nearly covering her. The impact against her bruised back made her suck air in.

We'll all die. "No," Haddie snarled. Her tone sounded above the ringing in her ears.

The grenade vanished among the metal filings. Cooper continued to fire, deafening them all.

Pain shot up her face. She cringed and her ribs reacted with sharp jabs until she couldn't breathe.

Trig's mouth hung open. He mouthed something, but she couldn't hear, then he turned toward the center of the room to where the grenade had disappeared. Confusion twisted a frown on his face when he looked back at her. His hand lifted off her shoulders and hung in the air.

She could barely stand against the pain. *Trig knows.*

The room turned dark with her visions.

CHAPTER 27

HADDIE GRIMACED as the gunfire of the battle outside the house crashed against her ringing ears. The visions left her heart racing. The cigar smell in the room reasserted itself, and she felt nauseous. Trig stood wide-eyed in front of her. *What does he think?*

Cooper swore and dropped an empty magazine to the floor.

The clatter turned Trig slowly toward the window. His head snapped back, and he studied her for a quick moment.

"Get down. They knew we'd come in here." He flipped the table onto its side and dragged it toward them.

She crouched with jolting gasps as pain ripped at her skin and ribs protested. *This had been another trap. Elon.* She hated the man.

Bullets dug into the brick outside, and the curtain swung as a bullet sailed in, fluttering a map beside Cooper. Stanton stood beside her, undaunted as he scrolled across the tablet.

Trig aimed his gun at the window. He spoke as if to

himself. "You turned blue. No — a blue mist came off your skin, for just a second."

"I'm sorry, Trig." Haddie couldn't be sure if she apologized for disagreeing with him, or for exposing what she was.

The gunfire outside diminished. Stanton focused on his tablet. "They're retreating back into the gully. We've taken severe losses. Do you want to follow?"

Follow? He had to mean the troops, her troops. Haddie shook her head. "I just want to leave."

"I'm having them prepare the second helicopter now. The first took fire. There doesn't seem to be any serious damage, but I wouldn't risk it."

Trig didn't move from his position; there was still gunfire to the north of the house. *I need to sleep.* She wanted to curl up with Rock in Sam's cabin.

Cooper stepped to the side of the window and moved the curtain with his gun. He flinched, then nodded to someone. "I'm assuming that's your people; they didn't shoot me." He turned to Haddie. "We should leave. Have the helicopter pick you up somewhere else."

Haddie bristled at his tone, but said nothing. She felt numb. *I need to tell Sam and Meg.* Maybe Liz could come out and meet them at Sam's cabin. Bruce's men wouldn't be looking for any of them anymore; Haddie just needed to avoid the police and FBI. None of that would likely go away with Bruce's death.

Trig stood and tucked his gun into his belt. "The detective is right. Let me get my people out front, and we'll head back to Kiana. We'll drive south, away from the activity. They can fight over the house if they want. We can —"

"Can you bring Kiana here?" Haddie asked. She shifted past him and stepped out the door to Bruce's office. He followed, but she wanted to be alone. Her skin cried against any movement, and the stiff jacket dug into her armpits.

Zipper came in from one of the rooms on the west side and nodded at Trig. "All clear," she said.

I hope they all made it. Haddie stepped to the window and looked toward the pond. Bodies littered the green lawn. Glass crunched under her feet as she inched closer to get a wider view. The left bottom pane of the large window had been shot out.

There had to be two dozen people dead or dying around the pond. To the right, a soldier stalked toward the short rise to the north and the treetops that poked above the gully there. The two people Trig had sent to the back were dead, and their Jeep had no glass left in the windows. *Glad most of Trig's people were inside.* Would Elon stop now?

Cooper walked to her side. "It's not safe here. We should go."

Haddie shrugged and regretted the stab in her ribs. "Leave. I'm not stopping you." Why did every man have to *tell* her what to do? She didn't really want him to leave, but couldn't bring herself to care.

She turned to find Trig on the other side, one step behind, watching her.

"Be sensible. This place isn't safe. Let me get you out of here," he said.

"Leave me alone." Haddie's voice came out in a growl. She drew in a deep breath and maneuvered between him and Zipper toward the map room.

Stanton looked up from his tablet, but didn't speak as she stomped past.

I just need a minute alone. The new helicopter would take some time. "I need to make a call." She closed the door to the map room behind her. The room stank of spent gunpowder. The thin man who had been sent to the garage stood there awkwardly. Haddie reopened the door. "Get out."

His expression darkened, but he left her alone. Haddie pulled out her phone and dialed Liz. *I'm being a bitch.* She needed to hear a friend's voice.

There was talking in the background, but Liz answered. "Hey. Glad you called. How is everything?" Her voice was too optimistic; it cut like a knife.

Haddie swallowed and tried to form a sentence. Her throat swelled and tears blurred her vision. "Dad. He's dead."

"No! Haddie, I'm so sorry. Are you okay? Of course, you aren't." A hinge squeaked, and the noise around Liz dulled. "Are you coming back? Do you need me to come to you?"

Haddie shook her head. "No, I'll bring him back to Oregon." She wiped her face and sat on the edge of the dropped table with a wince. "I'll let you know when and where. It would help if you could be there."

"Of course. Whatever you need. Physically, are you okay?"

Haddie pressed against her left side and grimaced. "Maybe a bruised or broken rib. Shot with a vest on."

"Not likely broken then. Bruised. I hear they hurt. Get the vest off when you can. Ice the area." Liz coughed. "Everyone else okay?"

Haddie stared at the map on the left wall. It had New York City with pins on it and a circle drawn in a red marker. "Cooper's fine. Same. He took a shot." She hadn't even asked him about it. "I killed Bruce — after he shot Dad." The declaration didn't bring any sense of justice or vengeance, just details and guilt.

"Well, I'm glad Bruce is stopped. So all this business of the collapse of civilization is done?"

Haddie stared at the map of New York. She'd have to ask Stanton. "Maybe. I'm supposed to use one of his helicopters to get Dad's body back."

"I'll be there. Wherever you tell me." A door to a stall slapped closed, and Liz dropped her voice to a whisper. "Wait, what? Bruce's helicopter?"

"His assistant is helping me because I'm the last of our kind. Whatever he thinks that is."

In the background, noises echoed. Liz probably had gone to the bathroom to talk. This time of the morning tended to be busy at the lab.

"I'll call you a little later, maybe lunchtime if I can?" Haddie asked.

"Please."

Haddie hung up and scanned the other maps in the room. She didn't want to go back to Bruce's office yet. *I could just wait here until the helicopter comes.* Why did they have to try and control her? Manipulated, tricked, and controlled. The urge to rip apart Bruce's maps flashed through her; instead, she opened a text to Terry and began taking pictures.

After seven pictures and before he had a chance to respond, she texted him. "Dad is dead. So is Bruce."

Her words seemed so empty and cold that she wanted to curl up in a corner. If she hadn't attempted a rescue, Dad might be alive. Of course, Bruce had expected it. *I'll ask Stanton about New York.* Everything Bruce had ever planned, she wanted destroyed. What would she do about Stanton?

Terry's text startled her; she'd been staring at a map of India. "I'm so sorry. What can I do?" he asked.

She'd needed to let Terry know, but couldn't handle more people at the moment. The helicopter ride, burying Dad, telling Sam and Meg, Kiana's reactions: they all seemed to weigh on Haddie, and she couldn't hold up under it anymore.

"I'll text you later. I can't right now. I'm sorry. I wanted you to know and have Bruce's maps."

I just want to hide.

CHAPTER 28

HADDIE MOVED to the window and pulled one side of the curtain open a couple inches. The soldiers outside spoke in terse, hushed voices while they prepared a makeshift bunker with a metal scoop from a bulldozer. They positioned themselves on the north side of the communications portable with everyone facing the gully behind the pond and house. Why did Elon still attack? *Vengeance.* She could understand his anger. Her jaw tightened, and she turned from the window to glare at Bruce's maps.

The door opened, and Trig stood respectfully without trying to enter. "I've got someone picking up Kiana; she'll be here in about forty minutes."

Leave me alone. Stanton stood close behind Trig. Cooper and Zipper glanced from their positions in the living room turned office. Haddie closed her eyes. They were trying to help. *I'm being unreasonable.* "Okay. Thanks. Give me a minute."

Stanton pressed in close to Trig. "Your helicopter can be here in fifty. I recommend a pickup slightly south of here to avoid Elon's troops."

"Yes. Yes." Haddie shifted to put her hand on the open door before Trig pulled it shut. She resisted the urge to kick it.

Heat flushed up her cheeks, aggravating her skin. Pacing, she pushed open the door to the dark garage. The air felt cool. She flicked a switch, and bright bulbs forced her to wince. It had been too long since she'd slept.

Parked near the door was a green '52 MG TD Midget in mint condition with a tan top. A workbench had little more than the tools needed to maintain the vehicle, and the metal shelving held oil cans and parts. The room smelled like Dad's old garage. He would have liked the car.

Bruce's car. Haddie marched to the door as her face tightened. Her fist clenched and she imagined punching in the window. As much as her joints ached, she resisted. Grabbing the mirror to twist it off, she winced as the cold metal bit into sensitive skin.

She spun toward the bench. A T-Handle wrench hung above, and she stomped over to grab it like a hammer. Cold and smooth, it had a solid weight.

The side window shattered into the driver's seat with old, original glass. *Nothing will bring Dad back.* She trembled with rage at the thought. Her wrist ached from the impact, but she swung a second time to punch a hole in the soft top. Her teeth ground, and she repositioned her grip. The next hit into the door reverberated up to her elbow and forced her to grimace as her palm flared in complaint. The wrench nearly slid from her grasp.

She imagined Bruce's bullet hitting her dad's face. *You took my dad from me.*

By the time Trig and Stanton made it to the doorway, she'd worked halfway across the windshield. A newer glass, cracks webbed out at each blow. "Get out!" she yelled.

Trig rubbed one hand across his bald head, in a move that reminded her of her dad. He opened his mouth as if to speak, then shook his head and strode over to the work bench. He came back with a ball-peen hammer. "Try this," he said and offered her the handle.

Haddie choked a sob and tossed the wrench to the floor with a ringing clatter. The hammer's wood was cold and hurt to wrap aching fingers around, but it put satisfying dents in the door. She took out the headlight on her side and smashed the blinker and mirror.

After two dents in the hood, she flopped onto the metal and started to cry. None of this would bring her dad back or punish Bruce for what he'd taken from her.

She flinched when Trig put his hand on her shoulder, but she didn't stop crying. Dripping tears and snot on the hood, she heaved with noisy sobs. *Nothing will ever be the same.* What was she supposed to do? Her life in Eugene was gone. Dad had been her anchor to any sense of home. *David?* She couldn't ask him to live in hiding.

Her hand tightened around the handle of the hammer, and she stood up, wiping her face on her sleeve.

Trig stepped back as she delivered another blow to the hood. She'd have to figure out the rest of her life once she got Dad buried. For the moment, she'd destroy anything Bruce had ever cared about.

PART IV

I missed Sam the most, but I sensed the tether of the blood and song bonds that had always existed with Thomas and Haddie.

CHAPTER 29

MEG SMILED as Milk ran across her shoulders on his way along the back of the couch. Louis yelped and struggled to join the game of chase. Curled with his chin resting on the edge of his hind paw, Rock watched the ruckus from his spot by the door. *He misses Aunt Haddie.* Sam had started lunch, and the cabin smelled like spice and onions.

Picking up a light lavender pencil, Meg drew careful lines for the wizard's cloak. The shade fit her image perfectly.

I miss the puppies and pens. She'd moved a lot since her parents had died. They'd been killed. The angels had known, even if Sam and T wouldn't talk about it. The kennel had been the most fun place to live, but it was nice here too.

"Sweet iced tea?" Sam asked from the kitchen door.

"Yes, please."

The music started around her, and she placed her pencil back in the tray. The angels had come. Milk bounced off her back as she shifted her sketch pad to the couch. She'd never heard them inside before.

"What is it?" Sam asked.

"They're here." Meg ran across the floor to her shoes by the door. "I'll be right back."

Sam peered at her and tucked her arms behind her back. "Lunch is almost ready."

"I'll be quick." Louis and Rock moved to the door. "We'll be back."

The day had turned warm, and sunlight beamed through the treetops. The pine trees sprayed their shades of green. Rock and Louis sprinted off, sniffing trunks and bright flowers. Pine and a sharp, fragrant blossom hung in the air. Insects buzzed around her as she ran toward the angels' music.

They waited for her on the side of the house, three glowing portals back to their world. She'd tried to understand where they were from, but it had been too much.

Their light fringed against the dark browns of the forest, swaying and fluttering as if a wind blew against them.

Meg froze. T was dead.

They had come to her so she would know. Aunt Haddie survived and would be returning soon. Her hands shook and Rock ran to her. He sniffed across her face as she began to cry. *I never told him I loved him.* She hadn't been able to say it. Why not? He'd saved her and always made her feel wanted.

How? The angels didn't answer. They never really answered. They just knew and she would understand, or not.

She felt weak. Rock whined and nuzzled her hand.

The angels believed she would be strong. *Needed to be.* She would have to be ready. Meg nodded, but didn't understand. Ready for what?

In moments, they began to dwindle, disappearing to their home.

Leaving her alone. *No, I have Sam and Rock and Louis.* She wiped her face and put her hands around Rock's neck. Louis pawed at her hips. *I have to tell Sam.*

CHAPTER 30

HADDIE STEPPED BACK from the wreckage of Bruce's car. Her panting emphasized the silence of the men standing at the door. The hammer rang on concrete as she dropped it.

Stanton bore no expression while Trig had a sorrowful, serious expression. Cooper just scowled.

Haddie's hands shook. She could barely open her stiff fingers. "Stanton, can you stop whatever was going to happen in New York?"

He coughed. "We have had trouble contacting our communications team in New York. Elon may have gotten to them."

"What do you mean?"

"His security forces were in charge of the device. He had a direct line to them."

Haddie ached and wanted to sit down, she settled on leaning on the car. "What device?" She couldn't be sure she really wanted to know. If she could disrupt any of Bruce's plans, she would.

"A nuclear warhead. It was designed to go off five days from now at 10:00 a.m. I am not sure if that will be altered by Elon's people. They still have to evacuate our resources there."

Haddie stood. "That's millions of people." They had to stop it. More than just destroying Bruce's plans, she couldn't let him kill all those people.

Stanton nodded stiffly. "Yes. Though the target is the UN, which is firmly within the blast radius." He gestured into the map room. "I can show you."

She motioned for him to lead and pushed past Trig. They could at least warn the government and evacuate New York.

Stanton moved to the map room, and she recognized the large red ring centered around New York City.

Zipper stepped to the doorway. "They're bringing Kiana in now."

The blood drained out of Haddie. She couldn't imagine facing Kiana. *This is my fault.* She reached back for her hair, but the cowl still held firmly under her chin and across her forehead.

She glanced at the map. "I'll be right back, Stanton."

Trig followed her as she headed for the front door.

"I'll be okay on my own." The constant guard had begun to chafe.

"There might be snipers."

She frowned. "What are you going to do? Take the bullet for me?"

He studied her. "Perhaps."

Would he? She opened the door, and the warm air made her uncomfortable in all her layers. The air still stunk of the fire, though no smoke came from behind the barn. Two of Trig's Jeep Wranglers remained parked across the lawn and drive.

Somewhere by the barn, someone pried metal in a dull

screech, and soldiers held positions along trucks or beside makeshift barricades.

The back of one of the Jeeps hung open, and the end of a black body bag waited alongside two pairs of boots. *Dad. Trig's people.* Where had they put the bodies she'd dismembered — and Bruce? Out near the fence by the dirt road, there were new corpses scattered in dirt and grass from the last attack by Elon and his men. *I'm lucky some of the men still follow Stanton.*

Haddie plodded to her Dad's body bag with dread and glanced south at a plume of dust following a truck. *Kiana?*

Men shifted in their positions along the fence, attentive but not training weapons on the vehicle. Her pulse raced. Would Kiana blame her? *She should.*

A young man with a trimmed goatee drove a dust-covered, white GMC Sierra up to the Jeeps. The back door behind him opened as he stopped, and Kiana burst out, shoving the crutch as if stabbing someone.

Kiana's face glowered as she hobbled over with her colorful cast, and her eyes flicked from Trig to Haddie. "What happened?" She swore and froze when she saw the body bag and the corpses of Trig's people. With a faltered start, she stepped toward the open hatch.

Trig approached, and she let him place a hand on her shoulder. Haddie stood awkwardly.

"I want to see him." Kiana touched the black bag.

"You don't," said Trig.

"Show me." Her face an angry snarl, Kiana pulled out of his grip, and moved to the back door of the Jeep. She leaned her crutch against the side, but it slid to the ground.

Haddie's stomach flipped as she remembered the bullet hitting her dad's face. She turned away, not wanting to see; Cooper and Stanton waited behind her.

Kiana wailed and Haddie couldn't hold back the tears. *She's going to hate me.* Guilt burrowed an empty hole in her chest. Loosing Aaron had been horrible, and Dad had been a thousand times closer to her. Nothing would make the pain go away.

She started when Kiana wrapped her arms around her.

"He wanted to find the children — that Bruce had taken. Did he find them?" Kiana spoke in broken spurts between sniffles.

Haddie blinked tears away. *Doesn't she blame me?* "It was all a trap, Kiana. Bruce wanted me to come so he could kill us both."

Kiana pulled back and wiped her face. "That sounds like the bastard. He didn't need to keep Thomas alive to do that, you would have come. Bruce knew that from the last time. You can't blame yourself for your dad's death."

A shiver ran down Haddie, despite the heavy clothing and heat. *I do.* "Stanton might be able to tell us about the children. We need to stop the bomb in New York. Elon controls that."

Kiana swore. "Who are Stanton and Elon?"

Haddie gestured to Stanton. "That's Stanton, Elon just attacked here. Stanton has been helping me — because I'm like Bruce. The last of something he calls Noveilm."

"From the letter." After she spoke, Kiana glanced toward Trig.

"Yeah." Haddie wiped her face and then peeled off a sweaty glove. "Let me show you the map, then we'll ask Stanton about the children."

Zipper and other members of Trig's team had come outside. Did Biff know? Most likely not. How would he handle this?

Kiana's face dropped and she nodded, looking back at

the Jeep. "Thomas would want us to do something about a bombing." She leaned forward and whispered, "Can you trust this Stanton?"

"I'm not sure, but Cooper and I wouldn't have survived if he hadn't gotten most of Bruce's soldiers to back me. And — he has a helicopter to get Dad's body back to Oregon."

Stepping forward, Kiana nodded, though she took a brief look at Stanton. "Let's see this map. What kind of bomb?"

Haddie raised her eyebrows. "Nuclear. Sorry, I thought I said that."

Kiana swore. "We need to warn people. Evacuate."

Stanton spoke. "If they follow protocol, Elon might detonate."

Haddie sighed. "We have only five days to stop it. Stanton has been trying to get through; he might still have some sway there." Was she going to try and stop it? She could just make it disappear. What about the radioactive material? How much was there and how far back in time would she have to spread it out? Maybe it would be better to remove the equipment that would make it detonate, then call the authorities once Elon or his men couldn't set it off. She walked past Stanton. *I can't just ignore it.* Liz or Terry might know about nuclear weapons.

Dad's body first. "We only have a couple minutes before the helicopter comes — for Dad."

Stanton spoke behind her. "Seven minutes. They are approaching in a wide arc from the southeast."

"Thank you." Haddie stopped. "Stanton. Bruce had children kidnapped, do you know where they are?"

Kiana studied the man, a grim expression spreading across her features.

"Yes. He's set them up in a home here in Amarillo, closer to the city."

"Are they safe?" Kiana asked. "From this Elon or anyone else?"

Stanton glanced at Haddie, she nodded, and he swiped across his tablet. The edges of his mouth softened. "Yes. I have contact with them. Elon would not concern himself with them. He had little to do with the project."

Haddie bristled. "Did that project include killing families?" *Meg's family?*

He nodded. There was no sense of remorse in him, nor enthusiasm. Purely professional, but perhaps closer to Josh's state than she cared to admit.

She sighed. "Give us some space. We'll be out in a minute."

HADDIE LED Kiana into the cigar-scented house. Trig said something as they closed the door, perhaps to his people, or maybe them. *Leave me alone.*

The bullet hole in the window became obvious from the entry. Men had taken positions outside, facing the gully beyond the pond. Some stood or patrolled, while others crouched at small barricades. What would they do when she left? *I don't care.*

Kiana hobbled to the window. "This is his office?"

"One, I haven't looked through the house. The map's in here." Haddie walked into the darker room and found the light switch below the map. A bright LED turned all the features crisp.

Kiana looked at the table on its side, metal filings scattered on the floor, and the open door to the garage. The ball-peen hammer lay beside Bruce's mangled car. "What have you been up to?"

Haddie flushed about her temper tantrum. "We'll have time for the story in the helicopter." She tapped the map. "I'm assuming this ring is the blast radius."

Resting on her crutch, Kiana leaned in. "Centered on the west edge of Queens."

"Stanton said something about the UN."

Kiana drew her finger west and tapped. "The General Assembly should be soon."

"Five days?"

"Possibly." Kiana sighed. "We need to warn the UN, at least."

Haddie nodded. *I should care — more — all those people in New York.* A few minutes earlier she'd cared and had been ready to charge in again. Now? She needed to get her dad to Oregon, somewhere safe and away from Bruce's place. *I'd be happy never to see this house again.*

Explosions from the back rocked the windows and walls. Haddie ran into the living room office. *Elon.* Dirt and water rained down from the edge of the pond. Gunfire sounded around the house. Smoke drifted from one of the simple barricades Stanton's soldiers had made, and a body lay sprawled a few feet away. Muzzles flashed from the berms at the gully.

Kiana swore as she hobbled in behind Haddie. "What the hell? We should have left."

Should have, Haddie agreed.

The pond rippled slowly from the explosions. Grenades? Why did Elon attack so quickly after the last time? Or why had he stopped earlier?

Kiana's crutch clattered to the floor. She pulled out her gun, her cast skewing to the side as she dropped to one knee. "Get down!"

Two of Elon's soldiers stood on the ridge, where the others had crawled to the edge or knelt. The pair faced the gunfire with two fat weapons on their shoulders. Haddie didn't know the equipment, but imagined they were like the rocket launchers they'd fired during the ambush.

A bullet smashed through one of the upper windows, opening a large hole and spreading a web of cracked glass to the frames.

Kiana's deafening gunshot echoed in the small room.

One of the attackers staggered back, his weapon pointed skyward as it fired in a plume of flame.

Again, Kiana fired. Haddie's ringing ears barely recognized the dull sound.

Around the weapon of the second man, a halo of orange light flared behind him. The rocket barely seemed to move, from her perspective. *It's coming directly toward me. Us.*

She imagined a cone in front of her that included the rocket and the men on the ridge. *Intent.* "No." Her tone rang out in the room, louder in her head than the ringing in her ears.

The rocket, branches of the tree, the men, and a swath of ground around them disappeared.

Kiana fired a third shot that sounded like little more than a pop.

Pain blossomed up Haddie's chin and spread to her cheeks. So close to the last use of her power, her skin felt as though it peeled away from her flesh. Her left knee gave out and she slammed to the floor; agony seared her palm as it slapped onto cool, polished wood. Glass shattered from either Kiana or the gunfire outside in a distant tinkle as it hit the desk and floor.

Her visions stopped all the sounds, and the wood floor turned to a dark forest that had the salty smell of a nearby ocean. A muzzle flare fired from across a glade, and Dad returned fire. The brush behind rustled, and she rolled over to catch a glimpse of a revolver. She barked an awkward yell at the red-coated soldier.

Daylight burst around her, and a rough looking man drew his blade from another's stomach. They stood across the road, and beside the stabbed man, a young boy watched in terror. The killer raised his knife to strike the child, and Dad yelled, "Stop."

The world turned dark as she huddled in a room. There were others hiding with her, the young and the old of the village. The door burst in, and sunlight silhouetted two red-coated soldiers. "Shhh," her dad said. The shadows of the men faded.

She returned from the visions to ringing ears, gunfire, and shattering glass with her nerves raging on her skin. Too weary, she couldn't push off her knee and stand. Kiana still fired single shots, quickly aimed. Bullets thudded against the walls.

A hand reached under her armpit and Haddie lurched.

Cooper grabbed tighter and shifted her away from the middle of the room. She gained control of her lethargic feet, turned sideways to hold his shoulder, and limped with him.

A sparse dining room with a small table and a single chair lay through the open arch from the office. Red flowers sat in a clear vase on the tabletop. A window looked out to one of the Jeeps.

"Wait here." Cooper pulled his weapon and used the archway for cover. He fired almost immediately.

Haddie leaned on the wall beside him, staring outside at the sunlit day with a bright blue horizon. The barn and truck were to the left side of the window. *Where Dad died.* She should be helping, but her body hurt so badly she could barely stand.

The kitchen was to the right of her, at the front of the

house through another smaller doorway. A hall beside her right hand led toward the back of the house, where most of the gunfire seemed to be concentrated.

I can't do this. New York, Elon, and all that Bruce had planned had to be destroyed. *It doesn't have to be me.* She dropped her head and stared at the black outfit Trig had dressed her in. Her heart thudded dully in her chest.

She flinched as a blond head eased around the corner from the hall, less than a foot from her shoulder. Angry blue eyes bore through the yellow haze of the coerced. They tightened into burning hatred.

Elon.

CHAPTER 32

As a knife flashed around the corner, Haddie blocked upward with her right hand. She grunted as pain raced down her forearm. He'd been swinging a wide arc aimed for her chest.

Elon wore soldier's fatigues, but she recognized him. The loose sleeve bunched as she slid her right hand up, searching for his wrist.

Old training pivoted her into the dining room, and her aching joints complied. Her fingers found his wrist and fought to get some purchase.

He had military training, though, and spun his hand to slash down. *Like Dad would have done.*

She had the height in this situation and stepped forward, not backward as he expected. Her left hand caught his forearm. Haddie slammed her right elbow into his solar plexus and drove her full weight into him. With her right arm sliding to his throat, he grabbed at her defensively.

Haddie stepped to the right and leaned in.

The back of Elon's head slammed into the corner of the hall doorjamb. Both of them jarred at the impact. He blinked and his eyes squinted into a glower. *Not hard enough.*

He hadn't been completely taken off guard; he buried his knee into her stomach.

Coughing through gritted teeth, she took the hit and thrust tighter. Her forearm pressed against his throat. He focused on his right arm, pressing the knife closer. *I'm going to kill you.* She couldn't stop his progress completely, and the tip crawled toward her shoulder. He expected her to be too weak. Her left arm didn't have the strength, and even her right wouldn't have been a match for him. Leverage kept him from plunging the knife through her vest.

Haddie bent and dropped her stance, relaxing the pressure against his legs and inviting another kick.

Elon obliged. His knee caught her stomach at the bottom of the vest.

She hissed from the impact, held her breath, and swept under his raised leg with her knee.

Their pinned balance shifted. His eyes widened as he slid off the corner.

Haddie would lose control of his knife arm. She rolled her right hand around to the side of his head as she dropped with him.

Momentum and his twisting body dropped his head into her control. Dad had taught her the move to lock in a choke hold, but he'd always warned that it could snap a neck. *Time to find out.*

Just before his back hit the floor, Haddie twisted and yanked up. The knife tapped futilely against her arm as Elon's neck popped.

She dropped him and jumped away, unsure.

His knife clattered into the kitchen. His arms flopped to his side, but he glared up at her.

Paralyzed?

At her right shoulder, Cooper and Stanton stepped up, side by side. They shot at the same moment, and she flinched away from the noise and blood.

"You okay?" Cooper asked.

She could barely hear him, and her own answer seemed no more than a whisper. "Yeah." Haddie shook. Fingers trembling and knees wobbling, she glanced over to the dining room chair. Outside appeared peaceful from this view, but the gunfire raged.

Kiana yelled something. Haddie couldn't make it out through the ringing.

"All clear," Cooper replied. He turned back and jutted his chin toward the hall. "I'm going to go check the back. We don't need any more surprises."

"Thanks." Haddie sucked in deep, slow breaths to calm her pounding heart.

Stanton slid his gun into an ankle holster. He'd never put down the tablet. *Does he sleep with it?* She hadn't known he was armed. If he wanted to harm her, he could have. *Can I trust him?*

Cooper stepped over Elon and crept down the hall. *I want to leave.* Could they just drive off with her dad's body and leave Bruce's soldiers fighting?

She stepped over to the front window and leaned against it with a sweaty palm, surprised that the glass was warm. Zipper and the thin man with the goatee used the Jeeps for cover, but they weren't firing. Dad's body bag waited in the back of the first vehicle. How was Biff? *I never asked.*

Kiana fired from the living room office. Stanton moved to her left.

"What's going on out there?" Haddie didn't turn from

the window. Her voice sounded dim. She asked more to do something and not fall to the floor than out of any expectation of knowing.

Stanton scrolled across the tablet. "Elon's men have taken heavy losses. They are retreating on the west side. They still hold the southeast corner of the gully to the north of us. Your troops are laying fire on them. We have men coming up from behind. It will be over soon. A communication trailer has been lost, which is affecting outside connections."

From the sounds of the gunfire, it didn't sound like anyone was retreating. However, she might be on the helicopter soon enough.

"What can you do about New York? The bomb."

"Little. You have teams you could send against Elon's men, but they might detonate upon a breach."

"Even with Elon —" Haddie turned to the body. "Dead?" Shouldn't she have some remorse or even satisfaction that she killed the man?

"They were not responding to any communication. Once we have our equipment repaired, I will try again." He pointed the tablet at Elon's corpse, and a flash blinked against the walls. "I cannot be sure they will not detonate when they find out their leader is dead. Elon may have left specific orders."

Kiana yelled from the room behind Haddie, "They're being pushed back!"

Haddie closed her eyes. *I need to get Dad home.* She wanted sleep and some tea. Her brain felt thick, her skin ached, and her stomach still churned. "Helicopter?" she asked.

"They are in a holding pattern south of here. I still have

radio signal with them. They will meet us once we set coordinates and time."

They should leave now. Haddie nodded stiffly and turned. Every part of her body hurt.

Kiana had managed to get up and propped herself with the crutch and wall. "Let's get out of here, Haddie. Anything we need?"

Haddie raised her eyebrows. She didn't want to bring Stanton, but he'd be useful with the New York bomb. She'd already sent Terry pictures of the maps. "I don't think so. Not right now. We can come back." Where would she go when this was all done?

Kiana's expression turned grave. *Where will she go? Back with Sam and Meg.*

The front door burst open, and Haddie stepped forward to find Trig marching in. "We need to move. Police have been spotted moving in. Fifteen minutes."

The backyard had bodies strewn across it. The scene could have come from a war movie. Stanton might have a more difficult time cleaning this up before the authorities got a good look.

"Let's go," said Haddie.

CHAPTER 33

HADDIE MOVED FOR THE DOOR, swaying slightly. Footsteps sounded on the stairs down the hall, and she stopped.

Trig pulled his weapon and positioned himself clear of Elon's corpse. Blood pooled on the floor and trickled down beige walls. The body had a grenade on its belt. *I hadn't noticed that before.* Their struggle could have gone differently.

The steps were distinct, plodding. "It's Cooper," she said.

"Clear," Cooper called out.

Trig holstered his weapon.

Cooper's voice grew louder as he walked up the hall. "There's a tunnel entrance down in the storage room. Lucky you didn't have an entire squad in here." He stepped over the body. "I closed it, best I could."

"We need to get her out of here. Your buddies are coming." Trig pushed past Haddie. "I'll be coming with you."

Haddie's cheeks flushed. *What is it with him trying to order me around?* "Me and Kiana. You get your people clear. Cooper, can you work with Stanton to find out what we can do about this bomb?"

The air outside reeked of spent gunpowder and a fire somewhere. A light haze hung over the ground.

Stanton spoke. "I should go with you."

Haddie faltered, her legs stiff. "I need you to get in contact with those people and stop this. Otherwise, I've got to at least warn the UN."

"Two members of the UN delegations were working with us. They might report to Elon's people. I will not be able to contact them until communications are back up."

Haddie nodded and motioned to him. "Exactly. I need you here to do that." She gestured randomly to the west. "Assuming you can get rid of the police."

"I will." Stanton's normally impassive face twitched, and the corners of his mouth threatened to droop. "Are you returning immediately?"

Am I? "Cooper has my number. Contact me once you have some news on communications." Either of them could call; cell service had been surprisingly good out here. She followed Kiana and glanced at Cooper.

His scowl had deepened, but he'd stopped following them. Would he stay and help?

Stanton still kept pace with her and swiped across his tablet. "I've alerted the pilots to look for the Jeep at these coordinates." He showed her the screen with a terse set of messages between him and the pilots. The last contained only numbers.

Trig growled, turned back with his phone, and typed at her shoulder. "Do you even know where you are going?"

Haddie drew in a breath. They couldn't get a helicopter near where they'd buried Aaron, and she didn't have a second location in mind. Her mom had been cremated.

Would Dad want that? It had never been a discussion. Why would it? *Hell.* They needed to decide in a hurry.

One of the soldiers jogged toward the side of the house. The portables had been seriously damaged. One had a gaping hole in the corner that Crow could fit through, and bullet holes dotted some of the sides.

"Are there any goons out there looking for me, my family, or friends?" she asked Stanton.

"Once you were identified yesterday, all contracts were canceled and assets recalled or relocated."

"So, other than the police or FBI, we don't have to worry?"

"Correct."

"Kiana, is there a place where we can land a helicopter on — the farm?" She still thought of the kennel and acreage as her dad's.

Kiana nodded as she hobbled for the Jeep. "Plenty." Her voice cracked, and she didn't turn.

Trig nodded for Zipper and the thin man to drive, then moved to her dad and carefully closed the hatch. Haddie faltered mid-step heading between the two Jeeps.

"Trig, we'll need help burying Dad's body. Do you have some people who can meet us there?"

His expression grave, he nodded. "I've got one man left there who's discreet. You'll have to help carry your father."

Haddie shivered at the idea of picking up her dad's body, but she would deal with it when she had to.

"How's Biff?" she asked Kiana.

"Luckier than he deserves to be. Bullet bounced off a rib and slid across his back muscle. Not one organ nicked. Crap-load of stitches."

Haddie kept walking around the Jeep. "It sounds

painful. How long will he be in there? Did he get any flak from the police?"

"The police seem to be buying his story. He's not under arrest." Kiana struggled into her seat. "I haven't gotten any updates otherwise."

"Eight minutes!" yelled Trig as he climbed in to drive his Jeep.

Haddie rounded the side and opened the back door. "I'll call him — about Dad. Thank you."

Zipper started the engine as Haddie crawled into the back seat.

Sweat trickled down her side and her ribs screamed at sitting. *I've got to get this vest off.* She started with the cowl. It fit stubbornly under the other layers with its extended shoulders. Her hair had been tightly braided, but now it frayed and tangled between the weaves.

As Zipper lurched them into motion following Trig, Kiana leaned her head against the glass of her window.

"You okay?" Haddie asked. She sucked in a gasp as she reached down to peel off the black long-sleeve shirt covering the vest.

"No." Kiana looked over and smiled weakly. "I've never been with someone like Thomas. Never thought I would." She jutted her chin at Haddie's struggle. "Let me help." She motioned for Haddie to lift her arms.

This is going to hurt. Wincing, Haddie lifted her arms, and her ribs jabbed into nerves.

Kiana strained against her cast and leaned over to grip the shirt in both hands. It tugged on the vest but came up quickly enough to Haddie's chin, then off over her head and arms.

Zipper turned at the road, and they all swayed to their

right. She gunned the engine to keep up with Trig, who had left them following in a cloud of dust.

The vest came off easier, leaving Haddie in a body suit and the black cargos. "Thank you." She hadn't realized how hot she'd gotten until the cool air of the Jeep washed over exposed arms. Her ribs hurt a little less in the competition of aches that was her body.

She slipped her hand gingerly into her pocket and pulled out her phone.

Terry had texted, "Reports of the Unceasing leaving New York. Evacuating?"

"Don't post this anywhere, but it's a bomb," she replied. "On that map, the circle is a blast radius."

"Couldn't. It would have to be nuclear to be that size."

"Yes. If anyone finds out and starts to do anything, they'll likely detonate. As it stands, we have five days."

"Impossible. They can sniff out radiation in any of the major cities. Biological or chemical though, that's different." He added an emoji bomb. Before she could reply, he sent another message. "Sorry. You okay?"

She thought of Kiana's reply, *no.* "The bomb is real." How had Bruce avoided detection? *Coerced?* "I have no doubt."

"We've got to stop it. What can I do?"

Terry might be able to help Stanton, but not until she knew it was safe. "Give me a bit to think about it. I'll text you soon."

If Stanton did get Elon's crew to stop the detonation, then she wouldn't have to do anything. She took a deep breath. Right now, she needed to get Dad buried.

It seemed so empty without Dad. "I don't know what to do without him."

Kiana took a moment to respond. "I know."

Haddie had almost lost David. It had been terrifying. *What would I be like if he'd died?* Her stomach twisted into a knot. She couldn't think about David.

"What do we do now?" Haddie's stomach tightened.

"What Thomas would have done. Stop the bomb. Save the children."

CHAPTER 34

Haddie sunk into her seat at the sound of sirens. Trig had slowed, kicking up less of a cloud. They reached the intersection where Bruce had ambushed them the day before. A plume of dust lifted from the two-lane highway. Only a day before, they had traveled along it to the city of Canyon. Zipper turned left at the crossroads, away from the police and following Trig.

Should I have brought Stanton? Her pulse grew restless. What if the pilots were secretly against her? *What choice do I have?* She couldn't bring herself to drive days in the same car as her dad, or have someone else take him. Exhausted, she found it difficult to think or even care about the pilots.

"Can you fly a helicopter?" she asked.

Kiana started. "What? No."

They'd have to risk it. Haddie wasn't about to drive.

She needed to alert Sam and Meg to return to the farm. Her phone felt heavy with dread. Sam might suspect that things could have gotten dangerous.

Stiffly, Haddie turned and peered out the back. The

Jeeps still kicked up dust, but she could make out blue lights. What if they followed?

She should call Sam. "How long do you think it'll take to get to Oregon?" *I'm procrastinating.*

"Ten, twelve hours. Depends on the helicopter. Did he tell you what kind it was?"

The police turned at the intersection, heading for Bruce's ranch. Haddie shook her head, lifted the phone, and dialed. *It's not fair to put this off.* Sam and Meg had lived with her dad for months. The image of Bruce firing into her dad's face flashed, and she winced. None of it seemed real.

Sam answered, sniffling. "How, Haddie? What happened?"

Did she know? Haddie swallowed. "Dad is dead, killed here in Texas."

"I know. Meg told me. I didn't want to believe her or these angels of hers. But it's true, isn't it?" Louis yapped in the background.

"Yes." Why would the angels tell Meg? Why were they involved? "Did they say anything else?"

The phone muffled, and Haddie leaned forward to look out the windshield. No helicopter.

Sam came back on with Louis barking. "No. They only knew about T."

"I'm bringing Dad back to the farm. It's safe now. We'll be arriving by helicopter. Can you meet us there? Kiana's with me."

"Yes, yes." Sam's voice grew lighter as she pulled away from the phone. "Get packed. We're going to the kennel. Haddie's bringing T back." She came back to the phone. "I'm sorry, Haddie. I've been nuts. I was worried about you and Kiana. Are you alright?"

Haddie touched her chest and winced. "Yes. Just upset. Text me when you get there, okay?"

"I love you, Haddie."

"Love you too, Sam." Haddie hung up, wondering why she hadn't talked to Meg. Their relationship had always been strained. *I was jealous.* She'd have to work on reaching out to Meg, the only family she had left.

Kiana wiped her eyes and looked over. "Sam and Meg okay? Are they going to meet us?"

"Yeah." She imagined dropping her Dad's body into a hole and grimaced. "Should we do a coffin?" Stanton could probably get her one, but she didn't want him involved.

"I don't think your father would care. He'd be more concerned with us getting his family safe. And the other children. I'll have to find out from Stanton what relationship Meg has with the great-great whatever of T's that Bruce took. I've been thinking we should bring them to the farm." Kiana tugged on her ear. "You have to accept that you might not be able to stop the bomb in New York, and things might get ugly for a while."

Would a bomb in New York cause the end of civilization like Bruce and the Unceasing hoped for? Not likely on its own. What else did Bruce have planned? Stanton would know. Haddie stared at her hands. Purpura had darkened them. It would fade. *Stanton has to stop that bomb.* Taking care of children who could grow up with powers hadn't been her plan. She didn't even know how many there were. *Explain that to David.*

Kiana seemed intent on it. She had called them great-great. Did she know how old Dad had really been?

"You know about his last wife?" Haddie asked.

"He's mentioned a few of them."

Haddie flushed. "He told you?" It had taken her forever to get the truth out of him. He'd known Kiana for months. "How old he was?"

Kiana's voice dropped to a whisper. "Centuries. He planned to outlive me." Her expression remained fixed. "Hard to explain Meg otherwise. He started with her being a cousin."

Could David accept Haddie like Kiana had Dad? "It didn't seem — unbelievable?"

Kiana snorted and glanced toward Zipper and the thin man in the front seat. "With everything else? Why not?" She gestured toward Trig's people. "We'll discuss later?"

Haddie nodded and leaned back in her seat. Dust flowed past, and she didn't bother trying to look for the helicopter. Zipper leaned them into another left and slowed.

They drove for a couple minutes in silence before they pulled off the road and bounced onto tan grass. The dust thinned immediately, and Haddie leaned over to look out the windshield. The helicopter waited for them. Sleek with sharp angles, it looked military. One pilot waited beside open doors leading to the back; the silhouette of the other sat in the tinted front.

Trig turned ahead of them and backed toward the helicopter. Zipper pulled their Jeep to a stop, and the thin man jumped out and jogged toward Trig.

"I don't suppose there's a toilet on board." Haddie had taken a tour of the Grand Canyon in a rounder helicopter that hadn't had a restroom.

Zipper grabbed a package of tissues from the console and handed them to her. "Use the back of the Jeep. Lean on the bumper." It sounded like she had practice.

Camping with her dad had taught Haddie to deal

without bathrooms. *I'm wearing a damned body suit.* She grabbed the tissue. "Thanks."

Kiana remained in her seat. "I better go too. Don't use them all."

Haddie slid out of the Jeep; except for Kiana still in her seat, the others were at the helicopter. Her clothes clung with sweat, and she'd begun to stink. Her left breast had angry red bruises flaring out from the bullets Bruce had fired at her. She stared across the plains. Would Stanton really be able to get rid of the police? *Should I have left Cooper?* At the time, she hadn't wanted anyone except Kiana around her.

Passing off the remaining tissues, she asked, "Do you need help? With the cast and all?"

Kiana shook her head. "Thanks, no. I got this."

They already had Dad's body in the helicopter when she returned. A brown-haired pilot offered a stiff salute. "Ma'am. We'll be making a stop in a couple of hours to refuel. There's water and food available in the back. Once we're in the air, we'll get coordinates from you."

Haddie didn't get the sense that this man begrudged taking her, or planned to betray her. "Thank you."

Trig stood back by his Jeep. "Okay if Zipper tags along?" He asked Haddie, not the pilot.

He doesn't trust the pilots. It couldn't hurt to have extra protection, but it meant inviting the woman into a private ceremony with Dad. Biff wouldn't be ready to travel; otherwise, Haddie would be happy to have him. *I can't forget to call him.*

Zipper stood with her hands clasped in the front of her black cargo pants. She offered a smile as Haddie studied her. "I'll keep out of the way."

Kiana limped toward them with her crutch, careful across the clumps of grass. She must have heard, as she caught Haddie's eye and nodded.

Haddie took a deep breath. "Okay."

CHAPTER 35

MEG GOT up from the floor of the van, sliding Louis out of her lap. He yawned and whined. Milk rolled in his soft carrier and peeked out at her. Rock sat beside Sam as she drove, and he watched the trees and sky rolling by the windshield. *He'll be happy to see Aunt Haddie.* The terrariums had a musty smell, sitting at the back on their padding.

Meg grabbed her sketchbook. She hadn't drawn since hearing about T.

Mrs. Mitchell will be surprised. Sam had been clear they wouldn't be stopping at the kennel, but surely no one would miss the big van driving by.

"Why can't we stop at the pens?" Meg slid into the passenger seat, Louis at her feet.

"We have to get the house ready for Haddie and Kiana."

They were driving up the last bit of pavement before they would turn and go down the bumpy dirt road that led to the farm. It might be spooky without T there, though he'd left them alone before. Kiana had been home. Meg had gotten used to being alone with Sam and the animals in the smaller cabin with the woods thick around them.

She would give Aunt Haddie a big hug when she showed up, and of course Kiana too. Aunt Haddie had lost her dad, just like Meg. *It hurt.* Hugs made it better, eventually. Love helped in life. It healed and created. The angels created with love.

Pine trees grew on both sides of the road in pale greens and browns. The light blue sky made them seem dark. She knew the river cut along the road to their left, but she only caught an occasional glimpse. T said it would get deeper in the spring.

Farms opened on both sides, and she craned her neck to see the river closer. Brown from this angle, it had cattails exploding in white fuzz along its banks.

Sam slowed as they passed the kennel. Mrs. Mitchell wasn't in the pens at the back, from what Meg could see. A blue car sat out front; perhaps someone was picking up their dog.

Tires crunching on gravel, they turned left into the woods and headed for the farm. They passed over the bridge, and the trees looked smaller and drier than she remembered. *I'll miss the cabin.* The pines had been so tall there. To the right, their farm opened into fields where wild-flowers had taken over, most of them white. Bees darted among them. Rock stirred as if he knew they were coming home.

The new trees that Sam and T had planted looked sick as they pulled up. "We should water the trees," Meg said.

"Yes, we should. Can you do that with Rock and Louis while I get everyone settled?" Sam acted as if she were okay. She'd stopped crying, but she hurt, just like Meg.

T had made them feel important and — right. It would be very different without him.

Meg would water the trees and keep Louis out of the

way. Later, she would have to help in another way. The angels had known that she would help.

CHAPTER 36

Haddie woke and yawned. Kiana snored quietly beside her. The air inside the helicopter had become stale, even sour. Dad's black body bag stretched across the seats, and Zipper looked over from the other side of Kiana. Haddie's head gear had shifted, and the thudding of the helicopter blades intruded. Outside was pitch black with only a couple dots of light in the distance.

She'd spent most of the time asleep. Her phone said 10:02 p.m. She adjusted her headset and switched on her mike. "How much longer?"

"Six minutes, Ma'am." The two pilots were polite and always offering salutes. *How am I supposed to react?* She wasn't about to salute back.

She texted Trig, "Almost there. All good?" He had decided to stay in case she came back, but he might be asleep.

He responded immediately, "Good here. Patrols report no sign of Elon's men. Believed dispersed. The authorities haven't returned."

Stanton had managed to hide the most obvious bodies

and convince the police that Bruce was off hunting some of the wild sheep that roamed the property. Bruce's contacts had reinforced his assertions, and the police had been turned away.

Haddie typed, "Thanks. I'll check in with you in the morning. What time is your man scheduled to come here?"

"Sunrise."

What were they going to do with her dad's body until morning? Coyotes and more roamed the wilder parts of Oregon. *I'm never going to get to sleep tonight.* She shifted in her seat and groaned. A bath would be good.

She considered responding, but there was nothing she needed to say. What little relationship she'd been building with Trig had changed. He seemed cautious around her. Perhaps for good reason, since she'd been nasty with him. She twisted her lips to one side and typed, "Sorry I was a jerk earlier."

"All good. Stress all around. You did good, considering." He sent the message then followed it with another. "I may not forgive you for leaving that cop here, though."

She smiled. Maybe he's not mad, just surprised about me. Her face grim, she turned to stare out the window. A city, perhaps Bend, stretched in a splash of tiny lights against the black. The angle slowly shifted; the helicopter was dropping altitude.

Zipper had noticed the lights as well, and stowed empty water and wrappers from a protein bar. From what Haddie could tell, the woman hadn't slept. She had a quick smile, but her expression usually remained stolid, and her eyes caught every move. Nodding to Haddie, she tapped at her pockets, sheath, and holster, as if inventorying.

The pilots circled a dark section west of the city where only a few lights dotted farms and roads. "We're going for the circular field." His voice sounded through the headset, and Kiana startled awake.

Haddie leaned toward the window and saw bright lights shine on brush below like it was daytime. As they neared, leaves blew and bushes bent. No one had discussed what to do with her dad's body. Her arms chilled, and she rubbed them. *I'm going to have to face Meg.*

When they landed and Zipper opened the side door, a cold, exhaust-laden breeze flowed inside. *Oregon.* Haddie wore only the bodysuit, cargos, and boots. Her top half would freeze until they got to the house.

Zipper helped Kiana stand, and the pilots moved a block to the door for them to step down. Lights flashed on their dark uniforms from the side, bouncing as if from a vehicle. *Sam?*

"White van?" Zipper glanced back at Haddie, a hand already on her holster.

Kiana waved in dismissal. "Sam and Meg. They were probably sitting up waiting for us."

Haddie made it to the opening as Sam backed the Transit to the helicopter. Her pink sleeve out the window, she looked back, focused on the blades. There was plenty of room. The second pilot, a small man with a pencil mustache and a nervous expression, waited for Haddie to exit. They needed to unload her dad's body. Hopefully, Meg hadn't brought Louis.

Hopping out, Haddie shivered and made her way up the side of the van after Sam came to a stop.

"I'm so sorry, Haddie." Wearing a pink and blue sweatshirt, Sam slid out of the driver's seat and hugged her.

Tears forming, Haddie held on. "I'm lost without him."

"You've got us. Come home. Are you going to stay?"

The van doors opened, and Kiana spoke with the pilots. They were moving Dad's body.

"Bruce is dead, but there's a nuclear bomb in New York. We can't let it detonate."

Sam pulled back. "Are you going — to New York?"

"I don't plan to, but maybe. Bruce's people in Texas are trying to stop it. There are some who are trying to continue, I think. We can't communicate with them."

Looking past Haddie toward the back of the van, Sam grimaced. "You'll end up going. You'll stop the bomb. T would have."

Haddie rubbed her arms against the cold. She might. Then again, Stanton was on it, and he seemed able work miracles. *I'm tired.* She'd slept between the stops to refuel, but didn't feel rested. "We'll see. I can't think right now." She turned as the mustached pilot disappeared behind the open van door.

Meg clung to Kiana. They both watched the procession.

"How's Meg?" Haddie asked.

Sam shrugged. "We've both been a bit of a mess. One of us cries and kicks the other off. I tried to distract her with cleaning, but it didn't really help. She's lost so much."

Haddie took a deep breath and plodded toward the back. *Why is it so hard for me and Meg?*

The taller pilot grabbed the door and started to close it, stopping to address her. "We'll head off and refuel. Do you have a time when you want to leave tomorrow?"

She hadn't thought that far ahead. Burying her dad had been the only focus. *Am I going back?* "I've got your number, I'll call."

He saluted and closed the back door to the van. "Ma'am."

Meg detached herself from Kiana and ran to Haddie.

With a wince, Haddie bent, and the girl wrapped her arms around her and began to cry.

"I'm glad you're okay." Meg spoke between sobs. "Please be careful."

Haddie raised her eyebrows. She'd assumed the tears were for Dad, but Meg's words surprised her. Did she know something? "Careful? Did the angels tell you something?"

Meg pulled back, composing herself and wiping her eyes. "They knew you would be sad, but they'd be there, and I would help. I think you have more things to do."

A nuclear thing. "Perhaps. But right now, we need to head back to the house, and then tomorrow we bury Dad."

Meg nodded seriously, and as Haddie straightened, the girl reached out and held her hand.

Kiana had already hobbled around to the passenger side of the van, and Sam climbed in to drive. Haddie ended up sitting with Kiana and Meg in the back while Zipper rode in the passenger seat.

"Sam, this is Zipper. She's Trig's friend. They were helping — us." Haddie stumbled over mentioning her dad. "Where can we put her up for the night?"

Sam started driving slowly across the grass, and the van shifted and swayed over the field. The headlights illuminated little other than brush. "Assuming you're taking the spare room, that leaves a couple couches. One in the living room and one in the den."

Zipper waved into the air. "I can sleep anywhere. Just put me someplace where I won't be in your way. I don't want to be a bother."

"No bother," Sam said. "Sweet tea, unsweet, or coffee?"

Zipper chuckled. "Coffee, black."

When the headlights lit stubby trees ahead, Sam pulled onto a dirt road, the van steadied, and she picked up speed.

The house came into view a moment later with its front porch lights that had been left on. Square, blocky, and wooden, it looked like a typical farmhouse.

"Are we going to leave T out here tonight?" asked Meg.

Haddie glanced at Kiana. "Probably best. Cold and protected from any animals."

"Where are we going to bury him?"

Haddie felt across her short, tangling braid. "Where would you want to?" She had no idea of the property. Dad had said that it was a farm, but that's all she knew.

"He liked the pines he planted."

Sam nodded in the front.

"Will that work?" Haddie asked Kiana.

"There's room. The ground is packed, but we didn't hit rocks." Kiana appeared somber, but attempted a smile when Meg glanced at her.

Sam pulled into a dirt drive in front of the house and parked beside two four-wheelers. Meg opened the side door, and Haddie sucked in a breath against the chilly, pine-scented air. As she stepped out, she glanced toward the back row of chairs. Dad's bag lay on the floor behind them; she could just make out the black plastic.

Haddie walked behind Sam to the front door. Someone had started a flower garden, but it needed water. "Trig's sending someone to help dig tomorrow morning. Sunrise."

Frowning, Sam glanced back. "We could have handled it."

"I wasn't sure we'd be up to it." Haddie paused at the door as Meg opened it to step inside.

Sam shrugged and motioned Haddie ahead of her.

Rock shoved past Meg and buried his head into Haddie's hand. Whining and snorting, his nails clattered on the wood floor as she rubbed behind his ears.

"I'm sorry, Boy." She pulled him to the side so Kiana could hobble in. Even as Sam bustled about getting everyone settled, Rock wouldn't leave Haddie. *I haven't been home enough.* Their life had been a daily routine. *And now . . .*

Jisoo seemed surprised to see her, but assumed it was for a feeding. Sam made Haddie tea, and she sat on the couch with the swirling warmth between her fingers while Rock curled against her thigh. Louis and Milk skittered up and down wood floors with the ferret taking an occasional run across the top of the cushions.

Kiana dragged out some clothes that somewhat fit. In the kitchen, Zipper chatted with Sam who made pasta, even though everyone had said they weren't hungry. The smell of garlic and onion started Haddie's stomach growling.

It was after midnight before hot water, bubbles, and solitude surrounded her aches. She stroked Rock's head when he laid it on the side of the tub

It would be sunrise soon.

Haddie woke to the sound of Louis yapping. The little room barely had space for the twin bed and a nightstand. The mattress didn't accommodate Haddie and Rock at the same time, but he kept her warm anyway; she lay diagonally with a bent knee and her other foot dangling off the mattress.

Outside the window was pitch black, leaving the clock to coat the room in dim red light. At a couple minutes past six a.m., a pan clanged in the kitchen while Meg called for Rock.

He lifted his head but checked on Haddie.

"Go," she said. "I'm not putting on more than a robe 'til I have to. It's got to be freezing outside." Kiana had lent her a dark purple robe and red slippers. Her fresh underwear were at the motel in Texas. The front door opened and closed, and she stretched.

Rock grunted and climbed off the bed.

They had an hour or more before sunrise, but Sam would have them fed before that. Haddie's joints still ached, but her skin wasn't as tender, except around the bruises on her chest and back. From what she could see, they'd turned darker with yellowish edges.

As she opened her bedroom door, the aroma of coffee greeted her. Jisoo cried from the kitchen.

Zipper wore the same uniform, though it looked fresh somehow. "Morning. Did we wake you?"

In a long blue T-shirt, Sam diced potatoes. " I'd have woken her up in a couple minutes anyway." She paused long enough to light the burner under a teapot. "I'm not sure Kiana's even slept. Shush Jisoo, you've been fed."

Haddie pulled a mug from the cupboard and ambled to the coffee pot. She'd need all the help she could get. Her eyes felt crusty, and her hair hung loose around her shoulders. "Can I help?"

Zipper snorted. "Best I got was to pull out some plates. She's a bit possessive about her cooking. I'm betting she'll let us clean up though."

Sam pointed her knife. "I'll send you both packing, if you get in my way."

"Don't test her." Kiana hobbled in with her crutch under one arm and a pile of clothes in the other, which she extended to Haddie.

Tucked under the shirt was a new package of undies. Haddie held the pile, trying not to let her tears well. The jeans looked like her dad's. *Focus, Haddie.* "Thank you."

"There's some jackets by the door."

Dad's jackets. No one else's would fit her.

Meg let in a breeze of iced air when she returned. She warmed herself with a hug from Haddie.

Everyone was fed and dressed by the time a bike sounded outside. Rock grumbled and stood. Haddie shooed him to the couch before the knock came on the door. A stocky man with a bushy, gray-speckled black beard waited outside. He wore a leather jacket and pants, and his helmet rested on a Harley-Davidson 1200 Custom.

"Trig sent me."

Haddie gestured him in. "Coffee?"

He stepped in and eyed Rock quickly. "Never touch the stuff. Name's Bill."

"Haddie." She walked over and sat by Rock, reassuring him.

"Figured. Trig described you. Hard to mistake you." Bill had an easy, confident way about him. His eyes smiled when he spoke, though the beard hid any smiles.

Sam came down the hall. "Good morning. Coffee?"

Bill nodded. "Black."

Haddie tilted her head in surprise, but some of Dad's friends were strange.

He smiled playfully enough that his whiskers splayed out as he ambled to one of the chairs. "Trig didn't say much about what I'd be doing. Said to bring a shovel and forget whatever I saw. Best I had is a collapsible doohickey, so I brought it. He thought you might have better — being a farm and all. A bad memory is part of my inherent assets."

Once Bill had his coffee, they all bundled up and headed into the cold. Rock kept close to Haddie even though he'd appeared to accept the new arrival. Someone had a fire going, as the hint of smoke hung with the scent of pines.

In the early light of a pale blue sky, Meg ran ahead to a patch of young trees. More than a dozen wilted in an area between the house and a disused shed. Another set of newly planted cottonwood or oak lined the outer edge of the young copse.

"Here?" Meg paced somberly at the end closest to the shed.

Haddie blinked. Far out in the fields, she spotted a pair of flickering white dots. She strode to Meg and jutted her chin toward the angels. There was no music. Too far away?

Meg reached for Haddie's hand, not taking her eyes off the lights. "Do you suppose they're here to say goodbye to T?"

Were these angels in actual heaven and the Bible? Why did Meg call them angels? Dad had never been religious, even if he often said hell and devil. Haddie swallowed "I don't know."

Bill coughed. "Y'all okay?"

She didn't answer and couldn't take her eyes off the angels. Did they have some answer to all this? Why did her dad have to die?

"Let me show you where we keep the shovels." Sam distracted him and led him off. Zipper offered to go with them.

Kiana worked her way up beside them, sniffling. "Angels?"

Haddie nodded and put her free hand on Kiana's shoulder. "Yes." She had felt something before and heard the music. *Nothing this time.* "Meg, do you know why they are here? Do you feel anything?"

Meg shook her head.

The two lights winked out.

Despite Kiana and Meg beside her, Haddie felt alone. Abandoned. She searched the area, looking for some sign of the angels. Sunrise approached, though the horizon to the east delayed it.

As the sun colored a few wisps of clouds, they both kept glancing into the field long after Zipper and Bill came out with a pair of shovels and began digging. Haddie tried to help, as did Sam, but Trig's people shrugged them off.

The more the hole took on the shape of a grave, the more difficult it became for Haddie to watch.

Meg motioned for her to follow along the thin woods at the edge of the field. "I know where there are some pretty flowers. T knew their names."

Sometimes Meg seemed to speak and act younger than her innocent age. However, she had a knack for knowing the right thing to do at the proper time. The trip into the woods worked perfectly for Haddie. Rock and Louis kept them company, and the light conversation about the plants kept Haddie from focusing on her dad's burial.

Meg led her to a knot of red flowers that bordered a pole and wire fence. The wind smelled marshy, and Haddie remembered Dad mentioning a river and reservoir. She wouldn't mind it if she moved here with Meg and Kiana. *Without David, most likely.* Maybe Terry and Liz would visit.

Louis yapped as they headed back, but Meg and Haddie didn't speak as they carried bundles of red and white flowers. *So many people died.* The carnage at the ranch flashed into Haddie's imagination like the visions that came after using her power. *More died there than at Albuquerque.* Crow had finally gotten out of the hospital. *Will this end with New York?*

Kiana with her colorful cast, Sam in pale blue, and slim, dark-clothed Zipper stood off to one side while Bill dug from inside the grave. A ladder rested on its side nearby. Earthy scents carried in the breeze.

When they arrived, Haddie gave some of her flowers to Kiana. "How's Crow doing?"

"He's fine. Overdid the meds for a day or two, but he'll be riding soon." Her eyes were puffy from crying. She looked down and tugged on her ear. "I wish we could bury him right, in a coffin and properly prepared, but I know Thomas wouldn't have cared."

"Zipper, ladder." Bill tossed his shovel out.

Haddie flushed. They were close.

Sam's voice faltered. "Should I — get the van now?" She carefully placed the flowers Meg had given her on the ground.

Zipper nodded with a grim expression. "It's time."

Haddie's chest fluttered as Sam ran off. Louis yapped, making the silence more obvious. *This is it.* Her dad was gone, forever. She choked in a sob and Kiana swayed at the sound. Haddie had the horrifying vision of them tossing her dad into the hole. *Discarded.*

Sam had to drive the van into the field to back up at an appropriate angle. Haddie found Meg's hand in hers once again.

Bill had left the dull aluminum ladder jutting from the grave. When Sam had the van parked, he and Zipper opened the back. Dad's body bag rested awkwardly on the floor behind the seats. He'd be heavy. Haddie imagined them dropping him and drew in a tight breath.

She handed her flowers to Meg. "Hold these for me."

Zipper glanced at Haddie's approach, and her lips tightened into a pained expression. They let her help. Gingerly, she took the shoulder opposite Zipper. Despite his weight, his body remained stiff in rigor mortis. The cold, thick plastic bunched in her right hand as she fought to hold him.

She'd buried a dog with Dad that they'd found on the side of the highway. It had remained frozen in a twisted position that even a beach towel couldn't hide. Tears dripped off Haddie's cheeks.

Once they laid the body down, Bill climbed into the grave, and Zipper stayed on the ladder. Haddie shifted her dad's body to waiting hands, and her teardrops left tiny puddles on the black plastic.

After they left his body on the bottom and removed the ladder, she stood between Kiana and Meg, taking her flowers.

Kiana hobbled forward and rested on her crutch before she sprinkled flowers into the grave. "You brought love into my life, Thomas. Far too short a time. You promised you'd be at my deathbed. I might never forgive you for that. However, our memories will always make me smile."

Zipper threw three flowers in. "For all of us you saved at Palo Alto, thank you. Clear skies and the wind at your back, T."

Sam choked as she dropped her bouquet in. "T, with you, everything was a miracle. You saw me and I won't forget."

Meg followed. "I love you, T."

Haddie shook as she dropped in her flowers. "I was going to quote someone from your books, Dad, but my mind won't remember them. I remember the rides in the mountains and camping beside streams. I can hear you telling me to stand up for what I believe, even when you knew I might change my mind someday. I can feel you holding me when I lost Mula. I know you loved storms and trees." She choked and forced herself to finish. "I will try and fix everything I can, to make your death worth it. I'll always love and miss you, Dad."

CHAPTER 38

Haddie sat on the couch with Rock's chin resting on her thigh; she scratched around his ears and rubbed the bridge of his nose. Louis chased Milk down the hall, nails clattering on wood floors. Sam talked with Meg on the floor, a sketchbook between them with a colorful butterfly drawn in blues and purples amid green leaves and a large yellow flower. Zipper, in one of the cushioned chairs, focused on her phone.

What now? Haddie's pulse grew restless. What was she supposed to do? Run back to Bruce's ranch? She couldn't bring herself to stare at Dad's grave any longer. Kiana had disappeared into her room.

Maybe Stanton had worked everything out. She pulled her phone out to call Trig, then scrolled to the contacts. She changed Biff from "Jerk" to "B" and dialed him.

"Hey, Haddie. How are you doing?"

"Biff, I'm sorry. I should have checked in with you earlier."

There was a long pause. "It's okay. Flesh wound."

Not from Kiana's description. "I'm glad you're okay. How long are you in there?"

"Gonna let me out tonight. Did you get T buried?"

"I'm sorry, I couldn't wait. He's — in the ground."

"Yeah. We'll come out there when this is all over." Biff's voice sounded thick.

"I'd like that," she said as her face twisted and tears welled. Sam glanced at her. Rock grunted and lifted his head. Haddie pressed him back down and stroked his eyelids. "I'm sorry." *I already said that.* "You'll call me when you get out?"

"I will, Haddie. Sorry about T. Are you okay? Can I do anything?"

"Yeah. Don't die, and stay out of jail." She hung up with Biff and wiped her face.

Meg colored, though she appeared more somber than her usual self. This had to be hard for her. Sam had barely spoken since the funeral.

Haddie glanced over to Zipper. "Thanks for helping."

Zipper looked up without moving her head and shrugged slightly. "Sure. Anything for T." She lifted her head. "Biff going to survive?"

"Yeah." Haddie stroked Rock.

"Too bad." Zipper smirked. "You should check on the boys. Men tend to get stupid ideas when they're left alone too long."

Haddie chuckled and scrolled through her contacts; she stopped at "DiCk" and dialed Cooper. "How's Stanton doing? Any luck?" she asked.

"No, but he's here. Want to talk with him?"

"Yeah. Thanks."

She waited as muted voices spoke.

When Stanton took the phone, he spoke quickly and

firmly. "We are still repairing the communications equipment. The servers with the personal information on Elon's team were damaged during the attack. We are trying to restore, but we lost one of the specialists who might have been able to fix it. We are no closer to reaching the people monitoring the bomb than when you left. The area is secure — for your return." The last part of his statement sounded almost pleading.

Haddie frowned. If Stanton wanted the bomb to go off, then he'd not be helping her at all. "I might have someone we can trust." Would Terry agree to it? Could he even help? "How fast can you get someone from Eugene?"

"Six hours, minimum. We have open contracts with a number of private jets."

"Text me a direct number for you. I'll let you know."

"I'll have a jet readied."

Haddie shook her head. "No, wait until I see if he can help."

"Better to be prepared. I'll cancel if your associate doesn't need the flight."

She raised her eyebrows. For the first time that she knew, he didn't comply with her statement. He was right, but it made her wonder what else he might do because he thought it best. "Okay. Hand me back to Cooper, please."

"Ma'am."

It took a second before Cooper came back on. "What's up?"

"Have you and Trig been able to keep an eye on Stanton?"

Cooper snorted. "Of course."

"Great." Haddie rolled her eyes. "Please let me know if anything seems weird."

"Weirder." Cooper corrected.

She hung up, patted Rock's head, and stood to pace. The house had started to get warm, but it had been chilly outside. Would Terry come out? The knot in her chest told Haddie that she wanted him to.

Haddie grabbed one of Dad's lighter jackets. "I'm going to make a call. I'll be back." Rock started to climb off the couch. "Wait here, Rock." Jisoo cried in response.

She dialed Terry once outside. The air had a crisp, fresh smell with a tinge of pine. Instead of turning toward the young copse where they'd buried her dad, she turned east toward the road.

"Hey, Buckaroo. How are you doing?"

"As good as it gets. I want to ask you a favor." She looked at her feet as she strolled, avoiding the rising sun.

"Shoot."

"Stanton, the man who's helping me try to stop the bomb, is one of Bruce's old people. For whatever reason, he's assisting. Trig, one of Dad's biker friends, and Cooper are keeping an eye on everything. However, during the whole mess, some of the servers and communications equipment were damaged. Stanton has people who should be able to fix, I think replace, their communications, but they lost the person who might retrieve the server data."

"Lost? As in wandered into the desert?" His tone suggested he guessed otherwise.

"Stanton thinks it's safe now." Maybe she shouldn't involve Terry. She had enough guilt over Dad, and she didn't need any more deaths on her conscience.

"Just kidding, Buckaroo. I can help. I'll see if I can get a flight out and call you back."

Haddie sighed and her stomach fluttered. Cooper would watch out for Terry. "There's a jet waiting for you at the Eugene airport."

"No kidding? Really? Yaass. I guess we know why they needed all that money. Other than buying bombs." He laughed and then coughed as if remembering something. "My job has a roll-out tonight. Is the Wi-Fi there decent? Even cell reception will work. It should go fine, I've just got to be available."

Terry interned remotely for a California company, though he rarely mentioned it. Haddie had reached the end of the drive. A wide field stretched on the opposite side of a two-story house at the far edge. *Am I right to do this?* Turning off a nuclear bomb seemed the best bet. Better than storming a building of fanatics who might be willing to die with it.

"I had great reception when I was there, and I had no trouble talking to Cooper this morning. I can check on the Wi-Fi if you want." She stood blinking against the sun.

"Don't bother. Just tell them I want chicken for dinner on the plane. How do I find this jet?"

Haddie chuckled, feeling a twinge of guilt. *I just buried Dad.* "I'll get you the information. Text?"

"Works, Buckaroo." He sounded excited.

She turned as they hung up. The woods to the left side of the drive were thicker than the sparse pines that led to the house. Haddie had only taken a single step before she heard the music. She recognized the angel's song. Three pinpricks of light looked like distant headlights on the drive, but they originated near the house. As before, they moved quickly toward her. Her chest tightened and she held her breath. In a moment they had moved close, and with them came their music and a serenity that let her breathe.

Like tunnels into infinity, they widened, grouped close together. Speeding ribbons flickered from eternity and back. White light peeled off their edges, feathering to the dirt and threatening to obscure the drive and house, but she could still see everything clearly.

They knew about the bomb.

"What do I do?"

She could sense distinct entities this time, but nothing changed with her question. They didn't answer. They just were.

Her eyes flicked at a motion. Meg ran down the drive, escorted by Rock's easy gait and Louis bouncing and skipping to keep up.

There was more that she could do, but they weren't ready yet. They felt her pain — her loss. Tears flowed down her cheeks, warm against the chill. *I just want to be alone.* Her body ached and she wanted to curl back into bed with Rock pressed against her.

She couldn't rest yet. There were things that needed to be done. They knew it, and now Meg knew it.

Meg stopped on the other side of the angels. Did they look the same from her view? Rock paused, watching Haddie.

What kind of world would Meg grow up in if the bomb went off in New York?

Dad wouldn't want that to happen.

PART V

We must be ready to aid the Seroveilm in defense of this world, both from outside and the Noveilm within.

CHAPTER 39

As the angels dwindled, Meg brought an excited, yapping Louis to Aunt Haddie. Rock trotted along the drive. The colors the angels brought faded though the fields where rich browns and golds were dotted by the occasional white or yellow flower.

Her heart raced. T had died, and Aunt Haddie was still in danger. *I'll be strong, just like them.* They had come this time for Aunt Haddie; she'd be leaving again. *The angels need Aunt Haddie and me.* Aunt Haddie had her work to do first, but they would need Meg soon.

CHAPTER 40

Haddie winced as she knelt to comfort Rock. Louis yapped as Meg ran over. The angels had withdrawn, but their somber tones hung in Haddie's soul. The road and farm looked dusty and dull without them.

Meg slowed. "Are you leaving now?"

There's little more I can do here. Stanton needed to get the people in New York to disable the bomb, then the authorities could move in. Terry might be able to help. *What good will I be?* Haddie drew deep a breath, trying to fill the emptiness in her chest. *Do I head back to Bruce's ranch?*

"I think I'll be leaving today. Sorry I couldn't stay longer. Maybe, when this is over."

Meg offered a comforting smile. "I understand. The angels need you."

It had seemed they had designs on Meg as well. Now that they were gone, she found that troubling. *Who were they? Who am I?* Anger flushed up her cheeks. She'd never asked for any of this.

Rock leaned in and nuzzled her neck. "I'll be back soon," she said, heading back toward the house.

Sam took it as calmly as Meg had, but there was an underlying sadness to her usual cheery demeanor. Jisoo complained.

Eyes red and puffy, Kiana came out and stumbled toward the kitchen with her crutch. "Shut up, Jisoo."

Haddie followed her in. "I'm going back to the ranch."

Kiana poured herself some water. "When do we leave? Do I have time for a shower?"

"You don't have to —"

"I'm going, Haddie." Kiana's expression hardened. "I'm so angry right now I can barely contain it. Don't treat me like I'm fragile."

Haddie nodded. She'd rarely seen Kiana like this, and then only for moments. Pulling out her phone, she dialed the pilot. "We're ready."

By the time she got information for Terry, and Kiana had packed some clothes for them, the helicopter thudded overhead. As if on guard, Zipper stood stiffly at the front door. Stanton had seemed excited to hear of Haddie's return. His usual monotone responses returned when he reported that he hadn't made any headway on stopping the bomb in New York. Trig confirmed that the ranch appeared safe. There had been no signs of the remainder of the men who had been attacking with Elon.

Haddie's pulse started to rise when she thought of going back. Dad had died there. Why would she want to be there? *Fix this first, then figure out my life.* She hardened when she thought of David. Could she watch him grow old and die?

The day had warmed, and the air smelled earthy. Instead of driving, they walked to where the helicopter had landed, pausing to look at the fresh grave. *I'll be back, Dad.*

Promise. Would they put a marker there? Haddie started to ask, but Kiana's dour expression didn't seem worth interrupting. The pilots waited outside the helicopter.

Terry texted a picture of the jet and Haddie sent an emoji. "Terry's going to meet us at the ranch. Stanton needs help fixing equipment."

Kiana frowned. "When?"

Haddie showed her the image. "He's getting on the jet now, I imagine."

"He'll be there ahead of us then." Kiana's eyes focused on her feet. "What's the plan?"

"Stanton hopes to contact the people protecting the bomb directly. They'll have regular communications up soon."

"Need to keep an eye on him."

"Cooper and Trig are on it."

The pilots had the block out and offered Kiana help inside. Zipper carried the small duffel they'd brought. The smell of exhaust hung around the helicopter. Haddie sighed. What am I doing? *I doubt I'll sleep through this trip.*

Terry texted another picture of the inside of the jet and an attendant. Haddie almost ignored his next text. "The Unceasing are posting pretty heavy. End of the world stuff. Are you sure about the timing?"

I wish I weren't involved. She had to at least try. Stanton and Terry were the key to fixing this, but they both would need her.

Leaving the pilots saluting at the door, she texted. "See you in Texas. Thank you."

"You got it, Buckaroo. Thanks for the sweet ride."

CHAPTER 41

As the helicopter approached its landing area at the ranch, Haddie focused on the ruins of the truck she'd dropped on Bruce. The dirt around it had tractor marks, and the cab was gone. The thudding blades above slowed as they descended, and dust rose to obliterate the scene. Stanton stood at the drive to the house.

Kiana had barely spoken during the trip. "I'm going to have Trig fill me in, then I'd like to find out about this children's home."

Haddie twisted her hair into a tight knot against her neck. "I want to check in with Terry." Her mouth felt dry, though she'd avoided drinking much until she knew they were a couple minutes from landing.

"Good idea."

Is this what the angels expected me to be doing? It had felt like something more. Terry would have an idea if they could move forward.

Haddie winced as they landed. The shot to her back hurt the worst, though her chest looked ugly.

Outside, Stanton strode toward their door clutching his tablet like a drowning man held a life preserver.

The pilot opened the door, and even in the late afternoon, warm Texas air flooded in with a disturbing ripe smell. The helicopter sat where Haddie had dismembered some of the demons. After Albuquerque, were there any left? She smiled.

Zipper looked quizzical. "What are you thinking about?" She grabbed Kiana's duffel bag.

"That there may not be any more demons left."

Zipper grimaced. "Those headless mutants in the pit?"

"Yeah." Perhaps the heads had gone in the hole first. Where were they buried?

Cooper waited by the house while Trig jogged toward the helicopter.

Moving to the door, Zipper shook her head. "I hope you're right about those — demons."

Stanton waited for Haddie to stretch. "Your man, Terrence, is hopeful about his progress."

"And then we call off this bombing?" She strode for the house.

"Hopefully. Elon's people can be difficult." Stanton's tone gave no hint to his hope for success.

Trig frowned. "He never told us you were about to arrive. He's slippery." He gave Stanton a dark look.

Stanton remained indifferent and swiped across his tablet. "Communications are due to be restored in three hours. We are waiting on one component. Patrols continue to report back that the perimeters are clear. Unless you have an immediate use, I'll send the helicopter for refueling and maintenance."

Haddie nodded and addressed Trig and Cooper.

"Thanks for staying here. I was half tempted not to come back."

Cooper grunted. "And not try to fix this?"

This isn't some obsession. She drew in a breath and faced Trig. "Dad is buried. I need to finish this."

"About that." A sly smile crept across his face. "I've been talking with Biff and Crow. Think a few of us could come by and pay our respects, once this is over?" He laughed before she could respond. "What we mean is light a fire pit and get drunk at T's grave?" He shrugged one shoulder. "If one drinks."

Haddie held back her tears. Kiana just stood to the side and listened with a somber expression. "If Kiana, Sam, and Meg are up for it."

"You'll barely notice we're there." Trig's smile suggested otherwise.

Kiana nodded. "First, care to walk me through what you've got set up here for defenses, Trig?" She motioned for them to head away from the house.

Haddie glanced at Cooper. He'd found a pair of fatigues to wear, and he appeared to fit the part. She led the way toward the house, and Stanton followed.

Cooper strode toward them, shortening the distance. "I see you brought Terry. You think he can fix this equipment?"

"If anyone can." She didn't actually know. Just because Terry could hack like the wind didn't mean he could fix equipment. However, she'd seen some of his set-ups, and they looked pretty intense. *I'm happy when the printer works.*

He studied her for a moment, then gestured to the side of the house where the portables stood. "Were you headed to check in on him?"

She nodded. The area looked deserted, except for the few guards posted at the corners of buildings. The bodies were gone, but she recognized blood in places. The window to the map room had been boarded up. The buried container was more visible. Whatever tarp had been covering the ramp down to it had been removed.

The wooden stairs and railing to the portable had bloody handprints and splintered notches missing, she imagined from bullets.

Inside, the gaping hole she'd seen earlier extended into the portable. The blast had torn metal and melted plastic into unrecognizable forms. Blood crusted the floor in pools. The room reeked of extinguished electrical fires.

Under a console, Terry worked on a rack of equipment resting on the floor. Wires wound up to components and a monitor on the tabletop.

"Pretty bad." Haddie drew in a deep breath. This would take longer than she expected.

"Hey, Buckaroo." Hair draped into his eyes as he looked up with a cheesy grin. "No, this is easy. I've got three different raids going on here. I'm not sure which ones are which, but I'll have a scavenged system up and running in the next twenty minutes. I can get Spooky Jeeves to identify them." He nodded toward Stanton.

"I will recognize the directory with the personal information quickly." Stanton didn't appear offended by Terry's moniker.

"Team Buckaroo." Terry tucked his head back under.

Haddie sighed and relaxed. *Finally, a break.*

CHAPTER 42

After spending a couple minutes but not wanting to delay Terry, Haddie walked down the steps. Two soldiers stopped talking as they passed the end and studied her quickly before they moved on. Somewhere in the fields, a four-wheeler whined, and the echo rung in the space between the portables.

She hadn't slept much on the flight until the end. Zipper had a few stories about Dad that Haddie hadn't heard before. *There's probably a lot of those.* When this was over, she planned on pumping Crow and Trig for more.

"Stanton, is there anything to eat?"

"I had them leave a plate for you in the fridge. I can heat it up."

She hadn't intended him to serve her, but ordering delivery seemed like a bad idea. "Thanks."

Cooper trailed to the side, looking at the western horizon with a scowl that intensified with his squint in the face of a lowering sun.

"How's your bruises?" She pointed to her own chest.

"Hurts. Stanton had a nurse check me out. Bruised ribs."

Caught up in her own loss, she hadn't really wondered what had happened to the wounded. Did Bruce have doctors and nurses on staff? If he planned a near apocalypse, wouldn't he?

On the front door, one of the windowpanes had a piece of wood tacked over it; she hadn't noticed it broken when they left, but there had been a lot of gunfire before they'd killed Elon.

Inside looked worse. Most of the windows in the office had been boarded up. The monitors and equipment were stacked to the side, and the desk was tilted forward. The room felt barricaded. The cigar scent dulled her hunger. She stopped at the arch to the dining room. Elon's blood still stained the walls.

"I will have someone in to clean up." Stanton passed her as he headed into the kitchen.

With all the damage to the house, where would she sleep? High up the wall, near the ceiling, she could make out a bullet that had punched through drywall. Perhaps this would all be over before she had to make that decision. She wanted her bed in her apartment that she probably could never visit again. *I want my own clothes.* She wore her dad's jeans with his belt and a black T-shirt of Kiana's.

Cooper walked across the floor behind her, and she felt trapped between ruined rooms.

I'm acting spoiled. Her phone vibrated, and she fished it out of her pocket.

Terry texted. "Tell Spooky Jeeves I've got the first raid up for him to look at."

Good. Haddie relayed the information. "Terry's ready for you to come look at the first server."

For the first time that she'd seen, Stanton had put the tablet down. He leaned over and swiped out a message. "I will have one of the technicians review the data. They know which files to look for."

Haddie walked across the office to the chair pushed against the wall. There wasn't any blood spattering the beige paint, just a couple of bullet holes. "Someone's on their way," she texted to Terry. Leaning into the chair, she peered out the left corner of the window where some glass remained intact. Blue sky silhouetted a dark green sprig of a treetop.

"Good news?" asked Cooper.

"Hopefully." Haddie stared at the leaves outside until they blurred. "Assuming we stop this, what will you do?"

"Haven't given it much thought. I've just been focused on surviving the last week. I don't have anything to go back to."

Cooper had obsessed on tracking down the truth when he came with them to Albuquerque. "Did you find the answers you were looking for?" she asked.

"Some. I think I understand what you were fighting all this time. Bruce and the Unceasing." He sighed. "Added a couple questions though."

She understood Bruce's plans and his beliefs, to an extent. *But, what are we?* He called them the Noveilm, which meant nothing. The angels were another mystery. When they were close, they seemed normal and reasonable. Perhaps some effect of their presence. What were they?

Haddie turned to him. "I've got some questions of my own."

CHAPTER 43

Haddie stepped outside and shivered.

Cooper followed. "Temperature's dropping. It'll be cold tonight."

Stars covered the southern sky. The floodlights from the side of the barn masked the horizon, but if she looked up, the night sky shone brightly. With some food and an hour nap, her mood had improved.

"Hopefully, Stanton has had some luck and we're done with all this." *He would have come and reported to me.*

The ground still stunk of rotting viscera, but the night breeze alternately pushed the reek away from her. Trig and one of his people walked along the drive in front. She'd noticed that his bikers were usually guarding close to the house. They wore black and stood out from the camouflaged soldiers under Stanton's — her — control.

Smaller floodlights lit the areas between the three portables, and two soldiers worked on the equipment atop the middle one. Their ladder leaned down, nearly blocking the steps.

Inside, Terry perched on a stool while Stanton stood in the middle of the room, looking up from his tablet.

"Outside communications have been restored," Stanton said.

Terry tapped on an empty soda bottle. "Not doing too well on the other front."

Haddie frowned. "What do you mean?"

Stanton remained impassive. "I have been unable to contact any of the people assigned to the device. I tried cellular, and now that communications are restored, I went through our encrypted connection. None of them are answering."

"There's only six of them in the building. I tracked their cells. The rest have hightailed it out of New York, along with the rest of the Unceasing." Terry shrugged with an apologetic expression "You need to alert the authorities."

"They will detonate if anyone attempts to evacuate New York, or if there is an attempted SWAT breach." Stanton's tone held no remorse or emotion. "That is protocol."

From Terry's expression, Haddie imagined they'd been having this conversation before she arrived. *What should I do?*

"Maybe they're rethinking their suicide options at this point," Terry said.

Stanton shook his head. "Three on this list are coerced, bound to Bruce. They will stick to the mission plans he laid out, and the protocols."

Coerced. Haddie drew in a long breath. No wonder they weren't responding. Were they disoriented now, like Josh had been?

Cooper spoke from behind her. "Options? Considering their protocols."

"A small force. I have mercenaries I can call in. If they

can disable the few key holders, then you might have a chance at stopping the device. Unfortunately, I lack details of the device's whereabouts or the organizational structure of the team." Stanton didn't sound hopeful.

Haddie didn't like the idea of risking everything on mercenaries she didn't know, but she couldn't gamble the lives of Trig and his people. "The building — is it abandoned?"

"No." Stanton scrolled across his tablet. "Twenty-three apartments are presently rented out. Should I prepare a team?"

Haddie shook her head. *I need to think this through.* They still had four days. "I need to wrap my head around this. How many floors? What's the layout? Who are the tenants? Families? Can you send details to my phone?" Maybe she should set up Bruce's office again.

Stanton focused on his tablet.

Terry nodded. "I've got my work thing to do in a couple hours. Where can I set up a laptop?" He motioned to the hole in the side of the trailer. "A bit drafty in here."

"There's a quiet map room in the house." A flush ran up her neck. *He'll look in the garage.* Part of her still held that rage. "I'm going to take a walk." Cooper stood too close behind her. She pushed past him. "Alone."

Cooper followed anyway. "I wouldn't walk around here without someone. I don't trust these people."

Blocking the bottom of the steps, she turned and faced him. "I can handle myself."

Cooper cocked his head to the side, nodding slightly. "You can. But anyone can be surprised."

Does he mean Dad? Heat flushed up her cheeks. "Just give me some space." She stomped past the end of the portables and turned south, toward the starry horizon.

I knew this wouldn't be simple. Frustration welled, and her stomach churned. There had to be a way to stop Bruce's bomb. She couldn't let all those people die. Trig patrolled to the left, and she veered right, heading toward the front of the silver building. The remains of the truck loomed in the lot ahead. *Where Dad died.* What would he do? He'd sneak off by himself.

Haddie turned left along the fence and stalked toward the back of the barn. She couldn't visit the spot where Bruce had shot Dad, not at the moment. Behind the building, the ground still smelled like the fire their explosives had started. All but one of the containers were torn to half their size or less and had melted along edges. The lights were dim in the back, so she could see the stars. Underfoot were shreds of metal and globs of blackened ash which crunched with each step.

Any choice she made, there was a risk of a nuclear bomb detonating in New York City. How many people would die? Her safest option would be to notify the authorities with as much information as she could gather. It likely still would be disastrous. Bruce would have prepared against the government, first and foremost. *Should I let Stanton send in a team?* That put more of the responsibility on her if it failed. *Am I afraid of the blame?* Haddie considered calling Liz or Sam; they helped her think through difficult situations.

A soft crunch sounded ahead and to the left, behind the shell of a container that barely came up head height. The noise echoed off the steel walls of the barn on her right side. Haddie stopped. "Hello?" Had Cooper followed anyway?

A chill rose up her back, and Haddie shivered. Beyond the wreckage a fence bordered a dirt road to the south, and to the west she could make out parked pickups, Trig's Jeeps, and four-wheelers. Someone could be hiding behind the remnants of the containers.

Kiana had ridden the extended perimeter with Trig, and she seemed confident of their defenses. Cooper had been the one to warn her.

Haddie's jaw tightened, and she took another step, then paused to listen. Lights moved in the distance and appeared from behind the edge of the barn as a four-wheeler bounced along the southern horizon. Its grinding and whining engine sounded as it cleared the building and cut westward.

Nothing moved around her that she could see. Taking a deep breath to calm her nerves, she strode toward the end of the barn and past the destroyed containers.

Metal clattered near the southernmost container. She stopped mid-step, her foot crunching into dirt and debris. There was barely enough metal wall left to hide a person. Perhaps an animal? *I'm being paranoid.*

Haddie walked forward, her eyes locked on the corner of the container, and stopped when she could see all the way into it. *No one.* She turned and looked behind her. *Nothing.*

Slower, she strolled the few steps past the end of the barn to the fence and looked at the stars. The four-wheeler had disappeared to the west. The round wood post felt warm and rough; barbed wire strung out from the sides, and dry grass plumed around the base.

A footstep rustled behind her, and Haddie turned.

A young man with a wide-eyed expression leaped to his feet from where he crawled in the shadow of the barn. The soldier looked more fearful than dangerous. His lips pouted.

He stepped toward her and fumbled with his holster. Both hands grappled clumsily at this side.

This is a kid. Most of the soldiers looked grizzled, in

their thirties or forties. College age and terrified, this man still meant to kill her. Haddie race toward him.

He pulled his knife out of his sheath with his left hand. His right hand found the grip to his gun.

Haddie leaped the last step and kicked with her heel. She caught him in the solar plexus with her full weight.

Exhaling a heavy grunt, he flew backward into the shadow of the barn.

Am I going to beat him up? She needed to get his weapons. Hell, Cooper had been right. Her teeth ground as she stalked toward him.

Knife lost, his right hand slid the gun awkwardly loose from the holster. The muzzle pointed low and to his side.

No. She couldn't face killing another person.

He kicked a heel into a clump of grass, pushing himself back, as if he were afraid of her.

Did he know?

The muzzle raised. Her hand reached out as if to stop his movement. Haddie screamed in anger and frustration.

CHAPTER 44

Haddie blinked as her tone rang in the air.

The boy remained. He let out a garbled cry. They both stared where the gun had been, his hand curled around a non-existent handle. She hadn't hurt him.

A mistake. Her skin prickled across her face and blue light drifted off her outstretched hand. The visions would come. She'd be helpless if he found the knife.

He sputtered and kicked himself back.

Haddie retreated a step, wincing at the pain of the purpura. The barn, the stars, and the shadow dimmed as the visions prepared to take her.

The pain across her skin vanished. The night turned vibrant; even the stars seemed to have blues and reds in them. Her faded blue mist lightened to nearly white and thickened to stream off her exposed hand.

She heard a winding tone, similar to her own. An angel was nearby. Close.

A plane of light passed through her, and vertigo nearly flopped her to the ground. She staggered, but her legs held. The angel itself carried a sense of being and place, of music, vibration, and light. Her skin still glowed, and white-blue wisps twirled off her, as if influenced by the portal. Even inches away from it, the ribbons defied definition as they moved as fast as lightning. Markings lined their surfaces and edges, indecipherable as they sped past.

The visions didn't take Haddie. Her skin felt chilled, but no new pain crawled across it. In fact, she felt none of her injuries or aches. Because of the angel? *Why is it here, now?*

She could see the boy running away, and sensed shapes and noises near the portables. It all seemed distant, as if it belonged to some other place, some other time.

The angel was now.

Haddie felt a knowledge of a distant place. A semblance of a vision, where it was cold and wet. *Dad.* Not as she had known him, but younger, not in appearance, but brash with youthful arrogance. Ice filled her veins. Her dad, before he'd ever used his powers or met her mother, was alive right now. She watched him around a fire with two other bikers, laughing and drinking without a care.

A sickening grief tugged at her face.

The vision changed. Outside of her interaction with the angel, she knew there was yelling and shapes moving in the real world. Then it disappeared and she saw him again. *Dad.*

She focused on the image that was not her now, but one of the times for the angels. It made no sense, but she knew this was a future, one of many. Sparks flew up from the side of a motorcycle as it dropped onto wet asphalt. A delivery truck, bulky and green, rumbled out of a driveway onto the paved road.

Haddie stood at the edge of the woods screaming, her tone a ringing peal.

The moment before the tires rolled onto her dad, he vanished.

No, she thought. *I won't.* All of his distant time in the past, had it been caused by her?

The image replayed, and she turned toward the truck as it rumbled carelessly down the drive, and she growled. It faded in excruciating slow eternity. With every molecule that drifted away, so did she. The vision popped away, and she sucked in cold air.

The angel sped into nothingness, a pinpoint on Cooper's chest as he ran toward Haddie. There were other figures and shadows ahead. People yelled, and voices echoed along the barn, but she couldn't focus.

Haddie sobbed and fell to her knees.

It was horrible. *Unfair.* If she saved Dad by stopping the truck, she couldn't exist to keep him safe, so she could only rescue him by sending him back. The angel knew and understood.

CHAPTER 45

HADDIE SOBBED and trembled as she knelt on the grass.

Cooper yelled as he sprinted toward her. "She's down here!"

He ran in the shadow of the barn, barely a silhouette, but she'd been able to identify him when the angel had been between them. Other figures scurried toward her from the left side of the barn.

She couldn't make the choice the angel had offered. Dad was alive, in his true lifetime, right now. *I could meet up with him.* If she stopped him from going on the doomed ride, she wouldn't exist. Wouldn't it all fall apart as soon as she was gone?

Cooper came to a stop past the corner of the barn. Floodlights far to the front illuminated a worried scowl. "We caught him. Are you okay? Did he attack you?"

I have no choice. Her knees shook as she forced herself up. "Yeah. I made his gun disappear. That doesn't matter. I've got to talk with Stanton, see if he can get me to . . ." Could she explain what she was doing without turning it into a debate?

"Get you where?"

She caught the glint of Stanton's tablet as he ran with others toward them. He wouldn't argue the situation. Haddie's face started to drain of blood when she thought of Kiana. *She can't know.*

"I need to talk with Stanton alone."

"About the device?"

Haddie shook her head. "This is not about the bomb in New York. I promise."

Cooper's scowl deepened. He glanced behind at the approaching people. "Stanton may have planned this whole attack."

Stanton had plenty of chances to kill her or get her killed. He acted like a fanboy, not a devious conspirator. "I don't think so."

Trig and Stanton came to a stop on each side of Cooper. Zipper stopped a few feet behind, weapon in hand and peering around the area.

Haddie waved off Trig as he started to question her. "I'm fine. The kid's more scared than I was." *At least of him.* The angel and her choice terrified her. "I need to speak with Stanton alone for a moment. This isn't a debate."

Trig paused, then sighed. "Can we at least get you inside?"

She drew in a tight breath, trying not to react to his need for control. *He means well.* Haddie knew the time and the exact location; somehow it burned inside her, like a lamp she was drawn to. She needed to act soon. Getting there would take time. Haddie gestured for Stanton to follow as she walked four steps toward the fence. Facing the stars, she spoke low enough that only he could hear. "I need to get to Iceland — the north side at 5 p.m. local time tomorrow.

Obviously, with a warrant, I can't go through airport screening. Can you get me there?"

He scrolled across his tablet. "We would need to leave tonight. I've asked your crew to ready the jet."

"No one except the pilots and you are to know the destination." Haddie turned back to study Cooper and Trig. *They won't trust that I'm not going to New York.* She marched back to the men, who had nearly matching scowls. "I need to go on a trip. It does not involve New York. Okay for Zipper to accompany me?"

Trig looked surprised. "Where?"

"I can go alone." Haddie motioned back toward the house and began to walk, passing Zipper. *Now I need to deal with Kiana.*

Trig swore, and Haddie thought she heard Zipper laugh. Despite the open air, the air was foul. The young, terrified attacker knelt amid the wreckage with two of Trig's people at each shoulder. The young man's eyes widened as she passed.

Haddie found Kiana at the front of the house leaning against her crutch, watching Trig's people and their captive.

"Trouble?" she asked Haddie.

Haddie twisted her hair back. "A little. But I need to leave — and I can't say why. A day, then I'll be back."

Kiana's head cocked to the side, then her lips pinched tight. "Why can't you tell me? I went through this with your father. I don't need it from you."

"I'm sorry. Don't ask me on this." Haddie blushed. *I can't tell her.* "It has nothing to do with Bruce or the bomb. I've seen something with the angels, and I need to deal with it. I can't . . ."

Kiana jerked her head and focused behind Haddie. "Cooper, give us some space." She threw both hands up.

"Whatever, Haddie. Stanton can show me the group home tomorrow."

"He and Zipper will be going with me. I'm taking Zipper so you all won't think I'm going to New York."

Kiana started to speak. Her lips tightened, and she nodded. Without another word, she spun and limped toward the house.

Haddie had thought to go in and get some clothes, but felt awkward following Kiana in. She turned to find the others waiting behind her on the drive. The cool air reeked from the death that had seeped into the soil, especially this close to the house. She'd be happy to go somewhere different. *I'll text Terry.*

In the same Jeep she'd taken to the helicopter, Trig drove them to the airport. Haddie sat in the back with Stanton. "I'm going to need some clothes."

He pulled up his tablet. "I'll find someone who can deliver to our first stop. Warm gear." He typed through a search and offered her a site. His first reaction was to hold onto the tablet as she looked at the clothing, but he acquiesced as she attempted to take it.

How cold would it be? She ordered layers of pants and shirts with a jacket. Zipper had a jacket, but she hadn't brought anything to change into. "Zipper, what size pants?"

Zipper leaned back and nodded at the selection. "Medium in most."

Haddie showed her a black shirt and received a confirming nod. She dug through and frowned. "Underwear?"

Stanton put his hand out for the tablet, did a search, and handed it back to her.

Trig cut through the back highway until they reached a more populated section with typical homes and manicured lawns, neon gas stations, and strip malls. A quick set of turns led to the airport. Stanton leaned forward and gave directions to a private gate. Past Trig's bald dome, she could see a man standing outside the guard shack. As he spotted Stanton leaning forward, he waved the man inside the small building to raise the gate. They were through without question.

The plane they stopped at had two female pilots waiting in caps and uniforms that differed only slightly from those of the men who flew the helicopter. The plane itself had five windows down the side and looked as though it could easily fit more than her, Stanton, and Zipper. Its wingtips were tilted up sharply at the ends.

Trig stepped out with them and approached Haddie on the tarmac. "Still don't like this." He shrugged. "You're a lot like your father. Be careful."

She fought tears. Dad had been a good man who shouldn't have died at Bruce's hand. The image of him skidding across the asphalt loomed in her mind. She imagined him, bike and all, disappearing and her tone ringing in the air. *I've made my choice.* Biting her lip, she nodded to Trig and strode toward the plane.

Haddie accepted another glass of iced tea. The attendant had made it as she described, and the glass felt both warm and cool against her palm. He'd asked about beverages when they first boarded the plane and seemed pleased when she approved. The plane's engines were winding down; one of the captains had announced they were nearing their first refueling. The jet had nine first class seats, and she faced Stanton. Zipper lounged to her right after leaning the chair back to serve as a bed.

"We're on schedule to be two hours early to your exact location." Stanton looked up from his tablet. "Weather is forecast to be cold and raining. I have taken the liberty of ordering hooded raincoats to go over your jackets."

She'd known the weather, but hadn't mentioned it to Stanton. He'd questioned her when she pointed to an exact location on a map, and then quickly retracted the statement, as if he'd insulted her. Anyone else would think she was crazy, pointing out a remote road outside the city. Where was Dad going? Why was he biking in Iceland? Of all the questions, she'd never asked that one. *Now, I can't.*

"A car is waiting at our final airfield, Akureyri Airport."

"There's no customs or anything to worry about?" Haddie took a sip. *An earthy tea, maybe even Pu'er.* She'd told the attendant to surprise her.

"We have a contact here, and diplomatic status. If there is any difficulty with local authorities, we have resources we can bring to bear."

The plane tilted, and the captain's voice came over the speaker. "We'll be circling in and have clearance to land in twelve minutes. Flight crew, prepare for landing."

Speckled lights marked civilization below while night hid this part of Canada. The pilots planned another refueling to get Haddie to Iceland well before Dad's accident. She hadn't asked the details.

Zipper straightened in her chair. "Never been to this part of Canada. I ride mainly the west coast. Calgary and Edmonton are about as east as I've gone."

"We ended up over the border a few hours north a couple times. Once, Dad took me up to Prince George, then west to Kaien Island. It was beautiful."

"I like that run. Rode that one with T two years ago. Great bar down by the ocean, and Kinnikinnick campground was always fun."

Trading stories with Zipper always gave Haddie a little insight into her dad. Considering the circumstance, it hurt a little, but she wouldn't have missed them.

The pilots stepped outside once they landed, and Stanton oversaw the provisioning. They'd passed midnight with the time change, and he still had people bringing him supplies. Somehow, he'd even managed to get their clothes. Haddie looked at the thermals and handed them off to the attendants. The chilled air coming in from the tarmac wouldn't last, and she'd be sweating.

Zipper held up the shirt and pants. "Thanks, I didn't bring enough clothes for this gig." She nodded toward the thermals. "Planning on riding or camping?"

At this point, it wouldn't matter if she knew or told Trig. "Iceland."

"Cool." Zipper smiled and shifted her braid out from behind her back. It stayed neat. Haddie's would have frizzed out.

Zipper changed into her new clothes when they were half an hour from Akureyri. Haddie spent most of her time staring at the rocky terrain. She'd be marooning Dad in the past. Had he always liked the mountains?

She'd gotten a couple hours of sleep, as had Zipper, and she might have caught Stanton napping at one point. Haddie jumped into the bathroom for a quick change when they landed. She planned on standing on the roadside, and the thermals would make it bearable.

When the pilots opened the door, she could smell the rain and feel a chilly wind. They had two hours to kill before Haddie had to be at the scene. Anxiety built in waves every time she considered what she had to do. *I need a distraction.* "Did you find us a place?" she asked Stanton.

"Yes. There are multiple bars that serve food in the city. Do you have a preference of menu options?"

"Surprise me." Haddie bundled up in the rain jacket he provided and tightened the hood over her hair.

She didn't recognize the model of the gray Volvo SUV sitting outside. A burly man waited at the end of the stairs with an umbrella; from his size, he could provide protection as well as drive locally. He was probably the type of man Bruce preferred to hire.

Haddie climbed in the back with Zipper, leaving Stanton in the front. The splashing ride through city streets, slick with rain, twisted her stomach, but she kept her face tightly under control. She hated everything about this.

Dad would die without her interference, so he wouldn't have lived in the past to marry her mother. *I'm doing the right thing.* It felt like she planned to attack him. She'd saved Kiana by moving her through time. *No different.*

The beer ended up being heavy and dark. Stanton didn't drink, and the tablet never left his lap. Zipper happily finished Haddie's fries. Haddie spent the last half hour comparing the campsites she and Zipper had been to in the northwest. A sizable number of them they'd both visited with Dad.

"Log House?" Haddie asked, knowing the answer.

Zipper sipped at her beer. She'd nursed the same glass throughout the meal. She wiped her lips, and a smile broke out. "Hell, yah. I'd say near every other year for the past fifteen. First year was when I ran away from home with Big Ben. You never met him, I bet. He took me up to Hell's Canyon. T always went up to Hat Point. I think it meant something to him."

Is that what Dad's here for — camping? Lousy weather. She'd seen wetter with him, but rarely this cold.

She hadn't applied any makeup to cover her markings, but would have if she had thought to ask for some. The waiter who spoke English was polite enough, but kept glancing at her, even as they left. *I must look horrible.*

The cloud-covered sun shone a dull gray and threatened to drop behind the western ridge as they headed out to the SUV. The driver got wet opening the door for Haddie. "You've got the coordinates to drop me off at?" she asked.

The man spoke passable English. "I do."

Stanton turned around in the front seat. "Are we dropping you off at the side of the road? Is that wise?"

None of this felt wise. "Do a lap. I'll tell you how long to take before you come back." The beer and food churned in her stomach. "I need to be alone for this." Did she not want them to know because of guilt?

She doomed Dad to centuries. From his visions, she knew that he lived through heartaches that she couldn't imagine. *I have no choice.* If she failed or bailed out, she'd never exist. That meant she couldn't not make the choice. There appeared no end to the circle, except for him to die under that truck. If she could choose her dad's present life over her own, that would steal everything else from him, good and bad. Bruce, in the meantime, might go unchecked and destroy everything.

He'd never know her mother, Meg, or Kiana. *Or me.*

Stanton looked worried as they left her on the side of the road.

She recognized the dirt drive that the truck would exit. Vaporizing a trench there would stop the driver and save Dad. He would survive a simple drop, but that would cause her not to exist. Because she wouldn't be born to save him, he'd die anyway. Her only choice was to send him back in time and let the circle begin.

Rain pounded against her, and her soul felt like it poured out into the rivulet that she stood beside. It wound along the road, heading toward the curve that her dad would come around.

The field on the driver's side of the road looked wide and empty except for a few small pines by the roadside beyond the dirt entrance. There was nothing that should have hidden the truck from her dad. The road curved just downhill, so from Dad's perspective, it might be obscured in the rain.

I should have called Liz or Sam. Wind buffeted her in a

sudden gust that pushed her back. The road curved. A good gust of wind, slick asphalt, and Dad might just end up dropping. She stepped back, nearly into the branches of the small pines that grew along the road.

Uphill, to her left, dim lights lit windows of a house. Was that where he was going? That close? *If I could, I'd fix his present life and end mine.* Would he have been happier?

The wind pressed against her, and thunder rolled in the hills behind her. Rain drove in a sheet, wetting her face and soaking into her shirt at her throat. It smelled like the ocean.

The lights of the truck bobbed in the field across the road from her. Her pulse quickened. Distant, they dimmed and lightened between waves of rain.

Haddie drew in a breath and glanced downhill, where she expected Dad. There was no light of a motorcycle, but over the wind, she imagined she heard a bike. Deep and rumbling. *Dad always runs his headlights.* He would never forget. Not her dad. *This wasn't Dad, yet.* The person she knew would take hundreds of years to become.

A sob escaped Haddie as chrome reflected off dim headlights at the corner. He pulled too tight, and she could hear the tire grab as he braked. He saw the truck. Why was he going so fast?

The front tire wobbled, and he went down.

Dim headlights lit the ground in front of her. The truck's wipers splashed water across the windshield, but it showed no hint of slowing. She sucked in a breath and turned back to her dad.

I don't even know his real name. Sparks flew off the side of the bike, doused by the downpour. A gust pressed against her side and threatened to topple her.

Her voice came out a mere pleading squeak. "No."

The rain slowed, turning iridescent. Her tone rang in

the air, amplified against the wind and weather. Blue light rose from her face.

An angel's tone mixed with hers and the panic, fear, and doubt faded away. The fields and truck became clear despite the downpour. Motion became curves and symmetry. Drops of rain appeared to pause.

A void in the symphony of splashing rain, Dad and his bike vanished.

The angel appeared in front of Haddie, and time resumed its usual pace. The raindrops glowed in colors as they passed its light. As time sped up, the driver, belatedly, braked the truck and dragged the rear tires through mud. She could see through the side window as the man rose in his seat.

He's gone. Twice. Haddie fell back into the short pines, but not from pain or visions. As before, the angel's arrival seemed to nullify the usual effects. She stared at the rain pounding and splashing on black tar where her dad had been and the front tires of the truck parked. Dad had told her the story. He'd tumbled into another world with no roads and no electricity. *I did this.*

The driver came out, peering at the road and under his truck, searching for a body he'd never find. He even looked in her direction, but never saw her.

Dad lived in another time. She'd abandoned him there.

CHAPTER 47

When the Volvo SUV pulled off the road to pick her up, Haddie didn't react until the doors opened. The engine idled two yards away from her. Exhaust broke through the fresh scent of rain. Stanton offered her a hand.

Zipper pushed through the pine branches. "Let's get you out of the rain." When she lifted Haddie's hood over her hair, cold water poured down her neck and back, waking her to reality.

In a moment, they were driving through the storm in the fading light, and Haddie stared at the back of the chair in front of her. She'd done what she was supposed to, and hated it.

Her clothes were wet, at least down the front and back of the shirt. The driver had turned on the heat.

"Back to the plane?" Zipper asked.

Haddie didn't really care where they went, but she didn't want to stay in Iceland. "Yeah."

At Zipper's prompt, she got out of the SUV clumsily. Stanton hovered as she made for the steps to board the jet. When Zipper insisted on getting off the rain jacket, Haddie stood in the aisle, staring at the attendant waiting in the galley.

He brought her a tea. "We've brought on some options for dinner . . ."

Haddie shook her head, holding the warming glass in both hands. "I already ate." The food from the pub turned in her stomach uneasily. "But, thank you."

When the plane eventually took off, Haddie reclined her chair, partially to avoid any conversation. She could not clear the image of her dad's crash and the moment he disappeared. The angel had returned. Why? *To make sure I did what I was supposed to?* What part did they have in all this? Or me?

Stanton caught her staring at the ceiling and reported on communications back at the ranch.

Haddie unbuckled herself and climbed out of the chair "Mm-hmm." She wobbled down the aisle to the bathroom.

Her phone had stayed relatively dry, and the Wi-Fi let her message Liz. "I just had to do something really uncomfortable. I still don't know if it was the right thing." She leaned against the sink, waiting for a response. The jet swayed against winds. *Hell, what time is it in Oregon?*

"Can you talk about it?" Liz texted.

"Not waking you up, am I?"

"At noon on a workday? Those days are past." Liz sent a laughing emoji. "Is this about New York?"

"No." Haddie drew in a deep breath. The bathroom smelled of sanitizer and urinal mints. *How do I say this?* "I just sent my original Dad, before he was my dad, back centuries in time. I started all this."

Haddie waited for the questions, then reread her message and added, "He was going to die. I couldn't stop the accident because then I wouldn't have been born to stop it. The only other choice I had was to let Dad die, but then Bruce would have done whatever he wanted to. Who knows what else would have been different without my dad having been through these past centuries?"

"Wow. I'm sorry. That had to be hard. Are you okay?"

"I don't know. Should I be?"

Liz sent a hug emoji. "No. But I think you did the right thing. Where would I be if you didn't exist? Especially if you can stop New York."

Haddie didn't really care about the bomb. *I should. Why is it my responsibility?* Hadn't she done enough? The jet bumped, and Haddie dropped the lid on the toilet and sat. "What if I can't stop it?"

"Then the world will be in chaos for a while. I can't imagine what it would be like. You've got to stop it. Call the authorities at least. Kiana must know which agency."

Bruce had always been a step ahead of them, both in Albuquerque and Texas. *I slid into his compound.* That hadn't worked out. Even then he'd had a backup plan.

She could spot the coerced in the building. Would that help? She imagined creeping in with Cooper while Bruce's fanatics were preparing to set off the bomb.

"I'll do what I can," Haddie texted.

CHAPTER 48

HADDIE STEPPED down the jet's stairs. The airport was quiet except for a fuel truck rumbling past the jet. The hot fumes of the engine wafted in the cool Texas air. The city lights clouded the night stars. Trig had parked close to the jet lounge and leaned on the Jeep with a white coffee cup.

She stretched as she walked over, carrying her bag of clothes. "Were you up?" It was after 2 a.m.

"I stayed up, knowing you were on the way back and due in soon." He finished his coffee and opened the back door. "Iceland? Everything go okay?"

"About as I expected." Haddie didn't feel comfortable discussing what she'd done with anyone. Liz had been different. *I needed to tell someone.*

Trig closed her door and opened his, sliding into the driver's seat. "Can we get back to the problem at hand? I've gone through the layout of this building, and we've got no idea where the bomb is. You've got trigger-happy people sitting on it."

"Suicidal, trigger-happy, fanatics." Haddie corrected.

He frowned. "Yes. The city's got to be evacuated. The

FBI or whoever can black out the area with some power outage, take down cell service, and blind them. Move snipers in, all that."

Stanton settled into the front passenger seat. "These are expected contingencies, in case we were exposed. We have contacts in the government to relay an evacuation order. I have control of most of those, or appear to. The fanatics, as you call them, are ordered to only preemptively detonate under certain conditions that Bruce laid out and Elon maintained. We wanted to make sure all the delegates were in the city at least, preferably on the UN grounds."

Trig started the engine, shaking his head. "We need to keep out of it, call in an agency. We're not equipped - look at the mess at the ranch." He seemed about to continue, perhaps blame her dad, when he glanced up at her in the mirror and shifted into drive.

Once they headed south out of the city, the stars shone across the horizon. Trig wasn't wrong. *We aren't equipped to deal with this.* Who was? They had two days. She'd hoped someone might have come up with a brilliant plan; she had none.

The ride turned bumpy, but her back didn't hurt as badly this time. Her face still looked frightful, but her skin didn't burn. The angels protected her somehow. Even her usual aches in her hips and knees seemed better. At this moment, if they had a plan about how to deal with this bomb, she'd go with it.

When Haddie arrived at the ranch and carried her clothes in the front door, Kiana was waiting in the boarded-up office. "Did you sleep on the plane?" she asked.

The room looked neater but still smelled of cigar. Zipper moved past toward the dining room and hall; she'd been sleeping with Trig's people in the basement.

Haddie nodded, her face flushed with guilt. "I did." Like her, Kiana would have struggled with the choice. The chance to meet even a different version of her dad clung as a regret.

Kiana obviously wanted to talk. "Good."

Haddie tilted her head toward the clothes. "Let me put these down, and we'll talk." She strode through the dining room. The walls had been scrubbed where Elon had been killed. No more blood splatter, but the paint had been dulled in an obvious patch. Haddie grabbed the sole dining room chair as she passed back through.

She paused at Stanton, who stood stiffly at the door with his tablet ready. "Would you mind making me some tea?"

His eyes flicked to Kiana, and he nodded. He'd give them a little space.

Kiana's head tilted back slightly when Haddie sat. "No comment about what you were up to in Iceland?"

Haddie shook her head and swallowed a sour taste in her mouth. *How can I? You'd hate me.* "Let's just focus on New York."

A false smile spread across Kiana's lips. Their relationship had darkened with Dad's death. "Okay. We need a plan, now. We only have two days."

"What do you think?"

"We have to risk Homeland Security. They'll be diligent and careful."

"And exactly who Bruce would expect. Won't his people know their moves?"

Kiana's face tightened. "They would have a playbook to go by, certainly."

Stanton stepped into the room. "We have their entire response scenario, if you care to see it. Three of our contacts are high within Homeland Security. Did you want tea as well, Kiana?"

Kiana's eyes grew colder and larger, her face darkened. "Do you still think a mercenary team is our best option?"

"Elon brought up the possibility of a small group of infiltrators, and it was dismissed." He paused behind Haddie. "Tea?"

"I don't want any damned tea." Kiana's face snarled in rage, then she covered her face and sobbed. "Dammit, Thomas."

Haddie jumped from her chair and knelt beside Kiana to hold her. Her own pain welled behind her eyes, but she said nothing. Stanton's footsteps drifted back to the kitchen. Kiana leaned in and smeared tears against Haddie's chest. Except for the small noises coming from the kitchen, the house turned quiet.

A minute later, Terry opened the door from the map room, and Kiana let go of Haddie.

"Hey, sorry. Everything okay?" He remained in the doorway, as if he might retreat.

"All good." Haddie's tone belied the darker mood in the room. "How did your work thing go?"

"Still running the roll-out, but no issues so far." He pointed toward the kitchen. "Just looking for something else to drink."

As Haddie sat, Stanton stepped into the room. He handed her the warming, swirling tea. "I procured more of that green soda you like. It should be cool at least."

"Awesome, Jeeves." Terry sped toward the kitchen.

From his footsteps, Stanton returned to his spot by the door.

Haddie turned. "Can you give us some time to talk? I promise I'll call you if I need anything."

He nodded. "I'll be in my room." He slept in one of the bedrooms, possibly his during Bruce's time as well.

Kiana leaned forward, her hands clasped and index fingers at her lips. "Do you have a plan, Haddie?"

"I'm beginning to think a small force is best, based on Stanton's comments."

"He could just want you to fail."

Haddie shook her head. "He could have had me killed after I dropped the truck on Bruce; there were troops by the house. Cooper and I never would have survived."

"What if he believes in Bruce's plan and thinks you will take up the reins if New York can't be stopped?"

Could he? He exuded a fanatical loyalty, but could it be to Bruce's plan and what he believed the Noveilm should be? "He put a lot of effort into contacting them. He seemed truly disappointed that he'd failed."

"He acts loyal, but we need our own information. Trig has set up people to get their eyes on this building."

Haddie raised her eyebrows. Despite how Stanton acted, she wasn't in charge. She couldn't expect them to wait for her while she took a day to go to Iceland. *And condemn Dad to centuries.* She looked away from Kiana. Would this always be between them?

Kiana leaned back and rubbed her ear. "We need to do something. If not my plan, then propose something tangible."

Terry stepped into the room, a bottle in each hand. "I'll go with whatever you come up with — whatever you need. I trust your intuition by now. Had me going a couple times, but Team Buckaroo." He lifted a drink in salute and took a sip.

"If you go with Stanton's suggestion, you shouldn't wait until the last minute to send in mercenaries. When Trig is set up to monitor would be the time." Kiana paused at footsteps from the dining area, then spoke quickly in a hushed voice. "Then we still have time to contact Homeland."

Still drinking, Terry turned.

Cooper, dressed in fatigues, came to the archway between rooms and leaned against the closer corner. "Maybe a joint team, with some of Stanton's men? Bombers are tricky, especially if they're suicidal."

Haddie bristled, unable to get a moment alone with Kiana. She imagined Trig or Zipper in the blast. *I don't want to risk anyone.* "Who are you willing to put in that kind of danger?"

Terry grimaced and made for the map room.

Cooper shrugged one shoulder. "Myself."

She shook her head. Perhaps Kiana and Trig were right to let the authorities handle it. "I don't want to be responsible for that choice." Someone had to take the chance, she just didn't want it to be anyone she knew. It felt cowardly.

Before Cooper could respond, Kiana stood up. "I need to get to bed. We can make the decision in the morning, but I'm not waiting another day." She wedged the crutch under her arm and limped around Haddie.

Cooper remained and waited silently until they could hear Kiana working her way down the hall. "How did Iceland go?"

Haddie shook her head. "Fine." Everyone wanted to know what she'd done. With the exception of Liz, she'd likely never tell another soul. "I need some sleep as well." She'd slept on the plane, but needed some space alone. Her phone buzzed, and with a sigh, she dug into her pocket.

"Of course." Cooper slowly rubbed his mustache as she passed.

Sam had texted, "It's midnight, and Meg just went

outside because of angels. I'm getting worried about all this. Should I follow her?"

Haddie slowed, but headed for the room Stanton had set up for her to sleep in. She'd guessed it had been Bruce's, with its own bathroom, but the furniture appeared sparse. A queen bed under a boarded-up window had a white dresser on the right side that served as a nightstand with a lamp. Boxes had been placed on the top; they looked like they held more clothes. On the floor was the backpack she'd worn to infiltrate the ranch. A ragged bullet hole shredded one pocket. The image brought back painful memories.

She reread Sam's concerns over the angels and Meg's midnight meeting. The angels didn't feel like a threat. Haddie sat on the bed and texted, "I wouldn't worry about it. I imagine Rock went with her?"

"Yes. Did I wake you?"

Haddie cocked her head to the side and dialed Sam. It would be good to hear her voice.

"It doesn't seem right that she should be out at this time of night, does it?" Sam paused and Jisoo cried in the background. "Am I being overprotective? She's barely a teen. Sometimes, she barely acts that old, then she runs out in the middle of the night to meet with angels."

"I wouldn't worry about her if Rock's with her. But head outside if you're concerned."

"Okay, I'm putting you on speaker so I can grab a jacket." Sam sounded like she'd been waiting for the chance to follow Meg.

There was some background noise, and Louis yapped excitedly.

"You're back," Sam said.

"The angels said I'll help Aunt Haddie." Meg sounded even younger over the speaker phone.

"What? How?" The door closed and Sam's voice grew louder, as if approaching the phone. "Aunt Haddie just called."

Meg's voice turned loud. "Hi, Aunt Haddie."

"Hey, Meg." Haddie swallowed. What help did the angels expect Meg to give her? "What did the angels say?"

Meg's voice swelled with pride. "They said I will be there for you."

Haddie couldn't be sure how to take the statement. It could mean Meg supported her actions, like sending Dad back centuries. It couldn't mean that Meg was coming to Texas; Sam wouldn't allow that.

"They're very happy right now." Meg had moved away.

Sniffling sounded at the phone that reminded Haddie of Rock.

The noise stopped as Sam took them off speaker. "Sorry I worried you. You've got a lot going on already. Have you figured out how to stop, you know, New York?"

No. The closest she could come was a small team like Stanton suggested. If Dad were alive, he'd go himself. *Alone.* "I . . ." Haddie faltered unsure what to say.

"The world's so broken, I don't think it would survive if something like that happened. I know you'll figure out a way to stop it. We're behind you."

Haddie deflated. "I'm sure." She didn't feel confident. Everyone looked to her for the answer, and she couldn't find one. Anger flushed against Bruce and all his demented plans. "I'll do something."

"Just be careful, and don't go to New York yourself."

Who was she supposed to risk? She couldn't ask anyone else, even Cooper. *I'd be the most obvious choice.* No one else could see the yellow haze of the coerced. If she got to

New York alone, she could contact Trig and get information from whatever investigators he'd set up.

"I'm not even thinking of going to New York," Haddie lied. Everyone would be livid with her. If she failed, then it wouldn't matter. If she succeeded, they could yell at her and then everyone could go on with their lives. It would be over. Meg and Sam would be safe. Liz and Terry. *David?*

"So, what are you going to do about New York?"

"Just take care of Meg. Keep her safe, no matter what. Okay?"

"Haddie? It sounds like you're planning something stupid — like you're saying goodbye."

I am. Haddie swallowed and tried to sound cheery. "I'm not."

CHAPTER 49

HADDIE STOPPED outside Stanton's door. Inside, he snored lightly. The house smelled stuffy with a tinge of cigar. She paused with her knuckles over his door; they trembled, hanging in the air. If Kiana were awake, she'd come out to see what was going on.

Haddie opened the door enough to put her mouth to the crack. "Stanton," she whispered.

He grunted and rustled.

"Shh," Haddie said. "Meet me out front, please." She left the door open and crept back down the hall. His footsteps followed by the time she quietly opened the front door. She'd dressed in the same pants and thermals she'd worn to Iceland and found a black shirt and jacket to match. Her hair was braided, and over her head she'd wrapped a black gaiter from their initial infiltration.

The door to the map room opened as she stepped into the cool air. She took quick steps to get out of view, in case Terry decided to ask what she was doing.

"Hey, Jeeves." Terry's voice carried outside, but he didn't appear to know she hid there.

Stanton closed the door, and she stepped out where he could see her. "Is there a concern?" he asked.

Haddie nodded. "My friend just called from Oregon. I've got to get out there tonight — this morning. I'll be right back. I just need to settle something. Can you wake up the pilots?"

He studied her all-black clothing and then nodded. "Immediately. I'll have the jet readied."

She couldn't have everyone wake up. "Can you get the keys to one of the trucks and drive me to the airfield?"

Stanton swiped across the tablet. "I will get someone to drive us."

"No. You can drive. I'm going alone."

He glanced up from his tablet. "Is that wise?"

Her cheeks warmed. Again, he questioned her. His unquestioning loyalty seemed spotty at times. "Of course. You trust the pilots, don't you?" She kept her tone even, not showing any frustration at his questioning her.

"Yes." He opened his mouth as if to say something, then led the way toward the portables. "The keys are inside."

The guards never questioned them where the trucks, Jeeps, and four-wheelers were parked; luckily, none were Trig's people. Some of the patrols near the road certainly noticed them, one shining a light in their direction, but no one stopped them. They likely knew the trucks kept at the ranch. If anyone did alert Trig, she'd be in the air by then. She sat stiffly in the passenger seat, her eyes locked on the crisp stars and heart pounding in her chest.

The same two women and attendant were waiting at the craft. Haddie smiled and thanked the man as he settled her into a seat.

She waited until the stairs had been moved and the door closed, then unfastened her seatbelt and jumped up.

The attendant looked mildly surprised. "Bathroom?"

Her stomach fluttering, Haddie shook her head and headed toward the pilots. "I need to speak with the pilots."

"Ma'am?"

Rubbing her fingers across the back of a chair, she repeated her request. He picked up a phone and called through.

One of the pilots came out of the cockpit with a puzzled look.

"Can I trust you to follow my directions and not inform Stanton?"

Stanton might still have some way of tracking them, but might not bother immediately. She glanced at the attendant, who stood listening.

The pilot's response seemed hesitant. "Yes. We can," she said.

Haddie sighed. "Good. We're going to New York. I want you to drop me off, then return to Texas immediately. Can you do that?"

CHAPTER 50

As her phone buzzed, Haddie righted her chair and heard the jet attendant start walking toward her. The cabin lights had been dimmed, and outside, the black night blotted all but a speckle of lights on the ground. She'd finished her oolong tea and refused more when he offered, but the sweet aroma hung in the air. Tilting, she reached into her pants pocket and pulled her phone out at a couple minutes after 4 a.m.

Kiana was calling.

Haddie's fingers dug into the arm of the chair. *Leave me alone.* She had hoped to get more than an hour out of Texas before they'd noticed. She hadn't asked Stanton to keep her flight secret; that might have caused him to guess her actual plans. His ability to question her actions worried her. He could have probably grounded the plane before she got to the pilots.

She waited as the phone rang until the call ended. Switching to text, she started typing to Terry. "Don't let anyone know I'm messaging you. Text me back when you can."

With tight lips, Haddie smiled at the attendant. "I've changed my mind. Yes, I'd like some tea."

Terry's text came before her drink. "What are you doing? Everyone is nuts here. They think you're committing suicide, going to New York."

Suicide. Her chest tensed. She didn't really care if she survived. *I have to, if I want to stop the bomb.* They didn't get to make the choice for her. "I'm not committing suicide, but I need help."

"Late for that."

"You trust me?"

"Of course." The message hung for a moment before a second text came through. "What can I do?"

"I need schematics of the building. Anything on the bomb as well. What should I be looking for? Shape, size, anything you think might be helpful."

"Kiana will string me up if she finds out I helped you. Why?"

"Why go to New York?"

It was Sam's comment, but Haddie couldn't blame her. Her muscles tensed in anger, at Bruce, for everything he'd done. She remembered his car. If she lived, she'd see it into a compactor. "Someone had to try and sneak in, without forcing them to blow the world to hell."

It took so long for him to reply, she feared he'd gone to Kiana. "Okay. I'm Team Buckaroo."

Haddie sighed, calming some of her anger. "Thanks, Terry." *Now, I just need a plan.*

Her hands trembled as she took the proffered tea from the attendant.

"Scottish Breakfast. Bold," he said with a proud smile.

Haddie stepped out of the cab in front of the brick building. Mid-morning traffic crawled and growled around her in a miasma of exhaust with sour, rotting notes. Thick clouds hung overhead, threatening a storm. From where she stood on the pavement, most of the side was twelve floors of glass. The stories tapered at the fifth row of windows, staggering up another section before an inset penthouse level that wasn't visible from this close. She'd studied the plans. Her stomach churned.

People jostled past as she calmed her nerves and searched for some hint of glowing yellow that would indicate one of the coerced. The restaurant at the corner had windows exposing tables full of people and staff milling about, but none of them gave her any concern.

The doors to the residences were tinted, but open to show an elegant sitting room with a maroon bench. The dark green canopy complimented the black trim and brick to signal ostentatious apartments.

To her right, the last section of the building looked like a travel agency with flashy posters of New York lining the windows and doors. In reserved lettering the advertisement offered luxury rentals. The rental office. Behind the picture-covered window, Haddie could make out a faint glow. *Coerced.*

She strolled toward the windows. Inside the main entrance, a man moved at a desk. He didn't appear to react as she passed him on her way toward the office. Why would he? People milled up and down the sidewalk. A third door with a lock and simple design that might be the stairwell sat between the main entrance and the rental office.

In a few steps, she disappeared from his direct line of sight and veered closer to the building, watching the yellow haze. It appeared stationary; she imagined the coerced to be ten or more feet from the doors.

Haddie put on a smile and opened the door. She couldn't be sure how her outfit would be received, but many of the people on the street wore all black.

The room had as many pictures of the building and apartments as the outside windows. A bell rang, and a thin man with tan skin, large ears, and a yellow haze across his eyes turned from a bank of three monitors. His eyebrows raised as if surprised, but he didn't act alarmed.

The desk appeared both elaborate and overcrowded. The room smelled foul, as if garbage rotted somewhere.

"Hi," Haddie said. "I'm wondering if you could tell me about the apartments. The luxury apartments."

He wore a black suit and smoothed the tie as he stood. "We don't have any rentals available at the moment." The bulge on his right side suggested a weapon.

"Oh, I don't mind getting on a waiting list." Haddie stepped up to the desk, searching for any keys that might get her deeper into the building.

"Alright." He frowned as he looked around his desk and found a business card. "You can apply online."

Would he have keys to show the apartments? She didn't plan on vaporizing a door if she didn't have to. More than likely, he had keys in his pockets. Her back straight and shoulders tense, she felt warm inside the office.

Behind the man, an open door led into another room, but she could only see part of it. There could be more people back there. A camera hung in the corner just right of the doorway. *What am I planning to do — kill him in cold blood? Perhaps.* If she could knock him out, she'd rummage for keys.

"Are there any apartments we could look at?" There had to be a master key.

His monitor chimed, he glanced down, and his demeanor and expression changed. A sneer grew on his lips as he pulled open his jacket. The holster rested where she'd expected.

Rage flushed up her cheeks. "Not today," Haddie said in a harsh voice.

Her tone rang out, sharp in the enclosed space. The man faded, leaving only his clothes. They paused in the air, then crumpled down into his seat, spilling onto the floor with a thud from his gun.

Her face prickled with pain, and she imagined purpura spreading across her cheeks. It had been a while since she'd used her power without the angels present. She gasped foul air and leaned on the desk, ready for the visions.

Sunlight drifted through a tall canopy, lighting a forest floor. A heavy man in a gray vest, white shirt, and an odd, knitted cap pulled a knife from a young boy's chest. Dad's son, Anders. She screamed, and Dad's voice rang out. Man, knife, and dripping blood disappeared.

The forest shifted as the sun, trees and leaves seemed the same, except the ground underneath shifted into a steep slope. Down the hill raced an angry brown bear. Dad's wife and child behind her, she shouted in his voice, "Stop."

The sky turned dark, and an explosion rocked the earth below her. A bayonet flashed as it stabbed into her leg. The soldier wielding the weapon wore a bright blue and yellow uniform, muddied with blood. Dad grunted when the blade pulled free of his gray coat; the weapon and man dissipated.

Haddie staggered as the visions faded. No one else appeared to be there. Wincing, she stumbled around the desk and peered into the office behind. It had two simple desks that looked unused and three doors, one with a keypad.

She turned back to find her face on the middle monitor with a flashing orange border. The picture flicked between a camera shot of her in her present outfit and what looked like her college ID when she'd had black hair. *Facial recognition. I should have thought of that.* Guessing, she tapped the space bar and the notification disappeared. Did anyone else receive this alert?

Each monitor had a dozen cameras on it, views of the residence. The coerced's clothing lay in stinking, wet lumps around his chair. Grimacing, she pulled up his soggy, black slacks and shook them, but nothing jingled. Her face tight, she slid her burning hand into a front pocket. *Nothing.* She shifted the pants around and pulled a slimy wallet out of the back. *A keycard perhaps?* She tossed it to the desk, leaving a red smudge. Squeezing the other back pocket, she found nothing. In the last pocket she found a keycard on a ring with a single key. *That's it.*

Just in case, she fingered open the wallet and looked for

any other keycards. Credit cards and ID mingled with a small amount of cash.

Most of the cameras were on the lobby, halls, and roof patios. The man in the lobby didn't appear alarmed. Nor did the doorman by the elevators. A female attendant cleaned equipment in a gym around two women on mats and a man on a treadmill.

In one of the halls, a couple left their apartment with a small terrier in the man's arms. A rock-faced man with a light brown beard, wearing a navy suit, sat in a lobby on a camera marked penthouse.

Any of the people could be coerced, except the man in the lobby next door.

She looked over her shoulder at the small back office and the door with the keypad. Where would you store a nuclear device? *I don't even know what I'm looking for.* Terry's information had been broad and vague in the end. She resisted the urge to call Stanton, though he might know. *I can do that later.* Did they have service corridors here, like at a motel?

Carrying the keycard in a wet hand, she entered the back office. The door to her left might lead to the lobby, from its placement. She stared blankly for a moment, searching for any hint of yellow haze. To the right was likely a closet. *The middle door?* Passing the keycard over the top of the keypad, a green light lit. Carefully, Haddie opened the door.

Yes. Boxes and bins, stacks of chairs, and random tables crowded the right wall. To the left, there was an elevator and two doors. At the far end, a single door stood with a pinhole of light in it.

She froze. Through the dirty concrete floor, she could see a pair of glowing orange demon eyes. Her chest tightened, and she scanned for more. *Just one.* Of course, what better to guard Bruce's device? And in a basement to avoid detection.

The door to her left had a keypad. She let out a breath and swiped the card over it. It unlocked, and she opened the door. She grimaced knowing she'd have to use her powers again.

A bank of electronic equipment glinted from the light in the corridor. There was a ladder up into a shaft and hatches on the back wall. *Elevators?* No demon, and nothing that looked like a bomb.

She let the door close and looked past the service elevator to the next door. There weren't a lot of options. Could there be another entrance, maybe in the stairwell?

The orange eyes moved under her, and she considered trying to kill it from where she stood in the corridor. *What if I miss and just make a way for it to crawl out? I need to see it.*

Haddie took a deep breath to calm her nerves before she swiped the card and the green light lit. She opened the door to a pit of darkness. Even the dim lights of the corridor barely showed her the concrete stairs leading down. Inside, she found a switch, already turned up. She flicked it down and up with no change to the maw of black. A damned flashlight — why couldn't she ever remember to bring one? The demon's orange eyes were still back toward the offices.

She clenched and shook her head. "Here goes."

CHAPTER 52

HADDIE STEPPED INTO THE DARKNESS, and her eyes adjusted. She flinched when one of the elevators started to her left and the machinery echoed from below. The air stunk like an unwashed kennel, distinct with the smell of demon.

She'd been in New York less than an hour and managed to infiltrate the Unceasing site without having them activate the bomb. *Not a suicide mission.* Her only obstacle now was the demon; she doubted there were any people hiding in the basement. *I just need to see it before it attacks.* The glowing eyes would help.

She checked to make sure the creature still hung near the offices. Maybe that was where the bomb was. *I'll need light at some point.* The walls on each side of the stairs were rough poured concrete. No light switches. Each step, she hooked a heel on the edge before she lowered her weight down. Breaking a leg would make her work difficult.

Her heart fluttered when her hand passed into open air as the wall to her right ended. *Stay calm, Haddie.* A landing appeared as she toed outward, looking for the next step.

The wall to her left turned a corner, and the stairs continued down another flight into inky blackness that even the dim light of the door didn't reach.

Debris crunched underfoot when she reached the bottom. The wall remained to her left, but she waved into emptiness on her right.

The glow from the demon shifted but remained toward the office.

Haddie turned to face it, moving her feet slowly and carefully. Wood or some other obstacle blocked her path, and as she reached out, she found the corner of the base to the stairs. Poking her foot sideways, she made sure she had clear footing. Once she could feel the corner of the concrete, she stood facing the creature. *An empty room?* Or were there walls? The orange glow appeared muted, as if she looked through something. The dim light from the door above did little to mark anything but the stairs behind her.

I've got to get closer. She could focus on the eyes and try to make the whole head disappear. It seemed to stand roughly her height. It could be some strange shape, like a flamingo with a four-foot neck.

As she stepped forward and sideways with her left foot, her toe caught debris and she felt it fulcrum upward from her weight. Without thinking she jerked her boot back.

Metal rang out; the noise echoed in the basement. *Hell.* Her heel caught something immovable, and Haddie lost her balance.

Flailing, her fingers traced against a flat surface, like a table. Her butt bumped against a corner, and she spun sideways. She fell with her arms outstretched, catching a pile of padding and metal towering just behind her.

Furniture that felt like cheap auditorium chairs toppled down on her, and glass shattered somewhere behind her.

Tangled in the legs of a chair, she landed sideways, her face pressed against a fat tube of cold metal.

Nails scraped on concrete.

Haddie scrambled. She tried to roll over onto her back, but stiff metal legs blocked her. With a swing of her left arm, she knocked a chair off her and a second leg slid into the side of her head.

A growl sounded in the pitch black. *Too close.* She rolled onto her face and pushed away from the pile to spin over. The demon reeked.

Before she could right herself, a nail pierced through her boot into her right heel. Pain shot up her leg. Through her teeth, she could feel the demon's claw dig through flesh and scrape against bone. It hurt, but her fists tightened as rage swelled through her. She'd made enough noise that surely someone would hear.

Her body jerked as the creature yanked her toward itself. The momentum flung her sideways. Smooth concrete scraped across her nose and cheek. Her fingers grabbed a moist chair leg.

Twisting, she tried to look at the creature. *At its eyes.*

A second nail caught her in the thigh, digging deep, and her body spun from the impact.

As the glowing orange eyes beamed down onto Haddie, she screamed.

CHAPTER 53

Haddie winced in the darkness as a remaining part of the demon rolled onto her leg. Footsteps ran on the concrete above her. Someone had heard her. She pressed a palm onto the cool, wet floor and tried to push up, but searing pain across her skin made her hand flinch. The smell of rotting demon hung in the basement.

I need to hide. Would they chance coming down here? She'd left the door open for light. Would they detonate? Part of the idea had been that a single intruder might not cause them to panic. If she were caught, Kiana could still call in Homeland Security.

Don't give up. She grimaced and pushed her torso up. Along with the purpura ravaging her face and arms, her foot burned, and the side of her thigh felt torn. Footsteps scuffed on the stairs as the visions took her. *No.*

Dad fought another war in some cold part of the world, possibly Norway. They used swords as much as rifles, and the battles she witnessed were bloody affairs. How had he always managed to find bloodshed. *How do I?*

When she returned to the basement, flashlights splashed against the walls from those who padded down the stairs. There was more than one person; it sounded like a whole team.

I'll have to use my powers again. The thought made her cringe, but she was so weary she could barely bring herself to panic. *Wait.* She'd have to take them all at once. Her heart pounded in her chest and her stomach churned.

A single beam flashed over her.

Wait.

"Are you alone, Haddie?" Trig spoke in a hushed voice.

Hell. She slid back down to the floor. What were they doing here? "Yes." How did they get here so quickly?

As more lights centered on her, she blinked repeatedly. Biff, Cooper, and Stanton walked down the steps, their guns lowered. None of them should have been there; Biff just got out of the hospital. *I didn't mean to risk them, too.*

Stanton's voice came close to her head. "Where are you hurt?"

Haddie snorted. "Everywhere." Part of her wanted to cry, grateful that they had come, and upset that they would suffer the same fate if she failed. *If we fail.* She tried to fully open her eyes, but there was too much light.

"Her leg. She's bleeding," Cooper said. "Stanton, hand me the med kit. How bad, Haddie? Bullet?" He moved a chair from beside her, and the legs scraped on concrete.

"Demon claw."

Something moved against her ankle. "Found its leg," Biff said.

Haddie winced as Cooper pulled at her pants, then cut along the wound. "I think the bomb's down here," she said.

"Got it," Trig said. "Zipper. Keep watch up top."

"Zipper's here?" Haddie asked.

"Kiana's setting up a sniper position, but the angle will only be effective on the west side. Crow's coordinating with the investigators and Terry."

Her skin chilled. "Kiana and Terry are here?" *In New York?*

Cooper prodded against her thigh and fire blossomed from knee to hip.

"Terry's back at the ranch. He's tracking cell phones in the building, and we just jacked in something for him back at that computer in the front office." Trig leaned in closer. "How'd you know to come in through there? I was trying to figure out where you'd breach."

"Blind luck." How did they know where she was? They had to have heard the demon attacking her. "How did you find me?" Haddie blinked, catching the biker's silhouette above her and Cooper kneeling at her side. Biff held something that could only be the demon's leg. He sniffed it, and Haddie felt her stomach roll.

Trig laughed. "Well, it was obvious as soon as we found out you took the jet alone." All except Stanton wore the same long-sleeved black outfits that they'd dressed Haddie in to infiltrate the ranch. "But here, in the building? You never turned your phone off."

He had used the app that they'd installed during the first infiltration into Bruce's ranch. She grunted as Cooper poked at her thigh and then lifted her leg to bind it.

"Is Kiana pissed?" she asked.

"She did mention killing you if we came out of this alive." Cooper wrapped a tight binding around her leg.

"Why are you risking this?"

"Fame and glory. What's up with your foot?" Cooper's tone barely hinted at humor.

"Demon claw in the heel."

"I'll leave it. Standing on it should cause enough pressure to slow the bleeding. If you can put weight on it. Any shooting pain up your ankle — tendon damage?"

"Not yet."

Tape screeched and he wound it over the gauze binding. "Want to see if you can stand?"

Haddie nodded and felt Stanton's hands at her shoulders. The heel hurt worse than anything she could imagine, but if she didn't put all her weight on it and stepped quickly with that foot, she could walk.

Trig's flashlight worked the far end of the room. The basement had random furniture scattered about, mostly near the stairs.

"We need to look for that bomb," she said.

Cooper flashed his light toward the stairs. "Take a seat. We'll check your boot when we're done looking."

Haddie hobbled over, and he kept the light on her until she sat. *Of course,* they *brought flashlights.* Cooper and Stanton began searching the piles of furniture. Biff headed toward Trig's end. *The bomb has to be down here.* Why else would Bruce have a demon here?

They'd done well so far. She'd gotten into the building without someone setting the bomb off, even if she wasn't in the best shape at the moment. One of the three coerced was dead. Haddie smiled and pulled out her phone. She'd forgotten about the app.

Opening messages, she texted Terry. "How does it look upstairs? Do they know we're here?" She doubted it, considering they were still alive and Zipper hadn't alerted them to anyone.

"I'm viewing their cameras now. I think I've identified staff, and they don't look worried." He added a second line. "Mad at me?"

"About?"

"I sort of folded when Kiana and Trig ganged up on me, demanding to know if you'd contacted me."

"No, we're good. Unless we all die, in which case I'll haunt you."

"I've got a Ouija board, we can text. Calling Buckaroo in the beyond."

Haddie laughed. She'd been so angry during the flight, at Bruce and herself. "Sounds like a plan." Her smile faded. She'd had no plan. No flashlight. Barely an idea of what she was looking for. She texted, "I wasn't prepared. Stupid. Not even a flashlight."

"Your phone is a flashlight."

I'm an idiot. She'd used it a couple times to dig through the back of her RAV4, not often, but she knew it was there. "Forgot."

Cooper and Stanton walked back toward her, their lights shining on the disused furniture and the legs of the demon. Wet remnants of the creature slicked metal and floor.

"Nothing," Cooper said. He glanced at her phone. "Crow?"

Haddie shook her head. "Terry. He's got cameras on the other Unceasing here. They don't seem alerted."

The stairs blocked her view of the basement where Trig searched the offices where the demon had been before she stumbled into the stored furniture. *I'm lucky to be alive.* The bomb had to be there. If not, then where?

Cooper took a few careful steps around the debris on the floor, heading toward Trig, then stopped. Light flashed over him, and he squinted. Had Trig found it and was coming back?

Trig made it to her and shook his head. Biff tapped the demon's leg with his toe.

"Where is it then?" she asked, then dropped her forehead into her palm. She sagged, feeling the weight of her arms and every wound and ache. They weren't done.

Haddie closed her eyes and sighed. Where? The men shifted in front of her, heels scuffing against concrete. It could be in any of the apartments, stored in a closet, or used as a nightstand beside a bed. Eventually, someone would try to reach the coerced she'd killed at the rental office.

They had to be guarding it. *We need to find it fast.*

She lifted her head. Trig stood closest to her, his face hidden in shadow. All of the men's lights tilted aside to shine on the furniture and debris.

"Terry is supposed to find us the vacant rooms, though we had to assume a subterranean placement to avoid radiation sniffers." Trig's phone lit up, exposing a grim expression.

"That might not be needed," Stanton said. "We were very careful to control key personnel here in New York."

"Yes, my fearless leader." Terry spoke on speaker through Trig's phone.

"We've checked the basement. I don't see any containers bigger than thirty by sixty inches, or any freshly patched concrete where they might have buried it. Do you have a list of rooms where we can begin our search?" Trig asked.

"I'd go with the sixth floor. It's all under construction, but I don't see any sign of that from the video feed."

Haddie grimaced, and stood. "Terry, you said you'd identified staff who could be our Unceasing guards. Are they covering the sixth floor?"

"No. I've got three on the ground floor. One at the desk, one cleaning equipment in the gym, and a guy at the elevators. He looks suspicious for sure. I've got two people, one on each of the two lobbies of the penthouse level, and a third that walked through, which is weird since Bruce has those suites to himself, and he's not there."

"No one on the sixth floor?" she asked.

"Not that I see, but the cameras aren't in the apartments, just halls and elevators. If you patch me into the elevator, I can see where the traffic goes."

Trig pursed his lips. "Maybe later. I think Haddie's right, we should check the top floor."

"Makes sense," Terry said. "The higher up the blast, the more damage."

"And how do we get into the penthouse without alerting the guards up there?" Haddie smoothed her hair; she'd lost the flimsy gaiter she'd used to cover it.

Trig patted his holster. "Silencers."

She drew in a slow breath. Terry had given her some idea of what to expect with the bomb. "Stanton, what do you know of the device? Like, how to disarm it?"

"Nothing, I'm afraid."

Haddie glanced at Cooper who just deepened his scowl. She didn't bother asking. *I'll revert to my original plan*. Send it back into time in millions of bits. She hadn't dared ask anyone, even Terry, about the ramifications. However, New York wasn't presently a radioactive swamp, so either she failed and they detonated it, or she sent it back far enough. If they found it at all.

"Penthouse," Haddie said.

Trig nodded.

She sighed. "With guns blazing."

"Team Buckaroo!" Terry yelled over the speaker.

Stabbing at his phone, Trig shook his head. "He is so annoying."

Haddie took a step and texted Terry, "Thanks. Text me if someone notices us."

As they reached the top of the stairs, Zipper leaned against the wall opposite the doorway. She smirked as Haddie came out, then her eyes tightened as she saw the taped bandage. A pistol appeared as she uncrossed her arms; the silencer on it doubled the length of the weapon.

Stanton moved to stand in front of the elevator. "This leads to the first level of the penthouse, though I have never used it myself."

"Laundry room or something enclosed?" Trig asked.

"There are laundry bins stored there, but I believe the actual laundry is on the fifth floor."

Trig almost seemed to growl. "Don't care where the laundry is, I just want to know if we can get out of this elevator without being seen by the guards in the lobby."

Stanton remained unaffected. "Yes."

Zipper took the lead, pressing the button up and stepping inside. Haddie limped, unable to keep weight off one wound or the other.

"Trouble?" Zipper asked.

"Demon."

"When do I get a chance with one of them?"

Haddie straightened. *I should be checking.* "Aim for the head." She spun slowly and stopped. "There's a coerced in the hall." Beyond the back of the elevator down to her left, a faint yellow glow shifted.

Trig peered at her. "How do you know?"

"I can see them, a glow." She motioned over her face, as if that would explain what it looked like.

"Of course you can." Trig swore.

Biff chuckled, and Cooper almost seemed to grin — at least the scowl lessened.

Throughout the trip up the elevator, she didn't see any sign of demon or coerced, until she got near the top. Through the back side of their elevator was a distant yellow haze.

Haddie motioned to Trig, pantomiming that she had seen a glow on someone's face. He already had his weapon drawn when the doors dinged open.

The coerced moved quickly, as if they ran.

She gestured in their direction, and Zipper and Trig ran into the utility room where rolling laundry bins cluttered the side.

A door opened nearly in front of them, and they fired a pair of shots each. There was no mistaking the sound, though the silencers didn't leave her ears ringing.

Haddie could hear the grunt and a body slap to the floor. The guard had never gotten off a shot. She'd expected it to go much worse. His feet lay inside the room, and the door rested open against the corpse.

Trig lurched toward the cloth bins as bullets ricocheted into the room. Gunshots echoed from the hall past the corpse. Zipper rolled back toward Haddie.

Cooper stepped forward and fired three times until the other gunfire stopped. He hadn't even tried to protect himself. They all likely had bullet proof vests on, but it wouldn't protect him if he got shot in the face.

Trig swore. "Great. A suicidal cop." He shoved one of the laundry bins.

Haddie's phone vibrated. She imagined Terry had seen them running. Hobbling, she followed Trig as he hopped out the door over two bodies. Stanton stayed at her side, holstering his gun to offer her a hand.

Trig and Zipper darted left through the door. Biff stumbled on an arm and followed. Cooper stepped over the bodies and nodded to Stanton, as if to confirm the area was safe for Haddie.

To the left, no one waited for them in the lobby outside the lone guest elevator. She recognized the view where the man in a green vest had been sitting in a chair. The room smelled of carpet cleaner.

The floors and even the walls were a beige marble. Centered on the elevator doors, the glassed-in room extended, furnished with chaises and comfortable benches. The windows looked onto a sun deck filled with umbrellas and chairs, but empty of people. The patio that stretched the entire west side of the building looked over city skyscrapers. It would have been a nice view, in different circumstances and better weather.

Haddie leaned against one of the windows at the corner of the lobby.

Biff peered out the glass windows of the hall.

Trig stalked into the middle of the lobby, examined the outside, then waved his gun toward double doors on the opposite side of the elevators. "Penthouse entrance?"

As Stanton opened his mouth to answer, the elevator

door dinged. The red arrow above pointed down. Someone had come from the second floor of the penthouse above them.

The glow of a coerced hung behind polished steel. Haddie signaled.

Stanton pulled his weapon as he stepped in front of her.

The gunfire had been heard. The Unceasing were warned. Would they detonate?

Cooper tugged at her arm, pulling them back from the elevators before gunfire erupted from Trig, Biff, and Zipper. Outside, a figure raced among the patio furniture on the far side of the lobby. How many were up here?

Past the door that led back into the service entrance, the hallway jutted inward, leaving a protected corner. Cooper pushed her there.

High on the walls she spotted a haze of yellow. She could see the coerced jostling upward. *Stairs*. Spinning, she found the door with the exit sign above and hobbled toward it as fast as she could. Her heel hurt the worst. Could they detonate remotely, or did they have to reach the device?

Gunfire rang outside, glass shattered, and the softer silenced pistols returned fire.

Haddie reached the door, and Cooper looked over his shoulder from where he leaned against the corner for cover. A bullet ricocheted off the marble near him. Glass shattered down the hall. She yanked open the door and heard footsteps above.

The stairwell smelled stale and slightly sour from old urine. Her heel and thigh screamed with each step, but she raced up. She made the first landing as the door above closed with a thud and fresh air wafted down.

Cooper entered below, and his steps followed. "What is it?"

"Someone running up to the roof," she yelled down.

When she opened the door she crouched down, expecting to get fired at. Gunfire sounded to her right, down on the lower patio where she imagined the others were. Cooper still climbed up the stairs as she let the door swing shut. If they detonated remotely, they were done. However, if the coerced above raced to the task, she had to stop him.

A low, brown, decorative fence surrounded the roof where she stood. A large air conditioner unit rumbled around the corner of the stairwell. A gate swung open in the hot wind and clapped. She sucked in a breath and pushed down the rising dread. The clouds were thick above and darkened the rooftop. She spotted the coerced's glow as it bobbed behind the border, running low and out of sight. Ahead, the building jagged inward, leaving him a tight corridor between the inner corner of the structure and her fence. Haddie turned right and ran parallel, hoping to intercept him where the corner and fence met. His goal lay somewhere toward the middle of the building. All she could see were more air conditioner units.

I'll have to use my power. She had no weapon, other than her fist, and the hole in her thigh would make tae kwon do difficult. Even the short fence looked daunting.

The glow stopped. A hair-covered piece of his head separated upward. She faltered mid-step. Blood sprayed and it took a second for her to realize he'd been shot.

A tablet, identical to Stanton's, clattered across the silver coated rooftop.

A gunshot echoed against adjacent buildings. *Kiana?*

Over the waist-high fence she could see along a silver stretch where air conditioning units dotted the roof. One unit looked new. It had an antenna. "No!" she yelled.

Her tone rang out. The edge of the unit began to fade.

Haddie heard the music of an angel nearby. Unlike her, it felt calm.

CHAPTER 55

HADDIE LEANED TOWARD HER TARGET, willing it back in time through the centuries. An odd rushing noise rose over her tone and the angel's music. In a flash, the gray-green metal had vanished, and a black spherical void floated in its place.

The world slowed, but the device hadn't vanished. Sparks flew from the opposite side and the cracks crawled along the silver roof. *It's detonated.*

The angel's presence calmed her, but panic still tightened her chest. Kiana was out there. Cooper behind. They would share her fate. *I have to hold on.*

Slow yellow flame sprouted from the building across the street. It burned along the window trim, and some curtains caught fire.

The angel had to be close behind Haddie. The brick looked rich in color, the oranges of the flames lit more vibrant than she'd ever seen. Her own skin sent out lazy wisps of blue-white light.

The roof below her continued to crumble. The wall

bordering the edge of the building drifted into open air. *It's not working.* She'd slowed the explosion, not stopped it.

The void hung in place. She sensed movement from it, but only an occasional spark escaped from the opposite side.

Help me, she thought to the angel.

It was. Whatever power Haddie tapped with her tone, it came from the same place as the angel's. She knew that now. They were linked in song, but it wasn't enough. Fires still sprung up on buildings, and the roof continued to crack and crumble at a slow, impossible pace. The thin outer metal of the nearby equipment sparked and warped.

Her skin burned. Not in the usual way. There was an actual heat to the sensation.

The roof had dropped below her feet. Haddie hung in the air, like the black sphere ahead of her.

The sensation of a vision ebbed at her mind. *No.* She'd been able to maintain in the cavern, holding the demons. *I can't afford to be distracted, not now.*

The lighting changed from dull gray to a yellow house lamp. She sat in Dad's office that served as their living room. Night hung outside. A young Rock nosed at her bare toes, making her giggle.

Dad had just brought the puppy home, and she had just named it.

Rock rolled over at her laughter, the whites of his eyes showing and his tongue lolling out. She rubbed his belly and he squirmed, acting as if he tried to bite her but just rubbing his face against her hand.

Dad knelt beside them and rested his hand on her shoulder, saying nothing but joining in her joy. He smelled of grease and metal. It was a warm smell that she would miss forever.

The vision ended, and she swallowed a sob. *I want that*

moment back. She found herself dangling a yard or more above the fragments of the roof. To her right she could see the edge of the patio becoming exposed as the penthouse collapsed.

Cooper had been right behind her. Trig, Zipper, and Stanton were in the building as it collapsed. Kiana was nearby; she had likely been the one to shoot the coerced. They would all die. *I'm not strong enough.* If Dad had survived, they might have worked in harmony and destroyed the bomb.

Dad is gone. It's just me.

Haddie cringed against the heat. Low, staggered rumbling joined the dull roar, her tone, and the angel's music. Her clothes smelled hot, like they got too close to a campfire. The world around her remained slow, while flames on the building across the street flickered and burned.

Sparks blew more frequently from the opposite side of the sphere. The rooftop crumbled, some pieces dangling in the air. *I'm losing.* The explosion that she worked to contain leaked out, causing destruction and burning her.

I need help, she pleaded to the angel.

They knew.

Her eyes flitted around, looking for more angels. Cooper lay in the rubble of the roof behind. Down on the patio she spotted gunfire and Trig's bald head. They couldn't do anything. *I'm alone.*

Do something.

The angel was doing what it could. It supported her body from the damage and maintained the bridge to their place for her power. Haddie could barely glimpse an under-

standing of their realm. Energy and light. They could not —
would not — manifest here on the material plane. That had
been the disaster that stranded Haddie's ancestors. The
Noveilm. It wanted her to succeed, but would not cross that
threshold.

Another vision threatened, and through the angel
Haddie knew that it truly was a moment of the past.
Unchangeable, but true.

Under a blue sky, she rode her first motorcycle down
the street behind Dad's garage. The small bike, a Honda
Silver Wing 305 Scrambler, didn't come near the big
Harley Davidsons that Dad rode. But it felt so free. She
glided down the road with the wind in her hair, and she
laughed at the pounding heart in her chest. That first
moment had been a nervous terror, then pure release as she
felt the control under her palms. She'd driven the truck, but
it was nothing like this. Would he let her take it on the
highway?

Haddie flicked back to the gray sky and scorching heat.
She blinked.

Other angels had joined them. There was pair to each
side of her and a fourth below her, level with the crumbling
roof. Haddie hung nearly six feet over the disaster.

Help.

She felt their songs join hers and the roasting of her skin
subsided. A new song rose, high and sweet. Haddie turned
down, knowing where it came from.

A white hand of light pushed out of the angel below,
then a shoulder, as a young woman appeared. She had
light auburn hair with gold highlights, at least it seemed so,
that close to the angel. As she stepped out, she looked up
with a smile. Perhaps eighteen or twenty, she looked
familiar.

Meg. Older, and here in New York. What had the angels done?

"Aunt Haddie. Follow my song." She wore a light-yellow dress, like sunshine itself.

Haddie knew that Meg had chosen this. Somehow, she had lived and learned with the angels, for this one purpose. *To help me.* A sob choked out of Haddie, and she nodded.

When Meg opened her mouth, she sang. Not a single note, but a melody. *Beautiful.*

Haddie quivered and tried to match. The physical song came nowhere near Megs, but their tones meshed. *Harmony.*

It's so peaceful. Time stopped. Haddie felt no need to breathe. Sparks no longer escaped the sphere.

The angels around her felt distinct. The one that had brought Meg turned somehow. It faced the void. They all knew that inside the sphere was pure energy. Haddie's attempt had increased the explosive interaction. *No matter exists.* It could all belong to the angel's realm now.

The black ball elongated, drawn toward the angel. A pointed tip pulled the sphere into a cone. It stretched out a misty dark tendril into the angel.

The rushing sound grew until it sounded like Haddie stood at the bottom of a waterfall. *It's dwindling.* As if the angel drank the void, it siphoned in, disappearing. The air wavered around it, and the colors around the angel grew lush and deep. The void didn't exist any longer.

It's gone. For a moment, Haddie hung there, floating in the music, then Meg stopped singing.

Haddie's tone ended. The world exploded into a rumbling cacophony, and she dropped. She sucked in hot, smoldering dust.

Her ankle hit a chunk of the sliding roof, and she lost her breath when she landed on her back. Meg had been close, her yellow dress shining near the angel.

A section broke beneath her and rolled Haddie sideways. She grabbed at sticky, silver roofing and found the edge of the slab she laid on. The stone crashed into a marble sink and blue walls buckled. The impact launched Haddie off the concrete, but a moment later she slammed back into it as they reached the floor.

A crack broke through the piece she rode, and the story below seemed to sag. Her stone threatened to fold together. Smaller pieces rained down from the sides. A head-sized boulder smashed into her hand, and she cried out.

In a second, it all appeared to settle. Dust hung, drifting away where the wind caught it.

"Meg?"

Haddie scrambled up. Her leg hardly hurt, but the middle finger on her left hand had turned purple and red. Slabs of concrete, some covered with silver roofing, piled waist high on the patio level. Meg?

The world hung gray overhead, and dust rose in plumes around her. Corners and edges were highlighted, but the depths were murky darkness.

"Meg, are you okay? Where are you?"

Motion flitted to the right. "I'm here, Aunt Haddie." Meg spoke with an older tone than Haddie expected.

"I'm coming." Haddie stumbled across the rubble, unsure if it would hold.

Meg's dress had been torn. A teen's dress on an adult barely fit anyway. Her leg had been scraped at the knee, and her calf was wedged between two cracked chunks of concrete.

"Are you okay? Is anything broken?" Haddie asked. She tugged at both pieces, but they didn't budge.

Meg smiled sheepishly. "I don't think anything's broken. Sorry, I bet you want to get out of here."

"Before the rest of the building collapses?"

"Yeah, that." Meg winced as she tried to pull her leg free. Edges of concrete bit into her flesh, reddening it further.

"We'll get you out, even if I've got to use my ability."

The debris appeared to be mostly concrete. To the west, she could make out the patio through windows that had lost their roof. An umbrella pole, perhaps.

"Haddie?" Cooper called from the north end of the building. His voice sounded raspy.

Had he been hurt? "Cooper, are you hurt?"

Before he could respond, Trig swore out on the patio. "What the hell did you do?"

"I need help," Haddie yelled out. It didn't matter which one came. Together they might be able to pull the smaller piece of concrete off Meg. "Meg's pinned."

"Who the hell is Meg?" Trig appeared in the opening where one of the windows had been. "Never mind, climb out of this rubble and get to the stairs with Zipper; Stanton and I can get her free."

Why did he always need to be in charge? "No." Her jaw clenched. "Please come help me."

Swearing and grumbling, he navigated through the debris. Blood smeared along his neck.

"You okay?" Haddie asked.

He cocked his neck as if testing it. "Good enough."

Haddie moved to the side of the smaller piece; it looked like something that might move. "This is Meg. She's family."

She tried grasping with both hands, but pain shot up through her wrist.

Trig frowned. "Name's Trig."

"Nice to finally meet you, Trig." She smiled shyly. "T said you're the most ingenious biker he's ever met."

He moved over to the other side of the concrete that Haddie held with one hand. "I like her," Trig said.

"Then let's get her out of here." Haddie pulled as he did and felt the stone shift. Grit dug into her palm and filtered through her fingers. "Move your leg as soon as you can."

Meg's calf tugged against the concrete, and she slid free, backing up on her palms.

Cooper crunched through wreckage toward them, his scowl edged with concern. "What do you need?"

"Back it up, Detective." Trig waved him off. He leaned down to scoop up Meg, but she moved to get up on her own. "We all need to get off this section of the building. I still ain't sure it won't all come tumbling down."

"Agreed." Haddie gestured for him to lead the way, and she offered her hand to Meg.

Holding Meg's hand, she followed across the uneven flooring. The patio had suffered less, but large cracks riddled the top. Would there be a way down?

Zipper jogged from the far side, meeting them near the lobby. "Stairs are a mess, but I think they'll hold."

Stanton limped toward them. Blood soaked his pants from the top of the right hip. He paused, still clutching his tablet, and waited for them.

"Who's the new girl?" Zipper asked.

"Family," Haddie said. She wasn't about to explain Meg's age difference if she could avoid it.

Zipper's eyes widened. "Who just happened to be here?" She flipped her hand toward the rooftop destruction.

Trig nodded. "That's what I'm wondering."

"Long story." Haddie raised the hand that Meg still held. "This is Zipper; she's nice."

Meg laughed nervously. "Good to meet you, Zipper."

Stanton's introduction went quicker as he asked no questions except about Haddie's finger.

Trig swore. "We'll get that splinted. I think you broke it." He stepped over a guard's body and aimed for the shattered glass doors of the lobby.

The windows around the entry were splintered and cracked, but the second floor rose to its original height about where the elevators stood. Perhaps the building was reinforced there.

The door hung open where Haddie and Cooper had chased the coerced. The stairs above had cracked and looked like they held by virtue of memory and bent railings. *Lucky we're going down.* They went single file, and Meg released her hand to go first. Stanton and Cooper followed.

Haddie's phone vibrated. The screen had a split through it, but it worked. There was a string of texts, the oldest from Sam. "Meg's gone!"

"Hell, Meg, we're going to have to call Sam. She's got to be freaking."

Meg turned around with a broad smile. "I love Sam." She wrinkled her nose as if pleased with herself. "Like, really. I can't wait to see her again. And Louis and Rock. It's been so long."

Haddie drew in a deep breath. She knew that Meg had lived with the angels, but couldn't comprehend what that meant. She looked at least five years older and half a foot taller.

Was it all over? "We'll get you home." It felt odd, calling it home. At least New York hadn't blown up, and life would be normal for Sam. Except for Meg.

Is that my home now? A farm and kennel in rural east Oregon? She wanted to go back to her apartment, David, school, girls' night with Liz on Fridays, and game night with Terry and everyone. Did it matter what she wanted? Bruce and his bomb were gone.

CHAPTER 57

HADDIE PUSHED ALONG with the panicked crowd heading down concrete stairs. She and Stanton sandwiched the wide-eyed Meg while the others packed around them. The stairwell echoed the hysterical racket of the rich tenants of the building. Sirens whined outside, dull through the walls. Everyone smelled of sweat and expensive perfume. Some carried pets; others clutched luggage or smaller items. One family clogged the exodus with a load of suitcases, the father actually carrying an espresso machine in one arm.

Wafts of fresh city air drifted up, and she imagined they were near the ground floor. *Almost there.* Despite the help of the angels, her skin had blistered along her hands and cheeks. *Radiation.* Dad had never gotten cancer, but had he ever been exposed like this?

The mob outside barely let the fleeing tenants out of the building. She followed Trig's bald head; she'd seen him talking on his cell. Stanton, too, had been working on his tablet. *They'll get us out of here.* She wondered if there were videos of her floating in the air with the sphere. Would this be one more investigation or warrant added to the rest of her record?

The sidewalk traffic thinned out a block from the building. Along a side street, Crow leaned against a white Dodge van. Haddie sighed and almost laughed in relief.

She fought tears when she saw Kiana's head lean out the passenger window.

Meg glanced over. Her eyes had Dad's shape, and her hair color was identical, but she didn't have the height that marked Haddie and her dad. "What's wrong?"

Haddie shook her head. "Nothing. I'm just happy Kiana's okay."

"Kiana is here?" Meg looked concerned.

Haddie pointed to the van ahead.

"Crow!" She smiled. "I've missed him — and Kiana and you." Meg jogged ahead and gave the surprised biker a hug.

Kiana's eyes widened, and she opened her door. She seemed to recognize Meg.

As Haddie arrived, Meg released Crow and beamed at Kiana.

Meg's smile dropped into a frown. "You still have your cast."

"And you have breasts. You can't be Meg. How?"

"Our friends." Haddie swallowed and glanced at the others filing into the van. "Maybe we can discuss it later?"

Meg shrugged and leaned into the passenger door to give Kiana a hug. "I missed you."

Haddie took the seat behind Trig as he climbed in to drive. Meg slid in beside her, and Crow closed the door behind himself and squeezed in with Stanton and Biff.

Trig adjusted the mirror. "Stanton, are we going to be able to get out of here? What airport?"

"The city has moved into a terrorist alert, as you can

imagine. I am working on Sikorsky Memorial. Head that direction." Stanton spoke as he worked on his tablet.

"Here I am, driving a white panel van loaded with people, in New York during a terrorist alert." Trig raised his hands, glaring in the mirror. "With a good number of warrants."

"I'll get us a limo," Stanton said.

"I'll go slow and keep to the back streets." Trig put the van into drive.

Haddie had gotten in and out of airports before without any checks on her ID. Would there be an issue with last-minute arrangements?

She turned. "Will we have trouble with the warrants?"

Stanton didn't turn up from his tablet. "I have requests out to three flight services that can handle those situations." He lifted a finger up toward Trig. "Take a right. Park anywhere you can. The limo will meet us."

Bruce was dead, and his plans trashed. Any coerced would be unattached, hopefully. They'd be like Josh, surviving on their last set of instructions. Did that include the FBI?

"Can we clear my problem with the FBI, now that they aren't connected to Bruce?" she asked Stanton.

"One way or another. I will work on it immediately." He continued to swipe across his tablet.

Haddie raised her eyebrows. That easily? She doubted it would be simple, but why hadn't he offered before? Because he didn't expect her to leave the ranch and go home. Adrenaline pumped through her.

"Kiana? Cooper? Terry?" Haddie spat out each name.

Stanton looked up. "Of course, if you wish."

Haddie sputtered. "Yes. I wish." This could all be over. She could go home and have a normal life. *David.* There would still be people who knew about her powers. Most were in the van. Maybe she shouldn't be too public. Her elation melted away. There had to be pictures and videos of a rooftop blowing up and her floating.

Zipper leaned up from the back, resting her arm behind Stanton and speaking into his ear. "I've got a slew of tickets in about six counties in California. How 'bout those?"

Stanton glanced at Haddie who shrugged and nodded. Why not?

"I'll need your legal name."

Trig came to a stop behind a large delivery truck but left the engine running.

Kiana peered at Meg, plainly suspicious. They would work it out. Haddie sat with Meg as Crow exited the side and Trig jumped out of the passenger seat. *Back to Eugene, or to the farm and kennel?*

CHAPTER 58

IN A LIMO BUS bigger than Dad's Ford Transit, Haddie sat quietly in the front beside Meg and across from Kiana, Trig, and Zipper. Padded benches lined the walls and chrome poles rose from the center. Lights flashed around the borders and lit a stocked bar. Biff and Crow laughed in the back, passing a bottle of whiskey. Haddie could smell the alcohol and the usual suspicious smells of a party bus. It reminded her of her senior prom. White lights trailed at their ankles under the benches and around the top, lighting the headliner.

Her finger, a radiation check, and a bind on her heel had been first on Stanton's list. Only when he finished, did Stanton reluctantly agree to lower his pants and let Cooper bandage his hip. Zipper started pulling out one dollar bills to throw at Stanton's feet and Trig followed suit.

Meg tried not to look, but she kept stealing glances.

Haddie couldn't help but examine Meg. *What had it been like, with the angels?* Were they anymore — human — in their world? Questions for another place.

Haddie texted Terry, "We're on our way back."

"Yaass. Crow said everyone made it okay. I'm going through the media now. Quite a ruckus there, Buckaroo. Heading back here, or Eugene? Or are you going to the farm?"

I don't know. She glanced at Kiana, whose frown had softened to a quizzical intensity. "Texas. We'll head out from there. Surely Livia is ready to have you back."

"Bring me a souvenir?"

Haddie smiled and took a picture of Cooper scowling at her, while Stanton stood sideways to her, his pants halfway down his butt. "Asked Jeeves for the bullet," she texted.

Terry sent a string of emojis; one hundred percent, a gift, and fire.

She had smeared some of the salve that Stanton had put over her hands onto her phone and wiped it off with her sleeve. Meg snickered at the photo. They'd called Sam and explained Meg and the angels as best as they could in a crowded stairwell of evacuees. It would still be as awkward as it was with Kiana.

"I'm okay," Haddie texted Liz. "Beers tomorrow, and I tell all?"

"Thank you. I'm crazy here. Have you seen what's happening in New York?"

"Unfortunately." *Close up and personal.* No mention of her flying over the building from either Terry or Liz. "All good though. Pick a place. I'll schedule later tonight."

Haddie texted David, "I'm safe. I'll be back to Eugene in a day or two. Want to meet up?" By the time she finished texting, she trembled and grabbed a water from the cup holder. She laid the phone face down so she didn't have to see how long it took for him to respond.

Meg reached down and held her hand. "Are you coming with us to the farm?"

Am I? She didn't want to commit. Days seemed to blur since the morning in the park when Cooper had her handcuffed and the FBI had issued a warrant. Even if Stanton did his thing and cleared them, couldn't some new evidence about Albuquerque, Texas, or New York pop up? Some random video that made the government want to dissect her? Did she want that risk looming over her?

She turned to Stanton. "Can we use the jet to get to Eugene tonight?"

He leaned against the pole. "Yes. It is your jet."

"Not really." It couldn't be like killing a boss in a game and getting all his loot.

"It is your property. I filed the paperwork in India, here in the US, and everywhere you now have properties and accounts."

Cooper motioned that he was finished.

Stanton pulled his pants up and primly took the seat beside her, separated by the cup holder. "You have some very large assets to control. You should become acquainted with them."

Haddie didn't want assets. *I want my life back.* The jet would be nice to use though. "You deal with it."

"I could manage everything on your behalf, if you wish." His lips pressed together. "I would need your approval, signatures on documentation."

He doesn't want me to leave. She took in a deep breath. His fanatical devotion had saved her, but now threatened to hound her. "Set up an office. I'll visit so we can go over business. Meg should be on it too."

Zipper waived a bottle in the back. "If you're looking for a partner in a multi-million-dollar corporation . . ."

Stanton studied Meg. Did he guess Meg had power, by Haddie's statement? *A Noveilm.* The angels' presence had left Meg's skin unmarred by purpura. *Good.* Haddie didn't want him to know.

As if discussing going to dinner, she asked, "What are you going to do, Cooper?" Her chest tightened. *I ruined his life; now he has to put the pieces together. Horrible question.*

Cooper remained standing, holding onto a strap above. "Even if there are no warrants with the FBI, there will still be issues with my weapon, among other things."

Zipper snorted. "Weapons get stolen or lost all the time."

Cooper ignored her.

If Haddie could return Cooper to his position as a detective, it might ease some of her guilt. "Stanton?"

Stanton leaned his tablet up and started swiping. "We will dispose of the weapon and have the evidence removed."

Cooper shook his head. "Even if you clear that, they've processed it and I'd need a damned good story to not be investigated. And I'd have no job, no matter how good the story. Best I'd get is security at the mall."

"We will hire an appropriate lawyer who will have everything else thrown out." Stanton didn't look up from his tablet.

Haddie swallowed. "Stanton, you're going to need security for this business, right?"

As little emotion as Stanton rarely displayed, he did not look excited at the prospect. His voice dropped. "Of course."

"Then he can head back with us on the jet."

Stanton seemed to recognize she'd included him. His expression lightened. "To Bend, then Eugene?"

Her phone vibrated in her lap. Her heart fluttered. "And Terry, Biff, anybody who needs a ride."

She flipped her phone over and read the text from

David. "I love you. Thank you for letting me know you're okay. Tell me when, and I'll be there."

Haddie's throat tightened. He hadn't given up on her. Meg squeezed her hand and leaned over so her head rested on Haddie's shoulder.

CHAPTER 59

HADDIE LEANED back in her seat as their New York flight landed in Amarillo. Meg let out a breath beside her and laughed. The engines whined as they taxied through a now familiar section of the airport. White domed hangars reminded her of a military base, but orange-vested employees lounged on carts outside. As they turned, she recognized the upturned wings of the jet — her jet that they would take to Oregon.

Meg had been nervous about the flight. She'd flown before, but long ago in larger planes. *How long had she lost with the angels, five years?* She could be in high school, maybe even college. *Did she regret the time she'd lost?* Would they need to hire a tutor? Stanton could provide one.

Zipper stood as the plane came to a stop. "You're not heading back to the ranch?"

Haddie glanced out the window as she undid her buckle. The cloudless blue sky hung over rounded, white roofs. "No. Headed for Oregon." She never wanted to return to Bruce's ranch.

"Crow's riding with us. Biff will take him in the truck,

and we'll head up to grab our bikes and come out for the biker's funeral you promised us." Zipper smirked and offered Haddie her hand. "You're definitely T's daughter. Good working with you. Thanks for not getting us killed."

Meg laughed and gave a surprised Zipper a hug.

When they walked onto the fuel-scented tarmac, one of Trig's Jeeps pulled up, and Biff offered Haddie a hug. He hadn't been that much of a jerk, this time.

"I heard you're driving Crow back," Haddie stated.

Terry climbed out of the jeep with a backpack and soda, nodding at her but heading toward Trig.

Biff shrugged and patted his hair. It had gotten a little ruffled during the cave-in of the roof, and he couldn't make it smooth without his boar-bristle brush. "You going to be okay all alone on your fancy jet?" He leaned forward conspiratorially. "I can't believe how hot Meg grew up to be."

Jerk. Haddie shoved her splinted finger toward his nose. "Keep the hell —"

He tapped her on the shoulder with his fist, grinning. "Just kidding." Biff turned to Meg. "Haddie says I'm too old for you, so you're going to have to call me Uncle Biff." He put his hand in the air in front of his chest. "I remember seeing you when you were this big."

Meg gave him a hug. "I remember, Uncle Biff."

Terry passed with a mock salute and gestured in the direction of the jet that Kiana limped toward. Haddie nodded.

Trig clapped Haddie on the shoulder, and she jumped. "Meet us out at the farm when we ride out for the funeral?"

Did he already assume she wouldn't be living there? "Wouldn't miss it."

He patted her shoulder. "Stay safe, Haddie." A genuine

smile, he seemed to have gotten over his initial shock at seeing her use her power. "I would be proud."

Stanton waited for them by the stairs of her jet. Kiana and Cooper were likely inside. "I took the liberty of having some new clothes waiting for you. In case you wanted to change. There is also the option of a shower inside the terminal, if you want."

"I can rinse in the sink, if there's something I can change into." Haddie raised her eyebrows at Meg, who nodded.

With some of the dust cleaned off, Meg grabbed Haddie's hand as they walked back.

Terry sat in the back, joking with Cooper, who just scowled, but noted Haddie and Meg coming through the door.

Kiana studied Haddie as she stepped inside. "Well?" she asked.

Where am I going? Is that what she was asking? It smelled like baked potato in the cabin. It was dinner time. "What?" Haddie asked. She sat down and strapped in as Kiana remained silent. "I'm taking Cooper to Eugene, after we drop you off in Bend, if that's what you're asking. I need to see David and everyone."

Kiana tapped the arm of her chair, remaining silent.

Haddie sagged. "I don't know."

"Want my opinion?" Kiana took a beer the attendant offered.

"Yes." Haddie nodded, holding her glass of tea and melting ice. "Thank you." Right now, she would appreciate Kiana's thoughts. *I can't make up my mind.*

"If Stanton clears everything, go back to school. Go back to your life."

Haddie snorted. "I've ruined school."

"No, you haven't. A setback, no more. Take the classes again. Move on for a bit."

The warmth of the tea reached Haddie's palms, and she ran her fingers along the condensation. Her mouth was dry. It smelled strong and earthy. "What if someone recognizes me, or finds fingerprints or something?" *I'm afraid to go back.*

Stanton had settled in their group of four reclining seats. "I'll be monitoring that carefully. Common practice."

She remembered the trouble Terry had retrieving images of demons. *Perhaps.* She just nodded, then quenched her dry throat. *I'm just afraid.*

"I'll think about it, Kiana. I'm nervous."

Kiana smiled. "You'll be fine, as long as you visit. Don't make me hunt you down. This cast won't last forever."

When the plane had reached a level that the pilots announced, she and Meg let the attendant begin serving dinner. Stanton had bought a huge selection of clothes with sizes that were an uncanny fit. Haddie had chosen a white tank top and black pants, while Meg found a purple dress with yellow flowers that matched her perfectly.

After dinner, Kiana didn't bring up the subject of where Haddie would be staying again, but focused on building relations with Meg. "Are you looking forward to working at the kennel again? You must have missed the dogs."

"I did." Meg smoothed the neck of her dress. "But Sam most of all. And you, and Aunt Haddie." She tilted her head. "I'll call you just Haddie, okay?"

Haddie smiled and nodded. *Aunt makes me feel old.*

Kiana chuckled, "Can I be Kiana, instead of Aunt Kiana?"

Meg's forehead wrinkled, then she shrugged it off. "Yes. And Sam will still be Sam."

Haddie glanced at Kiana. Meg's obsession with Sam appeared to be bordering, if not over the edge, of romantic.

"You're going to have to give Sam some time to adjust," Haddie said. "We've told her what happened, but the change is rather startling. Give her some space."

Kiana leaned forward. "She's right. I needed some time myself. It still feels weird."

Meg knitted her eyebrows. "You're right. She thinks I'm a kid. I mean, I was." She looked between them. "And she might find it strange if someone she thinks of as too young, a child, is suddenly in love with her."

Haddie pursed her lips and nodded.

Meg smiled. "I'll be patient. I always knew that she might not feel that — strongly, but I wasn't about to keep it from her. You're right. I'll take it slow."

She kept her word when they arrived at the farm that night. When they drove up, Sam was standing by the road, Louis yapping in her arms and Rock's collar firmly in hand.

Haddie had left Cooper, Stanton, and Terry at an airport motel. She planned on spending the night, and Sam had insisted on cooking a second dinner for them. The boys would have just made it an awkward situation. *Just family,* she thought as she stepped out of the limo.

The cold air smelled deliciously fresh and hinted of pine sap and a distant fireplace. Crickets chirped in the dark, though the twilight hung gray in the west. *A home, if not home.*

Louis squirmed at the sight of them, especially after Sam let Rock loose. Haddie knelt as he loped across the drive. He came straight for her with only a quizzical glance at Meg. Chest to chest, he nuzzled her neck and whined. "I'm sorry, Boy. Momma missed you, too."

The driver left, and Sam released Louis who danced

between them all. Kiana waited beside Haddie as Meg rubbed Louis and then straightened.

Sam took a step forward, blinking. Another step brought her to Meg. They stared at each other, in a deadlock of unreadable expressions. Tears rolled down Sam's face, and she pushed on Meg's shoulders. "You scared the hell out of me."

Meg staggered back a step, and her shoulders drooped. "I'm sorry, I had to help Haddie."

Sam frowned, glancing at Haddie who still held a squirming Rock. "I guess. But you could have said that you were leaving. And that —," she gestured at Meg from foot to head, "— this would happen."

Meg smiled coyly. "I didn't know how long it would take. They don't experience time like we do. I think they were surprised. I had to practice singing, to be ready."

Sam groaned. "Don't be all practical on me. I'm still mad." She grabbed Meg in a hug, tears still wet on her cheek. "But there's mac'n'cheese in the oven. I'm not that angry."

Kiana laughed and limped up as the two separated. "My hug." She grunted when Sam squeezed. "Not mad at me, are you Sam?"

"You two told me you were leaving. I didn't expect what I've seen on the news, though. I'm glad you're okay."

Haddie patted Rock and stood; he kept close by her side but sniffed as they passed Meg. Louis hardly seemed to care. Did they recognize her?

Sam grabbed a wincing Haddie in a hug, then pulled back lightly. "Sorry. Purpura?"

"Sunburn, I think."

"Yah, you're peeling. From Texas?"

Haddie shook her head. "New York. The nuclear bomb.

I'm guessing it'll be okay. Stanton checked me for radiation, and I was only slightly elevated."

"He brought a Geiger counter?"

"Had one delivered. Well, we picked it up."

Sam peered into Haddie's face. "Is it over?"

"I think so."

"Are you going back to Eugene?"

Haddie looked down to Rock, staring up at her with liquid eyes. "I think so." She needed to see Liz and David. "But, I'm just going to drop everyone off before I decide. Can you keep an eye on Rock for another couple days?"

"Of course. You aren't leaving right now, are you?"

Haddie raised her eyebrows. "And miss your mac'n'cheese?"

HADDIE STEPPED out of the black Ford Explorer. The rural highway along Goshen buzzed with afternoon traffic. Random clouds partially covered the sun. A cold front had moved in, preparing everyone for winter. She looked forward to snow. Maybe another ski trip with Liz or David this winter.

The garage smelled familiar with grease and gas. Her childhood. The RAV4 waited in the back, and she knew where the keys would be.

Stanton had driven from the airport, and she could tell he didn't look forward to releasing her back to her car, but he'd been the one to say that her warrants were clear. She trusted him. He barely showed any sign of being shot. The bullet had gone through the muscle, but he'd be okay.

Cooper peered around the area, as if still suspicious. His issues were still being cleared up, so he and Stanton would be hanging together for a while.

Terry rolled out of the front seat with leftover tacos and his backpack, his souvenir from the ranch. He'd been disappointed to find out he wouldn't be getting a bullet from Stanton.

"Later, Jeeves. It's been real." He faked as if to smack his behind.

Stanton stood impassively.

Terry saluted Cooper. "Keep your pants on."

Cooper snorted. "Funny. Take care of yourself, Terry."

Terry stopped. "That's all I get, no warning? Something about where I should stay . . . ?"

Cooper rubbed his mustache, almost as if hiding a smile. "Stay within the lines, Terrence."

"I feel safer just hearing you say that."

Haddie laughed at the two of them. They almost seemed friendly. Terry better not invite him to game night. "What about me? Any warnings?"

"Nope. See you at the office, Boss." Cooper smiled. He had teeth.

He proffered a hand, and she shook it. "Make sure you're there early," she said. Her smile faded as she turned to Stanton.

He waited for her with the tablet held tight to his chest. "I will check in with you as I make arrangements. I have some suggestions for liquidating certain properties that are no longer necessary, since conditions have changed."

"Like not blowing up New York?" Haddie nodded, ready to head out to meet Liz. She drew in a deep breath. "Kiana and the children?" Somehow, their care bound her and Kiana to her dad.

"Yes. I am working closely with her. We discussed a number of options. She is very passionate about their situation. Should I keep you updated?"

We'll take care of them, Dad. "Definitely."

He took a step forward, as if reluctant to end their

conversation. "There are some viable businesses that we can expand with the leverage we have."

"I'll let you work all that out, Stanton." She sighed as his face dropped. His expressions didn't change much, but she'd begun to read him. "Give me a couple days, then we'll sit down and go over everything. The highlights at least."

That seemed to please him. "I'll check in with you in forty-eight hours."

Haddie groaned with a smile, but she had said a couple of days. She lifted her chin at Terry, "Let's drop you off. Livia's?"

"Yeah, I better." He offered a goofy smile. "Can we hit the convenience store on the way, eleventh and eight? Amazing slushes."

The RAV4 smelled stuffy. She opened the window to air it out. Terry rolled down his as well and dug into his bag for another taco.

Haddie sighed. "What do you think, am I clear? Will Stanton keep any pictures out of the media?"

Terry shrugged. "I saw one already with you in it, though you can't tell. Security camera through a dirty window. Before the explosion there's a ton of dust, then a person flipping into the rubble. Slowed down, it was a fuzzy mess. The hair looked light blonde, not white. I was working with Stanton's people immediately on any images out of the New York terrorist attack. Most of the phone shots were too late to catch you up there. The media has it all wrong, but that might be Stanton."

She'd been hanging in the air for minutes, but time had slowed. "Send me that video, if you can."

"Starting a scrapbook?" Terry took a bite of his taco.

"Finishing one. I'm tired. I just want a normal week. Game night and nachos."

"I won't tell Livia you didn't mention her empanadas."

"Please don't." She pulled out of the drive and waited at the stop sign.

"Glad to have you back, Buckaroo."

Am I back? Haddie took a deep breath and pulled behind a beer truck.

CHAPTER 61

Haddie sat at the outdoor metal table by herself. Beyond the wrought iron rail, rush hour traffic ebbed and flowed. The air had a cold bite to it, but it felt good on her burnt skin. She'd been happy to sit outside, without makeup, but her purpura and peeling skin had the customers and servers on edge. She faced the street and doubted anyone bothered to look into the little beer garden.

Throughout her travels, the attendants and pilots had been restrained, helping her forget what she saw in the bathroom mirror. She'd forgotten until one of the busboys at the bar had dropped a tray the moment he saw her.

Probably should have gone to Liz's house. Her skin would clear up. It always did, unless her body wouldn't heal this time for whatever reason. *I'll worry about that later.*

"Here you are!" Liz called out from the door behind. "I swear I wasn't that late."

Haddie turned then winced as she stood.

Liz put down her beer. "Shit, Haddie, I could have brought makeup. I'd lend you mine, but you'd look like a pink clown." She sank into a hug and sighed. "I was really worried. That from the explosion? All over the news, but nothing about you."

They sat down, and Liz pushed hair out of her eyes and studied Haddie's hands. "Was it bright?"

"It was black. Like a night sky with no stars."

"Still could have been infrared; that might have caused the heat, sunburn, and blisters. We should get you checked for radiation."

"Stanton checked. A Geiger counter."

"What was the reading?"

Haddie raised her eyebrows and tilted her head.

Liz sniffed and lifted her glass. "Can you at least find out for me?" She took a long sip and leaned back in her chair. "Tell me all of it."

They talked long enough that Liz finally had to go inside to get refills; evidently no one wanted to come out and see Haddie's face. She returned with two heated pretzels and the spicy mustard Haddie liked.

"I'm really spinning on these angels." Liz took a sip of beer and held her finger up before Haddie could respond. "They live outside of our world, like in light and energy. What's with the tones and music? That requires matter. Unless their effect on the material world is to make things vibrate; can you ask them?"

Haddie pulled out her phone. "Let me text them and ask."

Liz lowered her head and glared. "I get it. But at least think about these questions the next time they're around. Like WWLA, what would Liz ask?"

"I hope not to see them again. They seemed focused on this one issue with Bruce and the bomb. I'll run next time they pop up." Haddie bit her pretzel. "I don't know if you'll get much more, but I'll ask Meg if she'd be okay with talking about her time there."

Liz nodded frantically, her eyes pleading. "Pleeease." She almost took a sip. "Oh! I know you're going to say no, but I was thinking inside — by any chance, did you save me one of those demon heads that you, uh . . ." She made a slicing motion across her neck.

CHAPTER 62

HADDIE TURNED her camera on and checked her makeup. The skin had peeled at her cheeks, making her look like a B-movie zombie. *He's going to expect me to be a mess.* He'd been caring and kind throughout the texts. She took a deep breath and knocked on his door instead of using her key. The sun had broken through the clouds by mid-morning. *A bit too bright.* She had a slight hangover from the night with Liz. They'd gotten a ride back to Liz's apartment when the bar cut them off. Haddie had just retrieved her RAV4 half an hour ago.

The lock clicked from inside. "Haddie?" David asked through the door, but opened it without waiting for her to answer.

"David."

He grabbed her into a hug on the threshold and pulled her tight. His hair smelled like soap with a faint orange to it. She rubbed her hands across his shoulders. His muscles were tense. She'd put him through so much over the past several days of worrying with no messages. Was that over? Could she have a real life with him?

No, she'd stay the same age and he'd grow old. Yet, Kiana had accepted it with Dad. David knew so much about her already, she could give him the choice.

He leaned in and tenderly kissed her lips. They were chapped, but she responded with passion. *I don't want to lose him.*

David pulled back and smiled, then drew her inside, "Your hand?"

"Bruised, not broken." She shrugged. "A little burnt in places."

David inspected her, noting the bulge of the bandage at her thigh. "And your leg?"

"Small wound. It'll clear up." She wanted to tell him all of it, but it would make her sound insane. A giggle escaped. *Like what I thought of Dad.*

"What's funny?"

"I'm nervous. Not sure you'll really accept me. I'm hoping the worst is over." She sucked in a deep breath. "How's work?"

"They've got me on leave for two weeks. They want to monitor me. I have to call in to a counselor every day, and we talk."

Haddie brightened. They could take some time off. She could work in a few conversations, maybe leaving out Meg and the angels for a moment. Just focus on the whole not growing old thing. That would be enough for one trip.

"What are you thinking about? I love you. I'm in this, no matter what." He pulled her into another hug, and she melted against him.

The picture of the pink blossoms caught her view. Wrong season. She pulled back and searched his brown eyes. "How's your Japanese going?"

"The lessons? Not great, I've been — distracted."

Kidnapped. She'd dragged him through all the worst of her life lately.

His eyebrows knitted. "What?"

"Want to take a trip to Japan?" Haddie reached back and knotted her hair around her hand. "I sort of ended up with this jet . . ."

If you haven't read the Origin story, *Shattered Blood*, then download a free ebook or purchase the paperback or audible on Amazon.

AngelSong Series

Penumbra - Book One

Red Tempest - Book Two

Coerced - Book Three

Demons' Lair - Book Four

Infrared - Book Five. (End of the AngelSong Series)

Website KevinArthurDavis.com

Facebook @KevinArthurDavis

KevinADavis on Twitter and Instagram.

Please join my mailing list if you'd like to be kept up to date on this series and the upcoming Khimmer Chronicles series.

I'm working on Khimmer Chronicles now. A first person, cryptid-filled, series that I'm told has an element of Isekai in it.

ACKNOWLEDGMENTS

My wife April is to blame for all of these books as I'm still trying to impress her. If she's not, she tells me. I still can't quite get her to cry through any scenes, but I'll keep trying. I appreciate everything she does and am really sorry that I sent the wrong file and she had to do the work a second time.

Robyn Huss, my editor, takes the wrong word and finds the right one to keep what I'm trying to show, and make it stronger. There are many times she'll find the right place for a sentence whether it is earlier in the paragraph, later on the page, or in a different scene. Besides that, she knows where commas go. She's amazing.

I miss David Farland and don't believe that will end soon. He was a tireless mentor and a caring man. Please pick up one of his books and enjoy the magic he endowed upon the world. Writers, study his lessons at Apex Writers.

Jody Lynn Nye's workshop will always be my recommendation for any aspiring writers.

Katharine, Mark, Rosemary, Tim, and Vail from my

JordanCon writing group (the infamous Fireside Group), Arrash and Michele from DragonCon, and Dianne and Brett from Apex are fundamental in making sure I keep on track with all aspects of storytelling.

Thank you.